GOOD GESTES

GOOD GESTES

Stories of Beau Geste, his Brothers,
and certain of their Comrades in
the French Foreign Legion

BY
PERCIVAL CHRISTOPHER WREN

Author of " Beau Geste," " Beau Sabreur,"
" Beau Ideal," etc.

" The Braves are gone to rest,
  The Brothers of my combats, on the breast
  Of the red field they reaped ; their work is done . . ."

WILDSIDE PRESS

WILDSIDE PRESS

Printed in the United States of America

CONTENTS

GOOD GESTES

GOOD GESTES

I

WHAT'S IN A NAME

1

THE three brothers sat in a solemn row upon Beau Geste's bed by the window in their barrack room, enjoying the blessed peace of a Sabbath afternoon.

John Geste yawned cavernously, and the pot-shot made by his brother Digby, with a small piece of soap, was entirely satisfactory—to Digby.

"The child seems bored," observed Beau Geste; "he must do more Arabic. Yes," he continued, "and I think I must institute a course of ethnological studies, too."

"Oh, splendid," agreed Digby, "I shall love that. What is it?"

"What I mean," continued Beau, "is that it would be rather interesting to see how many different nationalities we can discover in the Legion; how many different trades, professions, and callings, and—"

"And all that," said John, having completed another yawn.

"How is Beau like Satan?" asked Digby.

"How's he *un*like him?" interrupted John, ere Digby answered his own question with the statement:

"Because he'll find some mischief still for idle coves to do. They'll make him a sergeant, if he's not careful."

"Why mischief?" asked John. "Ethnology isn't mischief, is it?"

"It would be, my lad, if it took the form of going about asking personal questions of *les légionnaires*. They'd *do* you a mischief, too," was the reply.

"That's just the point," observed Beau. "No questions to be asked at all. See who can get the finest collection of nationalities, professions, home-towns and all that, without asking anybody *anything*. No vulgar curiosity. . . . All diplomacy, suggestion, induction, deduction . . ."

"Then production," murmured Digby.

"Quite so, my dear Watson. The one that gets the biggest bag, to give the other two a present. Splendid idea. Keep your young minds active. Train the faculty of observation."

"When do we compare notes?" asked John.

"When I think I've got the biggest list," replied Beau.

"And what if the same feller appears in more than one list?" inquired John.

"Cancel him out, or toss for him, or find who discovered him first, fathead."

"I'm afraid the idea's too late to save *you*, John," observed Digby—"mind dead already."

One evening a month later, the three brothers, sitting in a row as was their wont, with their elder and leader in the centre, adorned a broad, low divan in Mustapha's café.

"Well, pups, how's ethnology going?" inquired Beau, as he put his clay coffee-cup on the floor beside him.

"Fine," said Digby. "I'm a great man with a great mind. A diplomatist is lost in me."

"*Is* he?" inquired Beau, in some concern. "Let's get him out."

"No; you don't understand, Beau," observed John. "He means he *is* a diplomatist. He's right, too. Nobody but a clever diplomatist could hide the fact that he *is* a diplomatist so well as Digby does."

"Anyhow, I bet I win," said Digby triumphantly. "All authentic, too."

"Then you'll give us each a present," pointed out John. "Shall I choose a fiddle, or a free excursion-ticket, single, to—to—Brandon Abbas? Read out yours."

"No, we'll declare ourselves in order of merit," interposed Beau. "I've got a grocer, Bingen; a shipping-clerk, Barcelona; an officer of the Imperial Guard, St. Petersburg; a valet, Paris; a surgeon,

Vienna; a commercial traveller, Hamburg; a vendor of unpostable post-cards, valued and respected citizen of Marseilles; a stevedore, Lisbon; a street-corner fried-bean merchant, Sofia; a teacher of languages, Warsaw; a fig-packer, Smyrna; a perfectly good, nice-mannered, bloody-minded brigand, Bastilica—"

"There isn't any such place," interrupted Digby. "Where is it?"

"Nothing to be ashamed of in honest ignorance, my lad. It's right in the middle of Corsica, fifty miles from Ajaccio—according to the brigand," replied Beau.

"Isn't that where Napoleon Bonaparte was born?" inquired John.

"Bastilica?" replied Digby. "Why, of course; I remember the place quite well now."

"A restaurateur from Ancona; a rock-scorpion from Gibraltar; a Japanese barber from Yokohama —he speaks English with an American accent, he understands Russian, I know, and I'll bet you he could not only drill a battalion but handle a brigade or a division."

"Oh, you mean that chap Yato," interrupted Digby. "I've got him. He's a wonderful tattooer, too. He's going to do portraits of you two on my back, so that I can't see them."

"Will he, too, tattoo two, to . . ." murmured John sleepily.

"Cancel him out, then," said Beau.

"I've also got a Portuguese cove from Loanda. That's in Angola, Portuguese West Africa."

"Well, we know that, don't we?" complained Digby.

"No," answered Beau and continued: "A Swedish sailor from Göttenburg, and two frightful asses from Brandon Abbas."

"Rotten list," commented Digby; "barely a score."

"Well, how many have *you* got?" asked his brother.

"Oh, in round numbers, about a hundred."

"*Round* numbers? All round the truth, I suppose?"

"Well, listen and don't be jealous," answered Digby, producing a paper. "I've got a Russian banker from Odessa; an Italian opera-singer; a Dutch bargee; an Austrian count—or dis-count, perhaps; a Munich brewer's drayman; a Spanish fisherman; a Goanese steward; a Danish farm-boy; a beastly, bounderish, bumptious, Byzantine blackguard; a French actor; a schoolmaster from Avignon; a gambling-hell keeper from Punta Arenas—wherever that may be; a bank-clerk from Rome; a lottery-ticket seller from Havana; a hybrid Callao *maquereau*; another cosmopolitan gent from Sfax, who, on being asked his trade, always says, '*Je faisais la mouche*'—"

"But no questions were to be allowed," interposed Beau.

"I didn't ask any, clever; I overheard, see? . . . A Dutch Colonial soldier, a Bowery tough; a Dresden—"

"Shepherdess," murmured John.

"Wrong again," said Digby—"street-scavenger; a Finnish—"

"Time we got to the finish," murmured John again.

"Bloater-paster, or salmon-smoker—"

"Funny stuff to smoke," commented Beau, "but probably better than this French *caporal* tobacco."

"A colonel of Don Cossacks."

"From Donnybrook?" inquired John.

"Yes, and Donegal—or perhaps Oxford," replied Beau.

"A bootblack from Athens; a poor *fellah* from Egypt; a boatman from Beirut; and two frightful asses from Brandon Abbas. . . . Oh, and a lot I haven't written down. Tinker, tailor, soldier, sailor, rich man, poor man, beggarman, thief; painter, pander, pedler, parasite, printer, professor, prize-fighter, *procureur*, prefect, priest, pro-consul, prince, prophet-in-his-own-country. . . . Oh, lots. Get you all the names and addresses by and by."

"What have you got, John?" inquired Beau, turning as with bored distaste from the loquacity of his twin.

"I've got another Jones," replied John, alluding to Digby's *nom de guerre* of Thomas Jones.

"What *is* a Jone, by the way?" inquired Digby. "I ought to know, as I am some."

"Dunno. Anyhow, this is the only other Jones," replied John. "He's an Englishman—public-school, Oxford, and all that. Indian Army, too, poor beggar. In a rotten state, living on his nerves. Sensitive sort of chap. Shoot himself one of these days. This is about the last place in the world for a man like him."

"Sounds as though it *will* be the last place in the world for him," observed Digby. "Let's get hold of him and shed the light of our countenances upon him, thus brightening his dark places. Does he seem to be a criminal, like Beau?"

"No, nor a moral wreck like you."

"Moral wreck!" commented Digby. "Better than being an *im*moral wreck anyhow." And his look was accusatory.

"Neither criminal nor moral wreck," continued John. "Simply a gentleman, like me."

"Oh, a gentleman like you, is he?" remarked Beau. "Then I don't think we'll associate with him."

"Yes, we will. I'm bringing him here to-morrow night, to meet you two. He's simply longing to talk English to people of his own kind. And I'll tell you something else. Unlike most people here, he wants to talk about himself, too. He's in a queer state of nerves—neurotic."

"Poor chap, we must see what we can do for him," agreed Beau; and Digby nodded.

A lean, haggard man, his sensitive young face a mask of misery, old and lined, haunted and hopeless, arrived with John the following evening at Mustapha's café. That he was in a terribly nervous condition was all too evident—a reserved and reticent gentleman, devil-driven to be garrulous, talking the harder the more he was ashamed of talking. He seemed literally dying to express himself, to make a clean breast of something terrible, something that still stung and scorched and branded him.

His story, told in a swift rush and a curious metallic voice, without break or hesitation, greatly interested the sympathetic, silent brothers. It interested them yet more, next day, when they learned that, for some reason not divulged, he had shot himself during the night.

Five minutes after his introduction by John to Beau and Digby, he told them that his meeting with them was a godsend, for there was something he *must* get off his mind.

And a pitiful thing it was, to the listeners, prepared as they were to hear a dark story of vice, crime, ruin and downfall. . . . Pitiful, pathetic, tragic and ridiculous, like a torrent in spate, the absurd story came.

"Looking back and considering the affair again in all its bearings," he said, "I am still of opinion that I did my painful duty and nothing more; that I acted as a man of conscience should do, and that I have nothing whatever wherewith to reproach myself.

"Only the fool or the moral coward says, 'Am I my brother's keeper?' For what had my dear mother trained me, and my dear father in God developed my sense of responsibility to my neighbour and myself, but that I should act precisely as I did in that affair?

"I suppose it is the devil himself who is the *fons et origo* of those foolish, unworthy and sinful doubts that do sometimes try to raise their poisonous heads in my disordered mind when I look back upon the little incident.

"However, I will tell the exact truth as to what I thought and said and did; and you shall judge as to whether any high-minded, conscientious and morally courageous person could have done otherwise than I did.

"I was brought up by the best mother a man ever had, a human saint, and by a priest whose chief regret, I think, was that burning at the stake has become unpopular. No, he didn't want to burn anybody; he wanted to *be* burnt—for his faith. He sought a martyr's crown and found a comfortable living, much honour and preferment. Finding also that honour is not without profit save in its own country, he determined to go abroad and find profit to his soul among the heathen—and possibly the martyr's crown beneath the solar topi—it would look odd on top of one.

"And I went to India to join the Indian regiment into which I was exchanging, by the same boat that took him to join the holy army of martyrs, if he could contrive it. It was a great joy to my mother that I was to travel with the good man and not be left to stray alone into the detrimental atmosphere of Gibraltar, Malta, Port Said, Aden, Bombay or other such colourful, and therefore wicked, places.

"And on that accursed boat I saw my new colonel's young wife kiss another man. I saw him with his arms about her waist. I saw him go into her cabin, when the colonel lay snoring in a *chaise longue* upon the deck.

"When I heard them *plotting together to go off,* at Port Said, on Christmas day, my terrible struggle with my conscience was ended. My conscience had won, and I knew I must tell the colonel the horrible truth, however agonizingly distasteful and obnoxious this hateful duty might be. Yes, I was a Young Man with a Conscience. . . . But let me tell the facts in sequence as they occurred.

"My new colonel (of the regiment to which I was going), returning from leave and his honeymoon trip, was a grey, stern man; a typical dour Scot, very unapproachable, and the last man in the world with whom one would attempt to jest or trifle.

"His bride was a beautiful young girl who might well have been his daughter—as merry, frivolous and gay as Colonel Gordon-Watts was sober, hard and dour. Opposites attract—and it was plain that he worshipped her.

"I admired her greatly, and she was very kind to me on the one or two occasions on which I spoke to her. Sometimes I felt I would rather be promenading with her, sitting beside her deck-chair or playing deck-quoits and bull-board with her than eternally walking and talking with my good and kind mentor.

"But I was far too much his spiritual child, his acolyte and disciple, to think of breaking away from his control. You see he had educated me from childhood until I went to Oxford, and he had settled there, with those admirable Fathers irreverently known to undergraduate youth as the Cowley Dads, and continued to exercise his powerful influence upon my character. I was with him daily and much of every day, and, as you hear, even now that I was in the army—with a university commission, as my mother would never hear of my going to Sandhurst—and *was* going abroad into the wide and wicked world, he was with me still. Yes, I was a Young Man with a Conscience.

"No, I did not make any attempt to desert my mentor and cabin-companion in order to bask in the society of the colonel's wife; but while my ear listened to my spiritual father and my tongue replied to him, my eye undoubtedly followed her.

"Nothing happened until we reached Marseilles and the overland passengers came on board. When I went on the promenade deck that evening, one of them already sat beside her, and I was very sorry to see her accept a cigarette from him and smoke it. He was, like herself, young, and again like herself and most unlike the colonel, merry, frivolous and gay.

"They had evidently made friends very quickly and they were always together. Certainly they made a splendidly matched couple, and certainly she seemed far more merry and bright in his company than in that of her husband.

"*How* they laughed together!

"And the colonel seemed content. He would sit in the writing-room scribbling away, all the morning, at some military text-book or other that he was compiling; sleep all the afternoon; scribble again in the evening; walk violently round and round the deck, for exercise, before dinner, and go to bed quite early. I confess that I envied the handsome, laughing youth and that I often longed to talk to someone other than my spiritual father—someone like this merry, frivolous girl, for example.

"And on the second day out from Marseilles I received a terrible shock.

"Coming suddenly round the corner from the music-saloon, I almost ran into her deck-chair as she withdrew her hand from that of her new companion with the words:

" 'You are a darling, Bobby; you shall have a hug for that'—and, as I dodged the foot-rest of her chair, her eye met mine, even as she spoke. Did she look confused, uncomfortable, guilty? Not she! Her gaze was utterly untroubled, and it was evidently nothing to *her* that I must have heard every word she said.

"Perfectly shameless!

"And as for *him*—he had the effrontery to murmur quite distinctly, 'Hold up, old hoss!' as I stumbled and blundered past.

"Of the three, it was certainly I who would have struck an observant onlooker as the guilty one, as I flushed to the roots of my hair and hurried away, not knowing where to look.

"*Think of it!* Married a month, and the man had not been on the boat three days! I trembled from head to foot, and went straight to my cabin, feeling shocked to the point of physical sickness.

"Should I tell Father Staunton?

"Ought not I to tell her husband? Was not I an accessory after the fact, almost an accomplice, practically compounding a felony, if I stood by and said nothing? Was I my brother's keeper? I knew I was. I knew it was my duty to save the Colonel from shame; to save this woman from ruining her life; to save this young man 'Bobby' from himself.

"But I knew I was not brave enough to do it. And the devil tempted me with whisperings of *'Most ungentlemanly of you to tell tales of a lady!' 'Gross impertinence!' 'Colonel Gordon-Watts will refuse to believe you, but not to kick you downstairs.' 'Mind your own business, you young fool,'* and even: *'Make love to her yourself, since she's of such an on-coming disposition'*—whereat I jumped with horror and told myself I would do my painful, dreadful duty.

"That evening, while Father Staunton was un-dressing in the cabin, I went on deck. It was a glorious moonlight night. As four bells rang and the lascar look-out replied with his sing-song cry of *'Ham dekhta hai'* to show that he was awake and watchful, I was moved with an idle inclination to go right up into the bows and watch the phosphores-cence as the knife-like stem churned up the sleeping waters.

"I ran down the companion, crossed the well-deck, and climbed the iron ladder to the fo'c'sle.

"*He* and *she* were there, leaning on the bulwarks —and his arm was around her waist!

"Going up on deck early next morning, I saw them meet—*and kiss!* During that day, as on previous days, the young man (his name was Mornay, by the way) cultivated the society of other young women a good deal, presumably as a blind. But, as I sat reading in the lounge before dinner, Mornay and Mrs. Gordon-Watts came and sat down close behind me, and they made their arrangements for going off together, on Christmas day, at Port Said!

"They spoke with shameless openness and lack of decency; and I distinctly heard Mornay say: 'Slip away while he's writing, then,' and, a few minutes later: 'Bring *all* the cash you can scrape together, mind! You'll want it at . . . and I am nearly broke. I can't keep—' and her reply, with a heartless giggle: 'Suppose he comes after us!'

"I sprang up, and leaning over, said: 'Pardon— I am hearing much of what you say, and I shall—'

"With brazen effrontery, Mornay interrupted with, 'Right-o, old thing! Sorry if our artless prattle disturbed you,' while Mrs. Gordon-Watts stared at me as though she thought me eccentric.

"I rushed to my cabin.

"How shall I tell of the agonies of indecision, cowardice and self-contempt that I suffered, as I wrestled with my conscience once more. I *ought* to stop this thing. It was my bounden duty to warn the Colonel. Was I my brother's keeper? And so on, *ad nauseam*.

"And a thing which somehow, and strangely, seemed to make it all worse, if that were possible, was the fact that she was not the only woman that he pursued. He was a perfect Don Juan and made up to every pretty girl and woman on board, married or single.

" 'An arrant flirt,' thought I, 'a lady-killer; a heartless, conscienceless scoundrel.' And yet I could not deny that he was popular with all on board. He was in the greatest demand, always and everywhere —in fact, 'the life and soul of the ship,' as Mrs. Gordon-Watts truly said.

"And while I sat on my berth, and suffered, Father Staunton entered and I laid the matter before him. I weakly suggested that he, a priest, was the fitter person to intervene.

" 'No, my son,' said he, 'I go to no man with a tale about a tale. . . . And I shall leave it to your own conscience. Do what you think right, but be no self-deceiver. Be very sure of your motive before you act or decide not to act.'

"And I read this to mean, 'Do not stand by and see this happen because you are a coward while you pretend it is because you are not a busybody. . . . Do not shirk your duty because you have told yourself that this is not your business and that you have no duty in the matter at all!'

"I had no sleep that Christmas eve. I tossed from side to side, a prey to doubt, fear, self-contempt and indecision. I was stretched upon the rack of my Conscience.

"But in the morning, the glorious Christmas morning, I arose, calm and decided, and dressed as one dresses who goes to execution. Conscience had triumphed and I was going to do the right thing at any cost to myself—and the right thing in this case was, believe me, a loathsomely distasteful thing for me to do. I would go through with it, however—and I would do it openly and fairly, sparing myself nothing. I would tell Colonel Gordon-Watts, in the presence of his wife and her lover.

"There would be no backbiting, no 'tale about a tale,' no hole-and-corner sneaking about *that*.

"As the passengers trooped up from breakfast, I followed the Colonel, with whom were his wife and Mornay, on to the deck; and with beating heart and dry mouth, I went up to him and said:

" 'May I have a word with you, sir, on a matter of the most urgent and vital importance—and may Mrs. Gordon-Watts and Mr. Mornay be present?'

"The Colonel stared, looking more like a cold volcano than ever.

" 'What the dev—' he began, and I could feel my knees turning to tape and my heart to water, as Mornay interrupted with:

" 'If it's to form a syndicate for a bet on the day's-run sweepstake, on the strength of a tip from the engine-room, let us congeal ourselves and hist.'

"Mrs. Gordon-Watts giggled. If Mornay and she guessed at my business with the Colonel, they acted cleverly, I thought. There was no trace of guilty confusion. No; they did not *dream* of what was coming.

" 'Well? Out with it,' growled the Colonel.

"He had vile manners, as I had already discovered in my brief and rare encounters with him on board.

" 'It would be better for all concerned, if we were alone—we four, I mean,' said I.

" 'Let's go up on the bridge and ask the captain to clear out for a while,' suggested Mornay. 'He won't mind.'

"The lady laughed again.

" 'I am very much in earnest, sir,' continued I to the Colonel, ignoring Mornay.

"He saw from my manner, and probably from my appearance, that I certainly was very much in earnest.

" 'Come in here,' he said, indicating the empty smoking-room. All the passengers were crowding forward on the starboard side of the deck, to watch Port Said rising out of the sea.

" 'Sir,' said I, 'it is my unspeakably painful duty to tell you, before this man, Mornay, that I have seen him *embrace and kiss your wife*, have heard him address her in terms of intimacy and endearment, and have heard him *arranging to go off with her*—and with what money she could secure—at Port Said. I have said it and done my duty. My conscience is clear. . . .'

"The Colonel's eyes blazed. His wife and Mornay stared at me open-mouthed. Thus we hung for seconds that seemed like years, without sound or movement—till suddenly Mornay threw himself down upon the couch behind him and buried his face in a cushion; the Colonel raised a hand—not to strike, but to cover his poor twitching mouth; and Mrs. Gordon-Watts burst into wild hysterical screams of distraught laughter.

"And *I* had made this ruin!

"But I had obeyed my Conscience. . . .

"And *then*—and *then*—the Husband turned, first to the Wife, and then to the Other Man, and said:

" 'Is this thing true? If so, you are not to waste more than ten pounds in the shops, Lilian. And if you, Bobby, have been kissing your *own* sister for a change, it's a change in the right direction!' "

II

"I say," said Digby as he entered the Barrack Room, a few days later, and strode across to where Michael and John, sitting on the latter's bed, industriously waxed and polished belts, straps and pouches. "Did you see the draft that came in this afternoon from Colomb Bechar or somewhere?"

"No," replied Michael. "Why?"

"Well, they've got about the ugliest lad I've ever seen, among them. . . . *Awful* face."

"Worse than John's?" asked Michael.

"Well, you can't very well compare them," replied Digby. "John's ugliness is what you might call natural. He was born like it. This other fellow's is artificial. Been made like it."

"Got an artificial face, has he?" inquired John.

"Not exactly that either," replied Digby, pushing John off his bed, and seating himself by Michael. "It's the ugliness that's artificial. It's as though I didn't like your face—which I don't, of course—and set to work with cold steel and red-hot iron to improve it, or at any rate to change it."

"Wouldn't *any* change be an improvement?" asked Michael, looking up from the pouch that he was polishing.

"Well, I gather it wasn't so in this man's case," replied Digby. "His *escouade* seemed quite proud of his face, and one of them was telling me about it. He's an Englishman. It seems he got a poisoned foot and couldn't get his boot on. He fell behind, as they were doing a forced march to relieve a threatened post, and couldn't stop for anything or anybody. They hadn't even any mule or camel *cacolets* for the sick and wounded. He kept going, with the utmost pluck and endurance, sometimes hopping, sometimes using his reversed rifle as a crutch, and at last going on all fours . . . When he completely collapsed and couldn't even roll, the tribesmen who had been watching the Company and stalking this straggler, came down like a wolf on the fold and gathered him in—not without loss to themselves as they rushed him from all points of the compass.

"Well, it seems they were so annoyed with him, for shooting frequent and free, that they had a bit of fun with him, then and there, before taking him up to the *kasbah* or caves, or whatever it was, in order to let the ladies torture him properly.

"Apparently they slit his cheeks perpendicularly and threaded twigs through the lattice-work, so to speak, and did something similar with his forehead. An argument then arose as to whether the girls would mind if he were handed over to them without ears, nose, lips and eyelids. Some murmured *'Place aux dames,'* while others said, 'There will be plenty of him left for them.'

"Like the sensible fellers they are, they compounded and compromised and split the difference and said they'd just have his ears for luck, and for something to send in to the Commandant of the nearest Fort, on his birthday, or for Christmas or something.

"Well, one nasty man had just grabbed this chap's right ear, and had just begun to cut with a rather blunt knife, when round the corner came a policeman, and the boys had to run for it. In other words, along came a half-troop of Spahis who were following the Company.

"I gather that the Spahis were divided in their

minds as to whether it would be kinder to shoot
him, or to save him up, when the *vile corpus* or vile
body sat up and said that if anybody shot him, he'd
punch him on the nose. He said this in English, a
language understood by the *sous-lieutenant* of the
Spahis, so they pulled most of the brushwood out
of the lattice-work which was his face, tied his ear
on with string, mopped him up a bit, and put him
up behind a trooper."

"Poor devil," murmured John. "He must be a
stout lad."

"Yes, let's go and call on him," suggested Michael.
"He might like to have a jibber with fellow-coun-
trymen."

"We will," agreed Digby. "Better look him up
to-morrow, as he may be among those of the draft
who are being sent to Arzew to recuperate."

"Where's that?" inquired John.

"You're an ignorant lad," replied Digby. "It's a
health resort, on the coast, about one hundred miles
west of Oran. Didn't you even know that much?
I learnt it this afternoon."

The brothers found *le Légionnaire* Robinson to be
a pleasant English gentleman with a most unpleasant face, hideously scarred, and rather terrible to behold. It was obvious that he was still most painfully
self-conscious.

As the four chatted, Robinson sat with his hand

across his face, as does a weak-eyed person in a strong light. Although it was easy to see that the poor fellow was very uncomfortable among strangers, the tact, charm, sympathy and *savoir faire* of the three Gestes won upon him, and put him at his ease. Before long he was laughing and telling them the story of his ghastly experience.

"I suppose I'm a *légionnaire* for life," he smiled wryly and whimsically, "now that my face is my misfortune . . . This home of the Soldiers of Misfortune is the best place for it . . . the only place. Can't go about scaring women and children . . . Might get a job at a sort of Barnum's Show, I suppose.

"Rather hard luck," he added. "I had only four months more to serve. . . ."

"Rough luck," murmured Michael, "but look here, you know . . . I think you make too much of it. . . . What I mean to say is . . . it'll get a great deal better in course of time . . . scars do, you know, and these are very recent. . . . And then these great surgeons can do most marvellous things."

"Why, yes," agreed John. "It's astonishing what they can do in the way of grafting new flesh, and that sort of thing. I knew of a man whose nose was most hideously smashed . . . flat with his face . . . bone all gone—and they built him up a perfectly good nose."

"Sort of thing he took off at night with his wig

and false teeth?" inquired Robinson grimly. "I shouldn't care to wear a mask."

"Nothing of the sort," objected John. "This fellow's nose was not detachable. It was built up under its own skin, so to speak. I believe they inject molten paraffin wax, and mould it to the required shape as it cools—something of that sort."

"Yes," added Digby. "I distinctly remember reading of a great Viennese surgeon who practically rebuilt the shattered face of a man whose gun burst as he was firing it. According to the account they even made him a new jaw-bone, and grafted on to it skin which they took from his leg. There was a portrait of him, and he looked perfectly normal, quite good-looking.

"Why not take your discharge, and go to the best surgeon in the world? Costly job, I suppose, but if a loan . . . we should be . . ."

"Oh, I've plenty of money *now*, thanks," replied Robinson. "Reminds one of the Spanish proverb, *'God gives nuts to him who has no teeth.'* I hadn't a bean in the world. Partly why I came to the Legion. . . . But the day I came out of hospital—and had a good look at my face—I got a letter from home. Plenty of money *now*."

"Well, that's all right then," observed Michael, "and you can spend some of it to good purpose."

"My dear chap, it's hopeless. You know it is. It's most kind of you to be consoling and encouraging, and all that, but the damage is done, and it's irreparable. If the marvellous surgeon had been on the spot, I've no doubt he could have done something and made, at any rate, a tidier job of it than Nature and my comrades' dirty paws did. It's far too late now, and I'll spend the rest of my young life where nothing matters—thanks all the same."

"Well, anyhow," replied Michael Geste, "you see if I'm not right. Things would improve enormously in time. The scars will lose all colour and cease to be livid. They will become mere seams and lines . . . hardly noticeable."

"That would be a pity in a way, too," smiled Robinson. "My *escouade* would be disappointed. They would miss my face. Perhaps some sniper won't— if I can get on active service again."

§ 2

"Where's Beau?" inquired Digby one afternoon, a couple of months later, as he joined John at the trough in the *lavabo* where they washed their white uniforms.

"Dunno," replied John, "but he'll be in for evening *soupe* all right. Why?"

"A job, my little lad! . . . A *geste* . . . a deed . . . a do. . . . You know that dear fellow, Klingen. He was telling his gang an extraordinary yarn while we were peeling potatoes this morning. . . .

Reminded me of that lass who chased the Crusader home."

"What lass was that?" inquired John.

"D'you mean to say you don't know *that*, you un-educated worm . . . you worm that dieth not. No, that was a sharp-headed worm, wasn't it? Nothing sharp-headed about you, John Geste."

"We were talking about a girl," interrupted John coldly. "Who was she?"

"How the devil should I know?" replied Digby. "It's you who ought to know useful things of this sort, so that you can be helpful to Beau and me."

"You don't mean Mrs. à Becket by any chance, do you?"

"That's it, my lad," said Digby, smiting his brother with his wet tunic. "Why couldn't you have said that at once, without all this jibber. Thomas à Becket went to the Crusades and there picked up with a Saracen lassie."

"But I thought he was a turbulent priest, and a perfectly good Archbishop of Canterbury," observed John. "I think it was T. à Becket Senior, old Mr. Gilbert."

"No, no," replied Digby. "It was Tom Cantuar all right, and all this happened when he was young and merry and bright, before he had found grace. . . ."

"*Was* her name Grace?" asked John. "I thought it was Zuleika or Zenobia or Aggie."

"Will you shut up and listen, and improve your mind!" admonished Digby. "He took up with this young woman, and they were walking out . . . keeping company . . . *you* know . . . when T. à Becket's time expired, or else he was due for leave and furlough, and in the hurry of packing his kit and getting his papers signed and proving to the Quartermaster that he was a liar . . ."

"*He* was—or the Quartermaster was?" asked John.

". . . he quite forgot, or else mislaid, Grace or Zuleika or Zenobia or Aggie—and in any case he couldn't have taken her aboard the transport as she wasn't married to him 'on the strength.' Well, there it was. T. à Becket safe in England and poor Grace walking up and down the Pier or the beach at Acre or Joppa or Jaffa or Haifa weeping and wailing. . . ."

"Whaling?" queried John. "From a pier or a beach?"

". . . and Grace's Pa making kind inquiries for T. à Becket with a thick stick."

"How *do* you inquire with a stick?" asked John.

"I'll show you in a minute," promised Digby, and continued:

". . . When Grace found that Thomas had done a bunk—and she having nearly filled the bottom drawer and all—two of everything and all hand-stitched—she up and had an idea. Drawing her savings from the Post Office, she left Pa and Ma to scratch for themselves; she went down to the shipping office and just said 'Single, London,' and went straight aboard a perfectly good fifteen-ton lugger or yawl or scow or junk or barge or battleship and 'proceeded' to London, which she knew to be Thomas's home-town, as she had seen it on his washing.

"Safely arrived, she took a room in a perfectly respectable boarding-house in Bloomsbury, patronized entirely by clergymen's daughters, had an egg to her tea, and then went out to look for Thomas. . . .

"Now the artful dog, Thomas, had never given her his proper name and address, and she only knew him as Thomas, Tommy and Tom, and there were quite a lot of gents so named in London Town. However, she worked clean through the London Directory and the Bars and Night-clubs of the Shaftesbury Avenue District, and in the end, probably the West End, she met her own True Thomas, who promptly said he was just having a last drink before setting out to look for her, having been engaged hitherto in getting a home together. Whereupon they married and were happy ever after. . . . She was housekeeper at the Palace when he settled in at Canterbury as Archbishop, because you know how people talk and all that, when celibate clergymen . . ."

"But, my poor dear excellent ass," interrupted John, "what's all this got to do with the unspeakable Klingen and the deed we have to do?"

"Nothing, probably," replied Digby, "and then again, you never know. As I was saying when you interrupted, he was telling his gang an extraordinary yarn while we were peeling potatoes this morning.

"It appears that, last night, as he was strolling down the Rue de Tlemçen, a beauteous maiden stopped him and asked him if he was English. I gathered that he behaved precisely as Klingen would behave in the circumstances, and that she cleared off with her chin in the air, followed by Klingen with his mind in the gutter—until she went into the *Hôtel de l'Europe* and thither he could not follow her. Then up spake a lad whose name I don't know, and said he'd had a similar experience. A pretty girl had stopped him near the hotel, and, with blushing apologies, asked him if he were English. Apparently this chap behaved like an ordinary decent person—said he was sorry but he wasn't English. The girl then explained that she wanted to find an English *légionnaire*. Her idea seemed to be that her best plan was to find *any* Englishman, as he would be more likely to know *the* Englishman."

"Of course, the chap she wants will have changed his name, and her only chance—if the man has been transferred from Sidi—is to meet somebody who can identify him from her description," said John.

"Clever lad," approved Digby, "you've got it. Here's a girl looking for her Thomas, and hasn't got the vaguest idea as to what he now calls himself. She can't even go about like Grace or Zuleika asking for him by his Christian name, and, even if he's in Sidi, it's like looking for a needle in a haystack; and if he's in Morocco or the Sahara or the Sudan or Madagascar or Tonkin, she'd never find him at all. He *may* be here, of course. . . ."

"And that's where we come in," said John, wringing out the shirt that he had washed. "By Jove," he added, suddenly straightening himself up, "it couldn't be Isobel!"

"Of course not, you fat ass. That's what I thought the moment Klingen spoke. But it was only yesterday you had a letter from her. And if she came here, she'd have no need to stop strangers in the street and ask if they spoke English. She'd only have to send a card round from the hotel to the Barracks addressed to *Légionnaire* John Smith, No. 18896, saying that she was at the Hotel."

"Of course," agreed John sadly. "I spoke before I thought."

"People who never think, inevitably do that," observed Digby loftily.

"Now stop both thinking and talking and listen," he continued.

"La Cigale, who was standing there, peeling away as though he'd been a hotel scullion all his life, instead of a military attaché and ornament of Courts, suddenly said:

" 'Why! That must be the lady with whom I had so charming and delightful an adventure last night.' "

"You know how the poor old dear talks. He went on:

" 'I was sitting in the Gardens, not feeling very happy, when a lady came and sat down on the same seat. She was young, beautiful, and a gentlewoman. She paid me the compliment . . .'

"And here the poor old dear bowed most gracefully towards me—

" '. . . of asking me if I were English. I replied in French that I was not, but that I could speak the language quite well, and we had quite a long talk. I promised to mention to all the Englishmen whom I knew, that there was an English lady looking for a compatriot. But the whole matter had gone completely out of my mind until Klingen spoke just now. It must be the same lady. . . . This absent-mindedness is terrible. . . .'

"And the old chap went off into apologies and regrets that he'd forgotten to tell us."

"Hullo, here's Beau," interrupted John. "Beau," he added, "get some mutton-fat, or dripping or something, and make your hair extra beautiful. We're going calling on a lady this evening, at the *Hôtel de l'Europe.*"

Beau's eyes opened a little wider as he looked from John to Digby.

"Claudia here?" he asked.

"No," replied John. "Nor Isobel."

"Oh, no," added Digby. "It's Grace or Zuleika or Zenobia or Aggie or somebody," and he proceeded to tell Beau that there was an English girl who had the courage to walk the streets of an evening and stop passing soldiers, to inquire if they were English or knew any Englishmen in the Legion.

"We must go and put ourselves at her disposal," said Michael Geste.

§ 3

Helen Malenton, sitting at "tea" in her room, and honestly endeavouring to detect any remotely tea-like flavour in the luke-warm liquid that trickled reluctantly from a grudging coffee-pot, was losing heart and hope, if not faith and charity. From the day that Barry had disappeared, leaving only a letter of passionate renunciation of her, and even more passionate denunciation of himself, she had kept a stout heart, high hope and profound faith.

Being a firm believer in the great truth that Heaven helps those that help themselves, she had done her utmost to merit the help of Heaven, but hope had been deferred and undoubtedly her heart had grown sick—with apprehension, disappointment, and the feeling that the expected help had not been forthcoming.

She rose and went to the window that looked across a dirty street to a dusty garden, and, turning from the familiar and unsavoury prospect, began once more to pace the more familiar and less savoury room—hideously ugly as only the sitting-room of a provincial hotel can be.

"I *won't* give up," she said. . . .

"Faith as a grain of mustard seed . . . I *know* he's alive, because he could not die without my being aware of it. . . . My heart would die too. . . . Only believe and . . . if you want anything hard enough it comes to pass. Effort is never wasted."

Seating herself on an unbelievable sofa of stamped velvet, she stared unseeingly at the incredible carpet, her tense hands clenched on either side of her drawn face.

"Oh, God," she whispered aloud. *"Do* help me. Life isn't a welter of blind chance. . . . Oh, how long? . . . If there were a ray of hope. . . . A sign. . . ."

She sprang from her seat as the door opened and a dirty nondescript *garçon* of no particular nationality, and arrayed chiefly in a green baize apron, entered bearing an envelope in his grimy hand—an envelope addressed "To the English lady staying at the *Hôtel de l'Europe.*"

Murmuring that this was apparently *pour Made-*

moiselle, the youth explained that three soldiers were waiting below, for an answer.

Tearing the envelope open with trembling fingers, Helen Malenton read:

"Three English *légionnaires* would like to inquire whether they can be of any help to you; and, if so, will be delighted to put their services at your disposal."

Foolish and irrational hope sprang up in her heart.

An answer to prayer? A gleam of light in her darkest hour, the darkest hour before the dawn?

"Where are they, these soldiers?" she asked eagerly.

"Below in the *fumoir*, Madame."

"I will come down," said Helen quietly, and endeavoured to conceal the excitement that surged up within her, and caused her limbs to tremble.

Three handsome youths, obviously Englishmen, rose and bowed as she entered the stale and dingy lounge.

"Good evening. Will you allow our excellent intentions to excuse our intrusion?" said one of them. "I am—er—William Brown and these are my brothers Thomas Jones and John Smith."

Helen Malenton gravely shook hands with her visitors as Digby remarked:

"Same family, but different names. Curious, but quite simple—like us."

"Yes," agreed John. "William is curious and Thomas is simple."

"I think I understand," replied the girl. "My name is Helen Malenton, and I'm most grateful to you for coming. I most thankfully accept your offer of help. I have just discovered that a friend of mine—my fiancé, in fact—is in the Legion, and I've come to look for him. He disappeared suddenly. Nothing wrong; he is absolutely incapable of doing anything base or mean."

Her voice trembled.

"Look at *me*, Miss Malenton," smiled Digby. "You have but to glance at my countenance to be assured that I could do nothing wrong, and am absolutely incapable of anything base or mean. Yet I disappeared suddenly, and am in the Legion. And, in a lesser degree, this applies to my brothers—who also disappeared suddenly."

The girl smiled, and with regained self-control, continued:

"I am sure you all understand."

"Absolutely," murmured Michael. "We are in a position to do so, and may I add we quite understand that a man who is your fiancé must be an honourable gentleman."

"Oh, he's one of the noblest and bravest of men who ever lived," said the girl impulsively. "He hasn't a fault or a failing, except that he is headstrong and rash, and yet very sensitive really. You know how such a person can be beautifully good-tempered and yet—well—at times *hot*-tempered."

"Oh, rather," agreed Digby. "They are the best sort. Pure gold from the furnace—and with the warmth of the furnace still in the heart of them—noble, brave and generous. I'm like that myself," and smiled infectiously.

Helen Malenton laughed for the first time in many months.

"Oh, we'll find him all right," he added. "What's he like? Is he like me in face as well as character?"

"No," smiled Helen. "He's a very handsome man . . ."

Michael and John grinned appreciatively, and Digby looked sad, modest and embarrassed.

". . . but as dark as you are fair, I was going to say. Tall, broad-shouldered and spare. Extremely handsome—almost too much so, for a man—large eyes, silky black hair with a lovely wave in it, aquiline nose, small moustache, rather small mouth, a cleft chin. He had a complexion like a girl's. I used to chaff him about it, and tell him it wasn't right. He would laugh, and say it was due to his having been brought up solely by his mother, for his father died when he was a baby."

An awful thought struck Michael Geste. *Jones!* Of course it must be the poor chap who called himself Jones! Poor devil! . . . And oh, this poor,

poor girl! The unhappy, overwrought, devil-driven Jones, too sensitive, highly-strung and introspective even for ordinary life—much more so for life in the Legion—the very last place in the world for a man of his temperament.

Had they done their best for him? What more could they have done? They'd been most kind and friendly of course, and they had only got to know him on the day he committed suicide. It was Digby who had discovered him and brought him along. Had he said anything about a girl, in telling them his tragi-comic piteous story?

And he had shot himself.

The poor girl was just too late. . . . Ghastly . . . Oh, this was terrible.

He glanced at his brothers, and realized that the same thought had entered their minds. Digby was eyeing him apprehensively and he generally knew what his twin was thinking. John was looking very grave and thoughtful.

"You haven't told us his name," he said, for the sake of saying something while he considered the best way of breaking the terrible news to the girl, should his fears prove justified.

"Chartres," was the reply. "Sir Barry Chartres; but I don't suppose he would use his own name."

"I know the name perfectly well," remarked Beau, and added, "No, he wouldn't use it in the Legion.

You don't know what he calls himself now, of course."

"No," replied the girl.

"I wonder if he called himself Jones," said John, eyeing Michael.

"Quite likely," replied the girl. "Do you know an Englishman of that *nom de guerre?*"

"We *did*," admitted Michael.

"Did?" queried Helen Malenton quickly. "Is he . . . ?"

"Was Sir Barry Chartres ever in the British Army? Did he ever go to India?"

"Yes, yes, he did. He transferred from his County Regiment to the Indian Army, in the hope of seeing some active service."

The girl rose to her feet and faced them with shining eyes and parted lips.

"What is your friend like? You said '*did*.' Does that mean he has gone away from here? Where, where . . . ? Oh, it must be Barry! There wouldn't be *two* Englishmen here, who had both been in the Indian Army. Oh, *please* tell me quickly where he has gone?"

Seldom had the three brothers felt more miserably uncomfortable.

John and Digby looked to Beau for the next move, feeling that the situation could not be in better hands, and, while prepared to help him in every way, thankful that he was leader and spokesman.

What could he do? This was going to be really painful.

"Look here, Miss Malenton," said Beau Geste. "Suppose you leave everything to us. We are complete strangers to you, I know, but you can trust us absolutely. . . ."

"Rather," chimed in Digby and John.

". . . and we will do our best for you; we should love to. What I suggest is that you go back to England at once and we'll carry on. Do! I'll write to you immediately, when there is any definite news. It must be wretched for you here, and we three can do all sorts of things that are impossible for you. Go home to-morrow, and leave it to us."

"I don't know how to thank you," replied Helen Malenton. "But I couldn't, I simply couldn't. I *had* to come here, the moment I discovered that Barry had joined the Legion, and I must stay here until I am absolutely convinced that he is not in Sidi-bel-Abbès. And I shall only leave this place to go to some other in which he may possibly be."

"Suppose, for the sake of argument, he were dead," said Michael gravely.

"Oh, he isn't, he *couldn't* be," the girl protested.

"I want you to answer my question," replied Michael. "Suppose it."

The girl smiled through gathering tears.

"Why then, I could—and should—follow him, of course," she answered. "I don't want to talk wildly, and be melodramatic, but I am going to find him, either in this world or the next."

A silence fell upon the four. Digby wiped the palms of his hands with his handkerchief.

Suppose it had been Isobel looking for *him*.

"Please don't," murmured John, with the slight nervous cough which his brothers knew to be an expression of deep embarrassment at deep feeling.

Suppose it had been Isobel looking for *him*.

"Well, then," said Michael, "if you won't go home and won't leave here till you have a clue leading elsewhere, just remain quietly here, and let us work for you. We'll hunt out every English *légionnaire* in Sidi, and do our utmost to find out what has become of all those who have been here during the last five years. It'll be quite simple, for there are very few Englishmen in the Legion. We shall be able to eliminate most of them from the list very easily."

"Yes, but where *has* this friend of yours gone, please?" interrupted the girl. "You don't tell me. It is almost certainly Barry. I'll follow up this clue just as soon as I'm sure that Barry himself is not here—and that should be easy, now that you three are going to help me. I thank you a thousand times."

"Not at all. Pray don't speak of it," replied Michael. "It is both a duty and a great pleasure. My only fear is lest we fail or—or—have to bring you bad news. We'll go now, and start work at once."

And the brothers rose to take their departure.

"Where *did* your friend *go*, please?" repeated the girl as she extended her hand to Michael.

"That's what we're going to find out," was the reply.

§ 4

"A brave and charming gentlewoman," said Beau as they marched down the street from the *Hôtel de l'Europe*.

"Yes," agreed Digby. "If only the late Mr. 'Jones' had been as brave, and had stuck it out a little longer! How are we going to tell her he blew his brains out just before she came?"

"We aren't," replied Michael.

"You mean we're going to say he died fighting bravely beneath the Legion's flag?" asked John.

"I'm not sure we're going to tell her he's dead at all," was the enigmatic reply.

"Enlighten us, Uncle," said Digby.

"I'm not at all certain that poor old Jones is the man. I've got an idea."

"So have I," said John.

"The Man with the Face?" asked Michael.

"Clever lad," he approved.

"By Jove!" ejaculated Digby. "Of course! *Of course!* Brainy birds! I never thought of that.

He fits exactly, and of the two it's far more likely that *her* man would be the one who didn't commit suicide. I don't believe it was poor old Jones at all. Oh, brains, brains! I somehow feel certain it is the Man with the Face."

"So do I," agreed John. "Her description of the long-lost lover suits him even better than the late Jones. I got the impression of a big chap from her description, and Jones wasn't enormous."

"No," observed Michael, "but he wasn't by any means a small man, and I wouldn't build much on that particular point. I imagine that any average-sized ma is a fine huge hero to the girl who loves him."

"Yes, I suppose even we are," agreed Digby, his thoughts at Brandon Abbas.

"Yes," said Michael and John simultaneously, their thoughts in the same place.

"Still it really is an idea and a clue—and a hope," said Digby, "and we'll follow it up for all it's worth. I vote we now palter with the truth, and say that the ex-Indian Army man, to whom we referred, is at Arzew, and that we are on his trail."

"It isn't paltering with the truth so much as switching it over," said Michael. "A line of inquiry that was to lead us to the Legion Cemetery in Sidi-bel-Abbès, now leads us to the Convalescent Camp at Arzew."

"I say," broke in John. "There isn't very much

time to lose, is there? Didn't the Man with the
Face say his time was up, and that he was going to
re-enlist? Pretty rotten for Miss Malenton if he
did so, just before we told her we'd found him!"

"Yes, and that raises another snag," said Michael
loftily. "A point upon which I have been wisely
and profoundly pondering while you and your
brother jibber and jabber and gabble."

"A snag isn't a point, may I observe?" commented
Digby coldly. "A point is that which has no parts
nor magnitude."

"Like your brain, my lad," answered Michael.
"You call this unfortunate gentleman 'the Man with
the Face.' Well, does it or does it not occur to what
we must call your mind, that if he *is* the man, he is
certainly not going to bring his poor carven face and
lay it before his best girl?"

"By Jove!" said Digby. "I never thought of
that."

"What a ghastly position!" murmured John.

"But surely," he added, "the girl wouldn't turn
him down because he's hideously disfigured. Not if
she really loves him."

Would Isobel turn *him* down if his face were so
slashed and scarred that he was unrecognizable? She
would not.

"But it's not of the *girl* that I'm thinking at all.
It's the man, my good little asses. I believe she'd
stick to him if he'd lost both eyes, both ears, both lips,

and both nose. *He*'ll raise the trouble, not she."

"You're right, Beau," said Digby. "He will.
I've got the impression that he is the sort of person
who'd do just that. I believe he'd sooner meet anybody in the world than the woman he loved."

"I can quite understand it too," agreed Beau.
"He'd feel that she'd be repressing shudders the
whole time, and fighting a desire to scream. He'd
be afraid that, purely out of loyalty and decency,
she'd swear she not only still loved him, but couldn't
live without him."

"While, all the time, life was a purgatory to her—
a hideous nightmare," added John.

"Depends on the woman, of course," said Digby.
"There are women who'd honestly and truly love
their man all the more because he was a bit chipped
and cracked. Want to make it up to him, and mother
him."

"Yes," agreed John, "there are. And then again
there are equally fine women who simply could not
bear it—literally could not stand the sight of a face
like that, without being physically sick."

"And that's what poor old Carven Face will think,
I'm afraid," said Michael. "He'll write and tell her
he's not the only pebble on the beach and beg her to
acquire a nice round smooth pebble that has not been
carved—by Arabs. We'll do our best, anyhow, and
we shall have to be careful and clever."

"John, *you*'ll have to be careful," stated Digby.

§ 5

Le Légionnaire Robinson had returned from Arzew, his intention of re-enlisting confirmed by an offer of promotion to the rank of Corporal if he did so. He realized that he would probably regret the step when it was too late, but after impartially studying his terrible face, with the help of a good mirror, he decided that the best place for such a work of art was a desert outpost at the ultimate Back of Beyond.

"A pretty picture," he smiled grimly, as he regarded his reflection. "A picture which should certainly be hung," and he smiled again.

But only *le Légionnaire* Robinson knew that the facial contortion was a smile.

Seated alone in a dark corner of the canteen, on the night of his return to Sidi-bel-Abbès, his hand, as usual, across his face as though to shade his eyes, he saw an Englishman enter the room and approach him. Pulling his *képi* well down over his face, he turned away and appeared to fall asleep.

"Discouraging," murmured Beau to himself as he turned to the zinc-topped bar, and procured a bottle of wine and a couple of glasses.

Seating himself beside Robinson, Beau Geste poured out two glasses of wine, coughed slightly, somewhat in the manner of John, and remarked:

"As you say, Robinson, this is an unwarrantable intrusion."

"I haven't said anything," growled Robinson.

"No, not aloud," agreed Michael. "Very nice of you, but I am butting in nevertheless, and I apologize—and my reason is my excuse. I've got a most important message for you."

"Oh?" grunted Robinson, evincing no interest whatever.

"From a lady," added Michael.

"Yes?" growled Robinson, with the complete indifference of one who received messages from ladies every few minutes.

"From *Miss Helen Malenton*," enunciated Michael, slowly and distinctly.

Robinson's hand, extended to raise his glass, knocked it off the table.

"Ah?" he murmured, in the tone of one who was more than a little bored by Miss Malenton's attentions.

Watching the man's face as closely as was possible, Michael decided that it had shown no faintest sign of any feeling whatsoever; no slightest flicker of emotion; no shadow of change of expression, as he spoke the girl's name. But, as he told himself, he could not see the eyes properly, and the rest of the face was hardly calculated to register emotion of any sort. In fact, it was not a face at all, but a mask, a mask of tortured flesh, probably incapable of showing what its unfortunate owner felt, even when he wished it to do so.

Yes, decided Michael, *le Légionnaire* Robinson was well entrenched behind the double defence of the mask he wished to wear and the mask he *had* to wear. Only his hands betrayed him, as so often they betray the man who has perfect facial control.

This was going to be a difficult job, and Robinson was going to behave exactly as they had feared.

"She is here," he said quietly. "Here in Sidi-bel-Abbès."

"Yes?" was the discouraging reply, in a voice as cool and quiet as Michael's own.

"She wants to see you, Robinson," continued Michael.

"To *see* me?" asked Robinson. "Five *sous* a peep, or something like that? Have you gone into the impresario business, or what?"

The man was certainly bitter.

"Don't *you* want to see *her?*" said Michael patiently.

"Not the faintest desire, thanks," was the uncompromising answer.

Michael sighed, and picking up Robinson's glass, he refilled it.

"Let's drink to her health," he suggested.

"With pleasure," growled Robinson. He raised his glass, muttered something unintelligible, and drained it.

"She's an amazingly brave, staunch, loyal woman," observed Michael.

"I'm sure she is," agreed the other.

"And she's in a pretty bad way, too," added Michael somewhat sharply. And—

"Look here, Robinson," more sharply still, "at the risk of your considering me an impudent meddler, I really must say this—When a girl has suffered on a man's account as Miss Malenton has done on yours—and when moreover she has travelled to ·Sidi-bel-Abbès to look for him—I do think it's up to him to see her."

"Yes," agreed Robinson politely.

"Well, don't you think it's the very least he can do?"

"Oh, quite," agreed Robinson again.

"Then you *will* see her?" said Michael promptly.

"No, Mr. What-is-your-name, I will *not*—and we'll now close this somewhat boring conversation," yawned *le Légionnaire* Robinson, as he arose and departed thence.

§ 6

"Ah, this is a job that wants brains, of course," observed Digby at the conclusion of Michael's ac-

count of his discouraging interview with *le Légionnaire* Robinson. "Leave it to *me;* do as I tell you,
and all will be well.

"D'you mind if I visit Miss Malenton unham-
pered and unhindered—I mean, unaccompanied and
unsupported, by your two silly faces?" he added.

"Quite hopeless, my dear chap," said John, "even
if Miss Malenton were not absolutely wrapped up
in her lost lover. And, in any case, she would prefer
a visit from the nicest of us."

"We must try and keep him out of the sun,
Beau," urged Digby, surveying his younger brother
compassionately; "and while he keeps out of the sun
I'm going into the shadows—of the *Hôtel de
l'Europe* to propound a scheme to Miss Malenton."

"And why this sudden desire for a tête-à-tête?"
inquired Beau. "If you feel you have a Mission
and a Message and that we are neither worthy nor
competent . . ."

"Well, it's only partly that," smiled Digby. "But
I feel you'd be much more competent to play your
little parts in my plan, if you knew nothing about
it."

"Quite probably, I should say," observed Michael.
"What are our parts?"

"Merely to lend your countenances and your
money to my scheme. It's a dinner-party. We are
going to dine and wine Mr. Robinson. A dinner
to mark the occasion of his coming promotion and

re-enlistment—a most hilarious celebration and all that."

"Where?" inquired John.

"At the *Hôtel de l'Europe*," was the reply.

"He'd never go there," objected Michael. "He literally wouldn't show his face in a crowded café like that."

"We shall have a private room," said Digby. "He'll come all right. He's very fond of me—naturally."

"And if he does, what's the idea? Make him drunk and get his word of honour that he will at least consent to an interview with Miss Malenton before he re-enlists?"

"Wrong again," was the answer. "Now ask no more questions, but be prepared to dine and wallow in the wassail on Sunday evening with Robinson at the *Hôtel de l'Europe*. This is Friday, isn't it? I'm going to see Robinson to-night and Miss Malenton to-morrow, and thereafter you shall behold the wondrous works of your Uncle Digby."

As one man, his brothers emitted a loud derisive grunt.

The charming Digby charmed, and the morose and bitter Robinson succumbed, on learning that the dinner was to be held in a private room, and that absolutely nobody but the three Englishmen was to be invited to it.

"It's extraordinarily nice of you fellows," he growled, "and I can't refuse."

§ 7

The dinner went extremely well, for the Gestes were what they were, and Robinson strove to be what he once had been, a gay and debonnaire gentleman. The warmth of their kindly friendship unfroze the once genial current of his soul.

No mention whatever was made of Miss Helen Malenton, and when, at the wine-and-walnut stage of the feast, she entered the room, neither Michael nor John was greatly surprised.

The four men rose to their feet, and Robinson stared, his mangled face utterly expressionless.

Helen Malenton, her eyes shining, her countenance transfigured with emotion ineffable and uncontrolled, gazed at him for a moment, uttered a little gasping cry, rushed to him and flung her arms about his neck.

"Oh, *Barry, Barry,* my darling!" she sobbed.

Seizing her arms in his hands, Robinson removed them from about his neck and gently but firmly pushed her from him.

"I don't know you," he said.

"Oh, my own *darling,* my *dearest!*" cried the girl. "Your friend told me that your face had been wounded. . . . I was prepared for it. . . . My sweetheart, it is *nothing* to me."

"I don't know you," repeated Robinson, his out-stretched hand between them.

"Barry, my *love*, my *darling*, don't be so foolish! If such a thing be possible, I love you all the more! . . . How can you possibly think I should shrink from you? Why, my darling sweetheart, I used to think you were far *too* handsome for a man. . . . You were *pretty* almost. I swear to God that I like you better like this, even though I couldn't love you better."

The man's hand fell to his side in a gesture of resignation and acceptance, and the girl's arms were again clasped about his neck.

"I am *not* Barry," he groaned, and as, with the laugh of a mother humouring her child she drew his head down until their lips met, his arms went about her and crushed her to him.

Except for themselves, the room was empty.

§ 8

"Once again, good-bye, and God for ever bless you," said *le Légionnaire* Robinson, wringing the hands of the brothers, as the four stood at the bar-rack-gate.

"You'll keep your promise and visit us on the island that we are going to buy—one of the Islands of the Blest, of which we shall be the sole inhabitants, and where no one but her will see my face. . . . God! To think that to-day I should have re-enlisted and gone back into hell instead of going off into Paradise with this noble and wonderful woman. How can I ever *begin* to thank you?"

"No need," replied Beau Geste. "It's been the most tremendous pleasure. We shall always be happy to think that we brought you and Miss Malenton together again."

"You didn't bring us together *again*," smiled Robinson.

Surprised, the Geste brothers stared uncomprehendingly.

"I never set eyes on her in my life until last night," he said, and as he turned away added, *"But she won't believe it!"*

II

A GENTLEMAN OF COLOUR

I

L E LÉGIONNAIRE YATO was one of the quietest, most retiring and self-effacing men in the Company, and one of the most modest. It seemed to be his highest ambition—an ambition which he almost attained—to escape notice, to blush unseen, and to hide his light beneath a bushel.

And yet, to those who had the seeing eye, he was an extremely interesting person, and for many reasons. He greatly intrigued the Geste brothers, and in spite of his meek, self-effacing humility, they took note of him from the day he arrived, and watched him with interest.

At first sight, and to the casual eye, he was a poor specimen—small, narrow-shouldered, weedy, with yellowish face, a wiry scrub of short hair, and a silly sort of little straggling moustache, the loss of one hair of which would have made an obvious difference.

The mere look of him caused Sergeant-major Lejaune to feel unwell, and he made no secret of the fact. Indeed, he promised to stuff the little man into a slop-pail and to be ill upon him.

Never had the Geste boys, who were watching the arrival of this batch of recruits, seen so hopelessly dull, stupid and apathetic a face in their lives, as that of this recruit, while Sergeant-major Lejaune regarded it; never had they seen one more acutely intelligent, expressive, spirited and observant as Sergeant-major Lejaune passed on.

"See that?" chuckled Digby to his brothers.

"Yes," replied Beau. "If I were Lejaune I think I'd let that gentleman alone. Wonder what brought him here."

"He's come 'for to admire and for to see,' I should think," said John, "and come a long way too." And as the line of recruits turned to their left and marched off, he added, "His shoulders have been drilled too, and I'll bet you any amount he's worn a sword and spurs."

Other interesting facts transpired later. The mild little man could cut your hair and shave you beautifully, and he could speak your language if you were English, French, Russian or German. He could also sketch rather marvellously, and do pictures of surpassing merit in water-colour and in oil. He preferred to do these drawings and pictures out in the open air—the more open the better—and he had done some beauties of the country round Quetta, for example, and the Khyber Pass, showing all the pretty forts and things.

His manners were delightful, and he gave offence

to no man, least of all to those set in authority over him.

To their surprise, the Geste boys—who, during his early recruit days went out of their way to help this lonely little stranger in a strange land—discovered that he knew England fairly well, particularly Portsmouth, Plymouth, Weymouth, Rosyth, Aldershot and Chatham.

For the most part, *le Légionnaire* Yato's inoffensiveness, humility, excellent manners, and blameless conduct, kept him out of almost all trouble, official or private—but not entirely. Although a man may camouflage himself with a protective colouring of drab dullness and uniformity, which does indeed protect him by hiding him from general notice, it may not always suffice to hide him from particular notice. His very quietness and mild meekness may be his undoing through attracting the eye of those who need a butt for their diversion, and even more urgently need long-suffering meekness and mildness in that butt.

Two such were Messieurs Brandt and Haff, men who, themselves the butt of their superiors for their stupidity, slovenliness, and general worthlessness, must find someone to be their butt in turn. Almost a necessity of their existence was someone upon whom they could visit the contumely heaped upon themselves. Subconsciously they felt that, for their self-respect's sake, they must stand upon something lower than themselves, or be themselves the lowest things of all.

And this recruit, Yato, seemed so suitable to their purpose, so dull and stupid, so unable to protect himself, so harmless, helpless and hopeless, so proper a target for the shafts of their wit.

So they put thorn-brush in his bed, and unpleasant matter in his *képi* and on his pillow; stole his kit; put a dead mouse in his coffee; arranged a booby-trap for his benefit; fouled his white uniform after he had washed and ironed it; gave him false information, messages and orders, to his discomfiture and undoing; hid his brushes just before kit inspection; stole his soap; cut his boot-laces and generally demonstrated their own wit, humour and jocularity as well as his stupidity, harmlessness and general inferiority to themselves.

One day, Beau Geste and his brothers entered their barrack-room and discovered the cringing Yato ruefully eyeing *les Légionnaires* Brandt, Haff, Klingen and Schwartz—four huge and powerful men, who were proposing to toss him in a blanket, having first denuded him of all clothing. The bright idea had been that of Brandt. He had proposed it; Haff had seconded it; and the two, realizing with their wonted brilliance that a blanket has four corners, had impressed the services of the delighted and all-too-willing Schwartz and Klingen.

"Where shall we do it?" roared Schwartz, a great

bearded ruffian, strong as a bull, rough as a bear, and sensitive as a wart-hog.

"You won't do it at all," said Beau Geste, advancing to where the four stood about Yato's disordered bed, from which they had dragged a blanket.

"I do not like to be touched and handled," said Yato quietly, in the silence that fell upon the surprised bullies. "Please leave me alone."

"They are going to leave you alone," said Beau Geste.

"Yes! Watch us!" shouted Brandt, and sprang at the cringing little Jap as the mighty Schwartz turned upon Michael Geste, his great hands clenched, his eyes blazing, and his teeth bared. But as he raised his fist to strike, he swung about as something, or someone, fell against him from behind.

It was Brandt.

Using his right arm as though it were an axe, of which the side of the hand from little finger to wrist, was the edge, Yato had struck Brandt an extraordinary cutting, chopping blow on the neck, below and behind the ear.

As Brandt fell against Schwartz and to the ground, apparently dead, the Jap seized Haff by the collar of his tunic, where it fastened at the throat, and jerked his head violently downward, at the same time himself springing violently upward, so that the top of his bullet-head struck Haff between the eyes with tremendous force.

The huge Schwartz changing his line of attack, as he turned about, sprang upon Yato, as might a lion upon a gazelle. The gazelle threw itself at the lion's feet—but not in supplication. Before the astonished Gestes could come to the rescue, they saw Yato fling his arms about Schwartz's ankles, causing the upper part of his body to fall forward. And as it did so, Yato astonishingly arose, hugging Schwartz's ankles to his breast.

The result of this lightning movement was that the big man pitched upon his head so heavily that nothing but its thickness saved him from concussion of the brain, and it seemed impossible that his neck should not be broken. And, almost as the body of Schwartz reached the ground, Yato sprang at Klingen, who was in the act of drawing a knife.

Seizing the wrist of the hand that held this ugly weapon, the Japanese wheeled so that he stood beside Klingen, shoulder to shoulder, and facing in the same direction. As he did so, he thrust his left arm beneath Klingen's right, and across his chest, at the same time pulling Klingen's straightened right arm violently downward. There was a distinctly audible crack as the arm broke above the elbow.

Where four burly bullies had gathered about a cringing little man, three lay insensible and one knelt whimpering with pain.

"I do not like to be touched and handled," smiled Yato.

"I don't think you will be, to any great extent," smiled Digby Geste in return.

§ 2

But a man may be touched without being handled, and it was the dominating desire of Klingen's life to "touch" Yato.

It became essential to his continued existence that he should avenge his broken arm, his humiliating defeat and utter overthrow.

For Klingen was a conceited man, devoid of pride, but filled with self-esteem.

He was handsome and he knew it. But "handsome is as handsome does," and Klingen had done most evilly. It was, in fact, by reason of his last and most treacherous love-affair that he was hiding in the Legion.

He was big and strong and bold, and he had been made to grovel groaning at the feet of a man one-half his size. He hated pain, and he had been made to suffer agony unspeakable.

And so he was obsessed with thoughts of vengeance and lived for the day when the Japanese should make full payment for the insult and the injury he had put upon the bold and brave, the hardy and handsome Klingen.

Meanwhile, a certain poor satisfaction could be obtained by lashing the unspeakable Oriental verbally; for, curiously enough, the Japanese did not resent such abuse—apparently. So when Klingen came out of hospital he poured forth upon his quiet shrinking enemy all the choice epithets, insults, and injurious foulness that he had perpetrated, polished and perfected during the miserable leisure of his enforced retirement.

He assured Yato that he was a yellow monkey, a loathsome "native," a *coloured* man, if indeed he were a man at all. Klingen explained fully and carefully that he had always drawn the colour line, and had drawn it straight and strong; also that it was, to him, the very worst aspect of life in the Legion that one was forced to herd with coloured men natives, that foul scum (or sediment) of humanity which is barely human. He explained that while he hated niggers, abhorred Arabs, and detested Chinese, words utterly failed him to express the loathing horror with which he regarded Japs. Brown was bad, black was worse, but what could be said of yellow? That vile bilious colour was disgusting in *anything*—but in human beings it was . . . !

One could be but dumbly sick, and whenever his revolted eye fell upon *le Légionnaire* Yato, his revolting stomach almost had its way, and in crude pantomime Klingen would express his feelings.

And Yato would smile.

Furthermore, the good Klingen was at infinite

pains to indicate the private and personal hideous-
ness of Yato as distinct from his national bestiality.
He would invite all present to contemplate the little
man's unspeakable eyes, indescribable moustache, un-
mentionable nose, unbelievable hair, and unutterable
ugliness.

And Yato would smile.

But it was noticed that Klingen never touched
the Japanese, nor sought physical retaliation for his
broken arm. Nor did Messieurs Haff, Brandt and
Schwartz. In fact, these three appeared to enter-
tain feelings rather of reluctant admiration and
sporting acquiescence than of hatred and vengeance,
and when Klingen proposed various schemes for
Yato's undoing, they would have none of them.
They were quite content to regard him as a freak of
nature and a human marvel.

Of him they had had quite enough, and it was
their firm intention to leave him severely alone.

Not so Klingen. If Klingen were to live, Yato
must die; or, better still—far, far better still—suffer
some dire, ineffable humiliation, life-long and worse
than death.

.   .   .   .

Seated in a row, on a bench in the Jardin Publique,
Beau Geste in the middle, the three brothers contemplated the Vast Forever without finding life one
grand sweet song.

Life was hard, comfortless, small and monotonous; but quite bearable so long as it yielded a lazy hour when they could sit thus, smoking their pipes in silent communion, or in idle and disjointed conversation about Brandon Abbas. Frequently Michael would speculate upon Claudia's doings; Digby and John upon those of Isobel.

"Here comes old Yato," murmured Digby. "I'm going to hit him, one day," he added.

"What for?" inquired John.

"Fun," replied Digby.

"Fun for whom—Yato?" inquired Michael.

"Yes," replied Digby. "I want to see what happens to me."

"You won't see," asserted Michael. "You'll only feel."

"Well, you two shall watch and tell me exactly what happens," said Digby. "Then I can do it to you two."

"Good evening, gentlemen," said Yato, with a courteous salute. "Excuse that I approach you."

The brothers rose as one, saluted the tiny man, and invited him to be seated with them.

"Excuse that I intrude with my insignificant presence, gentlemen, but I would humbly venture to do you the honour, and pay you the compliment, of asking a favour of you. You are *samurai*. If one of you gave assent with no more than a nod of his head, it would be a binding contract. . . . Will you do something for me?"

"Yes," replied Beau Geste.

"You do not stop to make conditions, nor to hear what the request may be. You do not fear that it may be something you would not like to do."

"No," replied Beau Geste.

"Ah," smiled Yato, "as I thought. Well, I'm going a long walk one day soon, and I may want something done for me by a friend after I have gone. I do not *know* that I shall, but it is quite possible. . . ."

"We shall be delighted," said Beau Geste, and his brothers murmured assent.

Yato bowed deeply.

"Honourable sirs," he said.

"Better not tell us anything about your—er—long walk," said Beau Geste. "We shouldn't give you away, of course, but we're not good liars, I'm afraid."

"Oh," smiled Yato, "tell them anything and everything that you know, should you be questioned. The honourable authorities will be entirely welcome to me—if they can catch me."

And he rose to go.

"I will leave a note under your pillow or in your *musette*," he continued, addressing Beau Geste. "Good-bye, gentle and honourable sirs. May I have the distinction of shaking the hands?"

"Queer little cove and great little gentleman," observed Digby when Yato had departed.

"Yes," agreed Michael. "A very good friend and

a very dangerous enemy, I should say. I suppose he's in the Japanese Secret Service."

"I don't think I will hit him, after all," mused Digby.

§ 3

Colonel the Baron Hoshiri of the Japanese General Staff, and of the French Foreign Legion (in the name of Yato), made his way along the Rue de Daya with, as he would have said, a song in his heart. There was no smile upon his grim lips, nor expression of joy in his eyes nor upon his face. They were, in fact, utterly expressionless.

But he was very, very happy, for he was returning to his heaven upon earth, at the feet of Fuji Yama— the land of the cherry blossom, the chrysanthemum, the geisha, and the Rising Sun. He was leaving this land of barbarians devoid of manners, arts, graces and beauty.

Also, he had found a little friend, and she gave the lilt to the song that was in his heart.

A Flower from Japan.

Soiled and trodden and cast aside by these barbarian brutes, but still a Flower from Japan.

A pitiful little story—heartbreaking—but the little flower, picked up from the mud, dipped in pure cleansing dew, and set in a vase of fair water, was reviving.

He would take it back to Japan and it would bloom again and live, a thing of beauty and of joy.

Yes, a pitiful little tale.

Her parents had taken her to the *yoshiwara* to earn her dowry. There she had met her future husband, and thence she had been taken—rescued rather it seemed to her—by this man who so earnestly begged her to become his wife. He seemed a nice kind man, and her heart did not sink very much when he told her that they were going to travel to the wonderful West—for he was a merchant, and his business lay in Marseilles.

This was quite true, and in Marseilles, where his business lay, he sold her—in the way of business. Mr. Ah Foo (born in Saigon of a Chinese woman and a French Marine) did very well out of his little bride Sanyora—as he did out of all his other little brides, for he was what one might call a regular marrying man, and had entered the bonds of matrimony scores of times, and each of his wives had entered a bondage unescapable.

From Marseilles, Sanyora had been sold to a gentleman who travelled for his house, in Algiers, and had been taken to that house. Thence she had been appointed, without her knowledge or consent, to a vacancy (created by death—and a knife) in Oran. From there she had been sold into an even fouler bondage in Sidi-bel-Abbès.

Could she do nothing for herself? Yes—fight

like a tiger-cat until drugged, and scream appeals for help—in Japanese, the only language she knew.

And, in that language, Colonel Hoshiri had heard her cry to God for death, as he passed below the open shutters of a house in a slum of the Spanish quarter. He had entered, asked for the Japanese girl, made his way to her room, addressed her in Japanese, and told her he only wished to be a friend and deliverer.

And now Sanyora had her own pretty room in a private house in a respectable quarter, and the Colonel had a haven of rest and peace—a refuge and quiet place in which he could take his ease and hear his own language from beautiful lips. Between them, they had made it a tiny corner of Japan, and, day by day, Sanyora grew more and more to be the dainty, charming and delightful geisha, wholly attractive mistress of the arts that delight and soothe and charm the eye and ear—and heart.

.   .   .   .

As usual, *le Légionnaire* Yato was watched and followed by his bitter and relentless enemy, Klingen. A stab in the back, as he passed through some dark alley, would be simple enough, but it would be *too* simple. To a devil like Yato, it would have to be a death-stroke, and he might die without knowing who had killed him. That would be a very poor sort of vengeance.

What Klingen wanted was to hurt him, and hurt

him, and *hurt* him . . . humiliate him to the dust
. . . disgrace and degrade and shame him . . . torture him to death . . . but a long, slow, lingering
death. . . .

One night Yato might go to *le Village Nègre*.
Anything could happen there. There was no foul
and fearful villainy that one could not buy, and a
very little money went a very long way in *le Village
Nègre*. One could certainly have a man waylaid,
knocked on the head, gagged and bound and tied
down on a native bedstead in a dark room in a native
house. One could hire the room and have the key.
One could visit one's victim nightly, and taunt him
throughout the night. One could let him starve to
death, or keep him alive for weeks.

The things one could do! What about that lovely
trick of inverting a brass bowl on the man's bare
stomach . . . a rat inside the bowl . . . some red-
hot charcoal on top of the bowl. . . .

How long does it take the rat to eat his way into,
and through, the man? Might it not be too quick a
death? No, that was the whole point of it—a good
sound slow torture.

Klingen licked his lips and followed the distant
figure of Yato with his eyes.

Going to the same house again, was he? A pity
he did not go to *le Village Nègre*. What could be
the attraction here? A woman, of course.

Klingen pondered the thought. There might be

something in that . . . especially if he were fond
of her. An idea—of dazzling brilliance. Jealousy!
No vengeance like it—for a start. Get his woman
from him. Was there a girl alive who would give a
second glance at that hideous little yellow monkey
when the fine big handsome swaggering swash-
buckling Klingen was about? What an exquisite
moment when the girl (seated on Klingen's knee, her
head on Klingen's shoulder, her arms round Klingen's neck) turned languidly to Yato as Yato entered Yato's own room, and said to him in accents of
extremest scorn, "Get to hell out of this, you dirty
little yellow monkey. The sight and the smell of
you make me feel sick in my stomach."

That would be a great moment. And these
women could be bought.

· · · · · · ·

Ah, yes . . . the little yellow devil was turning
into the same house again. It *must* be a woman.

Klingen reconnoitred once again. The usual type
of house with a common stairway leading up from
a gloomy little basement hall to a rookery of rooms,
apartments and flats occupied by hard-working poor
people of the better sort.

Klingen hesitated, and for the first time entered
the house and looked round the dingy entrance-hall,
stone-floored, stucco-walled, gloomily lit by a smoky
oil-lamp hanging against the wall, and by the rays

that shone through iron-barred window-spaces from a street lamp.

Should he climb the bare, wooden stair that led to the floors above? Why not? Anyone might enter the wrong house by mistake when searching for a friend. Still, it was a pity Schwartz, Haff and Brandt could not be persuaded to come along and have some fun at the expense of the yellow monkey.

Footsteps. . . . Someone coming down the stairs. . . . A little man in seedy European clothing. . . . An idea . . .

"Excuse me, Monsieur," said Klingen, as the man reached the bottom of the stairs. "Can you tell me which is my friend's room? A *légionnaire*—a little fellow—Japanese."

The man shrugged his shoulders and made a gesture with his hands which showed that he was a Spaniard; also that he did not understand a word of what was being said to him.

Klingen mounted to the first floor, a bare landing, around three sides of which were closed, numbered doors. Should he tap at each in turn, and inquire for some non-existent person? And what should he do if one of them were opened by Yato? Suppose the yellow tiger-cat attacked him again? His mended arm tingled at the thought. What was he doing here at all? This longing for vengeance was driving him mad. . . .

Klingen turned back, descended to the street, and

took up his stand in a doorway from which he could keep watch upon the porch of the house in which was his enemy.

Another idea! . . . What about waiting until Yato left the house? He could then go in and knock at every door and ask:

"Is my friend *le Légionnaire* Yato here—a little Japanese?" If one of the doors were opened by some woman who replied, "No, he has just gone," he would know that he had found what he sought, and would get to work forthwith. He would soon show her the difference between a Yato and a Klingen. And if Klingen knew anything of women, and he flattered himself that he most certainly did, there was a bad time coming for the yellow devil. . . . He could almost hear the very accents in which she should say:

"Get out of my sight, you filthy yellow cur. I've got a *man* now!"

Yes, and Klingen would have his knife ready too, and this time he'd throw it, if Yato made trouble. And he also flattered himself that he knew something of knife-throwing.

. . . .

Ha! There he was. . . . Blister and burn him!

The retreating form of Yato turned the corner of the street, and Klingen darted across into the house. Running lightly up the stairs he knocked at the first door. No answer. He knocked again, and laid his ear against the wood.

Silence.

He knocked at the next. A fat, slatternly woman, candle in hand, opened the door and eyed him hardily.

"Well?" she inquired, running her eye contemptuously over his uniform.

"Monsieur Blanc?" inquired Klingen.

The woman slammed the door in his face.

The third and fourth rooms were apparently empty.

A child opened the door of the fifth, and seeing a *légionnaire*, shut it instantly. Hearing a man's deep growling voice within, Klingen passed on.

To Klingen's inquiry, at the sixth room, as to whether Monsieur Blanc lived here, the woman who occupied it replied that he did, but was at the moment in the wine-shop round the corner!

"Then may he sit there till he rots," observed Klingen, and climbed the second flight of stairs, and, arriving at a landing similar to the one below, repeated his strategy and tactics.

The first door was opened by a tiny dainty Japanese girl, and Klingen thrust his way into the room, closed the door behind him, locked it, and removed the key. He had found what he wanted.

The girl stood staring, between terror and surprise. This man was in a similar uniform to that which her lover wore. He must be his friend, otherwise how would he have known she was here? But her beloved had only just gone. Had something happened to him, and why had this man thrust in so roughly, uninvited? But they were rough and rude, these Western barbarians. Why had he come? Did he think this place was like one of those dreadful houses in Marseilles, Algiers and Oran? And she shuddered at the thought.

Oh, if she could only understand what he was saying and make herself understood by him! He seemed to be speaking of someone named Yato. Was it conceivable that he might understand a word of Japanese?

"I am the servant of the Colonel Hoshiri. What do you want?" she said in her own tongue.

And, for reply, Klingen snatched her up in his arms and kissed her violently.

Well, this was a fine *affaire!* . . . This marched! . . . She might, or might not, be Yato's girl, but most certainly she was. A Japanese would hardly be visiting a house in a Sidi-bel-Abbès side-street in which there was a Japanese woman, unless he were visiting her. Japs were not so common in the African hinterland as that. . . . But anyhow, and whoever she was, this was still a fine *affaire,* for here was Klingen the irresistible, locked up in a room with as pretty a little piece as he had ever clapped eyes on. And a very nice room, too, if a

little bare. Bed, cushions, hangings, flowers in vase
—yes, all very nice indeed.

And now for the little woman. A pity they could
not understand each other's language, but the language of love is universal. He could soon make
himself understood all right.

When *le Légionnaire* Klingen let himself out of
the room an hour or so later, he left a sobbing girl
lying upon the bed weeping as though her heart
would break; moaning as though it were already
broken.

But Klingen, as he walked back to barracks, smiled
greasily as he licked his lips, and encountering Yato
in the barrack-room, laughed aloud.

Yato was sitting on his bed engaged in *astiquage*
—the polishing of his belts and straps.

Having whispered his story, punctuated with loud
guffaws, to a little knot of his friends who evidently
enjoyed the joke hugely, Klingen went over and
stood in front of the Japanese, his hands on his hips,
and, rocking himself to and fro, from heels to toes,
leered exultingly. Without looking up, Yato continued waxing and polishing a cartridge-pouch.

Suddenly he stopped—remained perfectly still,
and stared at the floor between himself and Klingen.

Beau Geste drawing near, and watching carefully
as he polished his bayonet, thought that Yato sniffed
silently, as though trying to detect and capture an

odour. Yes, decided Beau, Yato could smell something, and that something puzzled him. Rising to
his feet, his hands behind him, and moving slowly,
the Japanese approached Klingen, his head thrust
forward, his nose obviously questing.

"What the hell!" growled Klingen, as Yato, his
face not very much above the big man's sash, deliberately smelt at him.

Yato returned to his cot without remark.

But it seemed as though a shadow crossed his face.
It was almost as though he changed colour.

§ 4

Le Légionnaire Klingen, smart in his walking-out
kit, a red *képi*, dark-blue tunic with green red-
fringed epaulettes, red breeches and white spats,
tightened his belt a little, pulled his bayonet frog
further back, and swaggered from the barrack-room.

It was "holiday" (pay-day) and he intended to
expend on wine the entire sum of 2½d. which he had
received. Thereafter, being full of good wine and
good cheer, it was his intention to see how the little
Japanese girl was getting on, and to cheer her loneliness with an hour of his merry society. He would
watch the yellow monkey go in, and wait till he came
out, and if the girl had locked her door, he would
tap and tap and knock and knock without saying
anything until she did open it.

What a fighting little spit-fire she was. But that was nine-tenths make-believe, and the other tenth was ignorance of French.

From his seat on a barrel, in the corner of a dark wine-shop which commanded a view of the street in which the girl's house stood, Klingen saw Yato approaching. Pulling down the vizor of his *képi*, and bending his head forward, so that his face was concealed, he waited until the Japanese had passed, and then abandoned himself to the pleasures of drinking, anticipation, and thoughts of revenge.

He was absolutely certain that the girl was Yato's, and, as he rolled his wine upon his tongue, he rolled upon the debauched palate of his mind the flavour of the lovely vengeance that combined the enormous double gratification of deep enjoyment to himself and deep injury to Yato. He honestly agreed with Klingen that Klingen was a great man, and never greater than in this manifestation of his skill—that made his own pleasure his enemy's agony at a time when his enemy's agony was his own greatest pleasure.

On the whole, it had turned out to be quite a good thing that Schwartz, Brandt and Haff had declined to take any further hand in baiting Yato. Any vengeance, obtained with their help, could only have been crude and obvious, and have contained but the single satisfaction of injuring Yato.

But this was subtle, private, worthy of Klingen.

"Yes, my friend," he mused, sucking the wine-drops from his moustache. "I hurt you by delighting myself, and you add immeasurably to that delight by being hurt."

And he laughed aloud.

A couple of thieves and their women, a fat person clothed from head to foot in brown corduroy, and an obese dealer in old clothes who wore a tarboosh (or fez) a frock-coat, a collarless blue shirt, football shorts, and a pair of curly-toed slippers, all turned to stare at the big soldier who laughed loudly at nothing.

"Mad," said a thief, and shrugged his shoulders.

"Drunk," growled the other.

"Mad *and* drunk," said a lady.

"*Que voulez-vous? C'est la Légion!*" observed her sister in joy, and drank to the health of *le Légionnaire* Klingen, in methylated spirit. As his tenth *caporal* cigarette began to singe his moustache, and the last glass of his third bottle began to exhibit sediment, Klingen again pulled his cap over his eyes, and dropped his chin upon his chest. A small figure in the uniform of the Legion was passing on the other side of the road.

Two minutes later, Klingen was knocking at the door of the room in which dwelt the Japanese girl. To his first knock no answer was vouchsafed; to the second, a thin, high, childish voice replied unintelli-

gibly. It might have been in invitation or prohibi-
tion.

Klingen turned the handle and, to his surprise,
found that the door was not fastened. Entering
the room, he saw a little figure on the remembered
bed, its back toward him, its head and shoulders covered by a silken shawl. Turning, he locked the door,
and slipped the key into his pocket.

The figure on the bed moved slightly and did not
turn to him.

The little hussy! What was the game? Perhaps-
I-will-perhaps-I-won't? Or was she pretending she
hadn't heard him come in? Going to make a scene,
perhaps, in the hope of extorting payment. Well,
she'd be a clever girl if she got money out of Klingen! The other way about, more likely.

With quickened breathing, gleaming eye, and
smiling lips, Klingen took a couple of steps in the
direction of the bed, and from it, casting off shawl
and covering, sprang Yato, lightly clad, his face devilish in its ferocity.

Klingen's right hand went to his bayonet and
Yato's right hand, open, shot upward, so that the
bottom of the palm struck Klingen beneath the chin.
As it did so, Yato heaved mightily upward, as though
hurling a sack of potatoes which was balanced on
his hand. It was as if the Japanese lifted Klingen by
the face, and flung him backward off his feet. But
even as his enemy was in the act of falling, Yato

flung his arm about him, and turning him sideways, fell heavily with him—Klingen being face downward. Instantly Yato, whose knee was in the small of Klingen's back, his right hand on his neck, seized Klingen's right wrist, and, dragging the arm upward and backward with a swift movement, dislocated his shoulder, and, as the prostrate man yelled in agony, Yato, with a similar movement of dexterous and powerful leverage, dislocated the other.

As Klingen again roared with pain, Yato hissed like a cat, and, with a grip of steel, dug his thumb and fingers into his victim's neck, with a grip that changed a howl to a broken whimper.

Five minutes later, Klingen's wrists were bound behind him with steel wire, his ankles were fastened together with a strap, and he was bound down upon the bed with a many-knotted rope, in such a manner that he could not raise his knees, nor his head, nor change his position by so much as an inch.

A large handkerchief or rag completely filled his mouth, and a piece of steel wire, passing round his face from beneath his chin to the top of his head, prevented him from ejecting it. In fact, the so-recently active and joyous *Légionnaire* Klingen, could now move nothing but his eyes, could only see and hear—and suffer.

What was this yellow devil going to do with him? Mutilate him as the Arabs mutilate *les légionnaires* when they fall into their hands? And Klingen shuddered, as he thought of the photographs that hang in every Legion barrack-room for the discouragement of deserters . . . photographs of the remains of things that have been men.

Was Yato going to carve and fillet him? Blind him? Cut his tongue out? Torture him with a red-hot iron? Cripple him for life? Destroy his hands, and so his livelihood? Or merely leave him there to die a dreadful lingering death of thirst and starvation?

He thought of what he himself had hoped and intended to do, if he could have had Yato waylaid in *le Village Nègre.*

And he could not utter a word of supplication or remonstrance, nor make offer and promise of impossible reparation and bribe.

What was the cruel, wicked devil doing now? Heating an iron, sharpening a knife, boiling some water? These cursed Japs were artists at fiendish torture, and had a devilish ingenuity beyond the conception of simple, honest Westerners with their kindly hearts and generous natures.

What was he doing? *Oh, God,* what *was* he doing? Something unthinkable . . . something unimaginable.

But, strangely enough, Yato was merely engaged in the exercise of one of his many peaceful and lawful pursuits. Seated comfortably beside *le Légionnaire* Klingen, to whom he addressed no remark of any sort, he was making a selection from a number of small objects neatly packed in a sandal-wood box. A faint, but pleasing odour came from this; also a small oblong cake of some black substance, in the powerful delicate fingers of the Japanese. Taking a tiny saucer from the box, he poured into it a little water from the flower-vase, and in this placed the end of the black cake, that it might soak while he dispassionately studied the contorted face of his enemy. Anon, taking the cake in his fingers, he sketched broad lines of the deepest black upon Klingen's forehead and cheeks. Klingen, expecting either burn or slash, winced and shuddered as the substance touched his face. Settling down to his work, unhurried, methodical, and calm, Yato rubbed and dipped, rubbed and dipped, until, save for the nose, the face of Klingen was as black as soot—eyelids, lips, ears, throat.

Having completed this portion of his task to his satisfaction, Yato again considered the contents of the box, and selected a small stick of brilliant vermillion. With this, he carefully and conscientiously painted Klingen's prominent and handsome nose, so that it glowed upon his face as a holly-berry upon black satin.

And then, changing his tools, Yato, with patient artistry, laboured long and well, to render indelible this striking effect. With a long-handled brush, whose bristles were needles of steel, he tapped and tapped and tapped at forehead, cheeks and chin, until the blood began to ooze. With separate and single needles, he worked faithfully and well, in the places where the broader tools would fail of full effect. . . .

And at last he rose, an artist satisfied, fulfilled, and gazed upon the face that, until the worms devoured it, would be a dark blueish-black—save for the nose of glowing red.

§ 5

Le Légionnaire Yato was not seen again in the barracks of the Legion. But, three days later, Beau Geste received a letter which reminded him of his promise to help his humble Japanese comrade. All the latter had to ask was that his honourable friend would proceed, forthwith, accompanied by his two honourable brothers, to a described house, and there, having asked a certain man for the key, go to room No. 7, and give freedom and assistance to an unfortunate man confined therein. Should they fail to do this, the poor fellow would starve to death. . . .

Michael, Digby and John did as they were asked.

"*Good God!*" ejaculated Michael, as they gazed upon the face of Klingen.

"Japanese vengeance!" murmured John.

"This is what they call a 'gentleman of colour,'" observed Digby, remembering certain things.

III

DAVID AND HIS INCREDIBLE JONATHAN

I

"READY, pup?" inquired Michael Geste, turning to where his brother John was endeavouring satisfactorily to arrange his hair by means of a brush originally intended for quite other purposes, and a mirror so small that the work had, as Digby observed, to be done by sections—if not by numbers.

As the three brothers looked each other over, in turn, with a view to avoiding unpleasantness at the gates, where a crapulous and arbitrary Sergeant of the Guard would turn them back if it were possible to find the slightest fault with their appearance, La Cigale approached them.

La Cigale, the Grasshopper, a nobleman of ancient family and once an officer of the Belgian Corps of Guides, was a kind and gentle madman, whose mental affliction had hitherto in no way interfered with his soldiering. At times he was quite mad, and at others appeared quite sane.

Returning to the *dépôt* at Sidi-bel-Abbès, from a long tour of foreign service, he had re-enlisted for

the third time, a veteran soldier *de carrière*. With
the Geste boys he was a favourite, as well as a source
of wonder, admiration and respect. Michael said he
was not only a noble, but one of Nature's noblemen,
as well as one of God's own gentlemen; Digby said
he reminded him of himself; and John, that he was
about the most lovable and pathetic thing in human
form.

And he had been for fifteen years a private soldier of the Legion!

"Are you gentlemen going anywhere in particular?" asked La Cigale with his pleasant, friendly
smile.

"No," replied Michael, "just going to walk
abroad, and give the public a treat."

"You were going alone, of course, a single and
indivisible trinity."

"We were," admitted Michael, "but we should be
delighted if you would care to join us."

"Charmed," murmured Digby and John.

"Thank you so very much," replied La Cigale.
"I'm sure that you mean what you say, and that
your politeness is not hollow. . . . Had you not
invited me, I was going to summon up courage to
ask if I might come with you to-night. . . . I am
frightened."

The brothers glanced at the old soldier's *Croix de*

Guerre, Médaille Militaire, and other medals, with incredulous smiles.

"And of what is the *doyen* of the First Battalion of the First Regiment of the Legion afraid?" asked Michael.

"Of loneliness," was the reply, "and of myself. It is terrible to be utterly lonely in the midst of such a crowded life as this, and it is even more terrible to be afraid of oneself—afraid of what one may do. I am haunted by the dread of doing something awful, horrible, disgraceful, and knowing nothing about it until it is too late. And I get these attacks—I can't describe them. I have one coming on now. Every nerve in the body tingles and burns, from the brain to the finger-tips and toes. Every cell in the body shrieks and screams, and I must do something, *do* something—something drastic, and do it instantly. But what that something is, I do not know. It is agony unspeakable. I would sooner have a dozen wounds."

"Come for a walk and a talk," interrupted Michael Geste, as La Cigale paused. It was obvious that the less he thought about himself the better.

"Let's go and find a quiet spot in the Gardens, and perhaps you'll give us the pleasure and benefit of hearing of some of your campaigning experiences? We should like to follow in your footsteps, you know."

"Rather," agreed Digby, "and get as many decorations among the three of us."

"Regard us as your sons, sir, and take us in hand," murmured John.

The quartette set forth, saluted the Sergeant of the Guard, and found themselves safely in the lane that separates the Legion's Barracks from those of the Spahis.

Having induced La Cigale to share a light and not wholly inelegant meal at the *Café de l'Europe*, Michael Geste proposed that they should adjourn and listen to the Legion's band as it played in the public Gardens.

"For myself—I dare not," replied La Cigale. "At times music has a terrible effect upon me. If they were to play a selection from a certain opera that was world-famous when I was a young man, I should go mad. I should completely lose control of . . ."

"Then let's go and sit on a seat in the moonlight, and you shall talk to us. We should enjoy that far more," said Michael quickly. "Come along."

"Not in the moonlight," objected La Cigale, "if you don't mind. Some nice dark place in deep shadow. I think moonlight is terrible—such memories."

.   .   .   .

"I can't tell you how delightful it is to me, to know you," said La Cigale, as they seated themselves on a bench in a dark corner of the Gardens. "Gentlemen and Englishmen. I've always been fond of the English. There was an astonishingly delightful Englishman here, who was a friend of mine for years. Killed trying to escape, with two compatriots —one of them a charming fellow—and a very attractive American.

"Then there was poor young Edwards—yes, he called himself Edwards, I remember."

"And what became of him?" asked Michael, as La Cigale fell into reminiscent silence.

"To young Edwards? Oh, it was a terrible tragedy. I will tell you."

§ 2

"David Edwards, as he called himself, joined the Legion some years ago, and was one of the most puzzling of the many people whose presence in the Legion is a puzzle to all who know them.

"He was one of the nicest fellows I've ever known, and it was impossible to suppose that he had left his country for his country's good, or had chosen the Legion as a refuge. It was quite obvious that it was not poverty nor vice, crime, debt, disgrace nor anything of that kind, that had been the cause of his coming here. Nor did he strike one as being of the born soldier type—one of those men who are cut out for a military career, and are fitted for no other. And he wasn't one of the wildly adventurous sort, mad-cap and hare-brained. It was my good fortune to be put in charge of him when he arrived, that I might show him the ropes, and instruct him as to *astiquage*, *paquetage* and so forth.

"We had much in common, including one or two acquaintances, for I knew the part of England from which he came, and he knew Brussels, where his father, evidently in the Diplomatic Service, had been stationed.

"He was extremely kind and friendly to me, but his *real* friend, pal, and *copain* was, extraordinarily enough, an astounding rascal of the name of Jean Molle.

"It was indeed a case of the attraction of opposites, for this man Molle was all that Edwards was not—the one a gutter-bred rough, the other a public-school man of family and refinement.

"It was really interesting to watch these two, and try to discover what it was in each that interested the other. One would have supposed that Edwards would only have seen in Molle a coarse ignorant ruffian, devoid alike of manners and morals, and that Molle would have seen in Edwards a white-handed, finnicking fine gentleman, full of irritating affectations and superiorities.

"Molle, who had been a Paris market-porter at his best, and a foot-pad *apache* at his worst, was a huge powerful person of most violent temper, and an uncontrollable addiction to drink. But he was droll, I must admit—really very funny when half-sober or half-drunk, and a born mimic, clown, and buffoon. I should think that he must have been attached to a circus in some such capacity, or perhaps was born in one, and he made David Edwards laugh —laugh until the tears ran down his face, and he had to beg Molle to stop impersonating a *curé*, a *cocotte*, a Colonel, an old market-woman, a Sergeant-Major, or whatever it might be.

"Yes, Molle was very good for Edwards from that point of view, for he kept the Englishman laughing—and laughter is the salt of life, both as savour and a preservative. And, of course, Edwards did not understand the vileness of one half of Molle's remarks, spoken in his almost incomprehensible and wholly untranslatable *argot* of the slums and *halles* of Paris.

"And Edwards was good for Molle in every possible way, and gave the creature ideas such as he had never before dreamed of, standards and ideals hitherto unglimpsed by this sewer-rat.

"Surely a more ill-assorted pair never foregathered, even in the Foreign Legion. I think Edwards grew quite fond of Molle, as the benefactor often does grow fond of the beneficiary, and undoubtedly Molle really loved David Edwards. He would have thrashed anyone who said a word against him, and killed anyone who injured him.

"They quarrelled, of course—as friends must do —generally on the subject of Molle's drunkenness and debauchery. He was one of those *canaille* who simply must, from time to time, give way to the demands of their gross appetites, slink into some horrible hole, and drink themselves insensible.

"Edwards was really wonderful when his friend eluded him and got drunk. He would go from wine-shop to wine-shop in the Spanish quarter, search the houses that are in bounds for troops, ransack *le Village Nègre* itself, and when successful, be rewarded by a torrent of oaths and a drunken blow. Time after time he was punished with *salle de police* for coming in late, supporting his drunken friend, whom, for hours, he had been trying to get back to Barracks.

"Never did he desert the drunken brute, even though it meant being out the whole night and returning too late for parade, but not too soon for severe punishment.

"I myself, when on guard, have seen them at the gate in the small hours of the morning—Edwards, who was a teetotaller, by the way, bleeding about the face, and with torn and muddied uniform, supporting and endeavouring to control the singing, shouting, raving Molle, and striving to prevent him from assaulting the Sergeant and resisting the Guard.

"After these disgusting, disgraceful affairs, Molle would be tearfully repentant, grovelling in apology, and loud in self-accusation and promises of reform, and for a time he would behave well, would walk out with Edwards and return quiet, clean, sober and punctual for roll-call.

"Nevertheless he was always extremely dangerous after one of these orgies, for his terrible temper would be in a highly explosive condition—a thing not to be wondered at, in view of the fact that he had consumed gallons of assorted alcohol, and been knocked on the head when fighting like a wild beast to prevent being thrown into the *salle de police.*

"I never ceased to admire the moral and physical courage with which Edwards would come between Molle and his desires when the evil fit was on him, and tackle him when he was in the surly and quarrelsome stages of drunkenness. Undoubtedly, Edwards saved Molle from three times as much imprisonment as he got, and Molle was the cause of practically every punishment awarded to Edwards.

"Can you understand such a friendship between two such men—between a cultured man of breeding and a dissolute brute like Molle? But there it was. And the only explanation I can offer, is that Edwards imagined himself more or less responsible for this creature who had attached himself to him as a stray and homeless mongrel dog will attach himself to a man, and who loved him as such a dog will do.

"Some men will risk their lives to save a dog, and

thereafter be very fond of it, and I suppose it was in some such spirit that Edwards risked his life in *le Village Nègre,* and his peace, prospects and reputation in the Legion—and became fond of the dog Molle.

"And then one night the tragedy occurred, strangely, suddenly and unexpectedly, as tragedy does occur.

"Molle had been drinking. After evening *soupe* he had evaded Edwards, slipped out by himself, and gone to drink in a low wine-shop. Unfortunately he had not the money to buy enough liquor to make himself drunk, but merely sufficient to see him through the successive stages of hilarity and despondency into that of a quarrelsome moroseness.

"Making his way back to Barracks when his money was gone, and carrying, with the air of a dour teetotaller, enough assorted liquor to intoxicate half a dozen, he strode past the Guard Room across the Parade Ground, and up to his Barrack Room. Here he sat himself down in morose and sulky silence, and sullenly cleaned and polished his kit.

"As he sat, gloomy, heavy and repellent, a dangerous and ugly customer to tackle, Edwards came into the room. He was wearing walking-out kit and overcoat.

" 'Oh, there you are,' he cried, on catching sight of Molle. 'I've been looking for you everywhere.'

" 'Am I a dog that I should be hunted? And by

a thing like you?' growled Molle, glaring angrily at Edwards.

" 'Yes,' replied Edwards pleasantly. 'A dirty dog,' and strode across to where Molle sat.

" 'Oh! I am a dirty dog, am I?' muttered Molle quietly, without looking up.

" 'Regular mongrel,' agreed Edwards, 'but full of clever tricks. . . . Sit up and beg. . . . Up, Fido! Beg, Fido!'

"Molle rose to his feet obedient—and spat in Edwards' face.

"I told you he was a creature of pleasant habits! And I told you Edwards was brave.

"Although Molle was about twice his size, and four times as strong, he let drive instantly with all his strength and landed Molle as fine a smack in the eye as ever I saw a man receive.

"Molle struck back, hitting Edwards with such force that both he and Edwards fell to the ground.

"At that moment there was a cry of *'Fixe!'* and every one sprang to attention, as our Major came into the room. Molle, full of liquor though he was, scrambled to his feet, and stood like a statue at the foot of his bed, steady as a rock.

"Edwards lay where he was—on his face—gasping and coughing.

" *'What's this, then?'* snapped the Major, a man who was always in a terrific hurry. He occasionally made these sudden inspection raids, and indiscriminately dealt out severe punishment to all and sundry.

"Edwards gasped, groaned, and partly raised himself on his right elbow.

" 'I am drunk,' he said clearly, and collapsed.

" 'Drunk and fighting in the Barrack Room,' shouted the Major. 'Assaulting your comrades. No one else here is drunk. A drunken, quarrelsome disturber of discipline. . . .'

"And more of the same sort of thing, ending up with an order that the drunkard should be removed immediately and thrown into prison.

" 'He is not drunk, *Monsieur le Majeur*,' interrupted Molle, stepping forward and saluting. 'It is I.'

" 'Four days cells for daring to address me, for contradiction and attempted interruption of the course of justice,' roared the incensed officer, as soon as he recovered from his shocked surprise at Molle's temerity.

"I would have spoken up for Edwards myself, but for the absolute certainty that I should also incur a sentence of imprisonment without the slightest possibility of doing him any good. Quite the contrary, in all probability.

"Edwards, really looking the part of quarrelsome drunkard who had been badly knocked about, was carried off and dumped in a cell, while Molle was led away to the *salle de police*.

"That night I was on guard, and as it happened, it was I who first entered Edwards' cell in the morning, to take him the loaf of bread and drop of water that would be his food for the day. He was lying face downward on the dirty floor, his left arm bent beneath him, and his right extended, the hand touching the wall of the cell. Just above it, I could see, in the dim light, smears and smudges, such as might have been made by a child playing with a housepainter's brush on which still remained a very little half-dried red paint.

"Just so might a little girl, named Susan, have tried to write her name upon the wall—for the first smeared hieroglyphic was a crude but unmistakable *S*, followed by what was almost certainly the letter *U*.

"A finger, dipped in blood, had made the rough double curve that was an S, had twice made a stroke beside it, and, when a little more of the slow and painful medium was available, had joined the bases of the strokes with a curve.

"I saw this much, at a glance, as I knelt to do what I could for David Edwards. He was quite dead, and had obviously died from loss of blood, after having stabbed himself, or having been stabbed, in the left breast.

"Yes, my friend was dead; I could not be mistaken as to that—I who have seen so many die.

"I looked again at the wall. *'SU'* he had painfully scrawled while still comparatively strong. I think he had then fainted, or perhaps had waited. . . .

"So much of the blood had been absorbed by his clothing, and the pad he had made with his neck-cloth.

"Oh, yes, he had done his best, poor boy, but had probably grown too weak to do any more for himself than to staunch the flow of blood.

"Yes, as I read the signs, he had fainted, had revived, and realized that he was dying; had painfully scrawled the first two letters, and had then collapsed —probably through fresh hæmorrhage caused by the effort.

"For there was a space after the *U*, and then a straight stroke, followed by a curved one. Near the top of this was a single finger-print. Evidently, with failing sight and ebbing strength, he had tried to make this curve into the letter *C*, and, ere the heavy hand fell from the wall, he had smeared the beginning of another stroke.

" *'SUICI'* had been accomplished, and he had then either rested from these last labours of his brief life, or had again been overcome by that dreadful sinking faintness that attacks us as the life-stream ebbs from wounds.

"Once again he had recovered. This time he had made a mighty effort, and had been but too well provided with the dreadful medium in which he worked.

"Below the other letters, and a foot to the right of them, shakily but clearly were written the final *D* and *E*.

"*Suicide!*

"*Why?* And with what weapon? And where was it?

"He was not wearing his bayonet, of course. Had he a dagger or clasp-knife which he had returned to its place of concealment, after inflicting upon himself a death-wound? And if so, why?

"And then again, why spend his last minutes of terrible agony—as he lay upon the very brink of the grave, and imminent dissolution was upon him, in such work? Why, I asked myself, should he have been at such pains—such unthinkable pains—to smear this dreadful writing on the wall, in his own life-blood?

"When a *légionnaire* commits suicide, he commits suicide, and there's an end of it. He doesn't trouble to write about it. It is obvious. If he should have anything to record about his death, he would write it before killing himself, wouldn't he?

"Reverently I assured myself of the fact that he had no concealed knife or dagger, and then that there was, in the cell, absolutely nothing of any sort or kind with which he could have inflicted this wound upon himself. A man cannot give himself a neat and clean stab, three quarters of an inch long, a quarter of an inch wide, and deep enough to kill him, without a knife, or something that can be used as a knife blade.

"Men have hanged themselves with their braces, strangled themselves with their boot-laces, opened veins and arteries with a nail, and battered their heads against their cell walls. There is always a way for a determined man to put an end to himself, but he can't fatally stab himself—without at least a piece of glass, or of hard and pointed wood.

"Could David Edwards have had an enemy who had entered his cell and murdered him during the night?

"Absurd nonsense! How could such a man get into the cell, unless it were the Sergeant of the Guard himself? And, if a prisoner were murdered in this way, would he write 'Suicide' upon the wall as he died?

"It has taken me some time to tell you all this, but I don't suppose it took a second for these thoughts to flash through my mind.

"And then I decided that when a man, at such terrible cost, proclaims the fact that he has committed suicide, he has almost certainly not committed suicide at all, and of course I was confirmed in this belief by my absolute certainty that there was nothing in the cell with which he could have stabbed himself.

"Although I knew that it was perfectly useless to do so, I opened the door of the cell, and exam-

ined the floor of the narrow passage outside.   As
you may not be aware, those beastly cells have no
window, grating, nor aperture communicating with
the open air.   There is nothing but the grating above
the door that opens into the passage.   It was just
conceivably possible that Edwards had stabbed himself with a knife, and had then contrived to throw it
between the bars of the grating, so that it fell in the
passage without.

"Apart from the fact that this would be an extremely difficult thing to do, and that the sentry
would hear the knife fall, why should a suicide do
such a thing, particularly when he intended to take
the trouble to proclaim the fact that it was suicide?

"Surely it would be obvious enough that he had
taken his own life, if the knife were found lying beside him, or gripped in his hand, or sticking in his
chest.   On what conceivable grounds should a man,
after inflicting a mortal wound upon himself, proclaim the fact of suicide and carefully conceal the
means whereby it was effected?

"Life has presented me with some sore puzzles,
my friends, but I think this was the most insoluble
problem with which I had been confronted.

"Well, there it was, in all its stark simplicity of
fact.   Edwards was dead, with a stab near the heart;
there was no knife or other weapon in the place, and
he had written the word *'Suicide'* in his own blood.

"And there it was in all its bewildering complex-

ity, its incredibility, its sinister insoluble impossibility.
And there I left it.

"I reported to the Sergeant of the Guard that the
prisoner in No. 1 had committed suicide.

"The body was carried to the hospital for autopsy,
and thence to the mortuary, in the kind of coffin they
give the *légionnaire*.

"Next day, David Edwards was buried in the
Cemetery of the Legion, and doubtless one can still
find his grave—for it became rather famous, and
probably the *légionnaire*-pensioner in charge of the
Cemetery, looks after it. In the past he must have
made quite a few *sous* by exhibiting it.

"No, it was not the mystery attaching to the death
of Edwards that made his grave a nine days' wonder. No one takes much notice of the suicide of a
légionnaire, however interestingly he may contrive
his death.

"It was what happened, a week after he had been
buried.

§ 3

"When Molle came out of prison, his first thought
was of his friend, and he hurried in search of him.
I was in the Barrack Room when he entered, looking
all the worse for his term of *cellule* punishment.

"He stared in astonishment at seeing another man

sitting on Edwards' cot and obviously occupying his place.

" '*Here, you—where's Edwards?*' he said, approaching the newcomer, a big Alsatian named Gronau.

" 'Dead and buried,' growled the fellow, with an ugly laugh.

"Molle planted himself in front of Gronau, his big hands tense, flexed, about to clutch. . . .

" '*Where's Edwards?* I asked you,' he said.

"I got up with some idea of getting Molle away, but Gronau answered again.

" '*Dead*, I tell you! . . . Dead and buried. Dead and damned.'

"And Molle sprang upon him, literally like a wild beast.

"It took half a dozen of us to get him off Gronau before he had choked the life out of him.

"The Alsatian, although a big powerful fellow, was like a child in the hands of Molle.

"We got him down and held him down, and for a time it was more like holding a horse than a man.

"Then suddenly he fell quiet, as though all his strength had gone out of him. And it had.

"His attack on Gronau was his last activity—his last effort, if you understand me.

"He had grasped the fact that David Edwards was dead, and it broke him, mentally and physically.

Yes, that is what he was, a broken man—heart-broken and broken in spirit.

"For a few days he moved about, doing things automatically. He reminded me of those stories, that one has heard and read, of the dog that loses its master and straightway loses all interest in life, refuses food and pines and droops. Sometimes such a dog will go and lie upon its master's grave and refuse to be moved.

"Such a dog was Molle.

"He never spoke: he never smiled; scarcely did he raise his eyes from the ground. He did not sleep; he did not eat, and, marvellously, he did not drink.

"What would one have expected such a creature to do? Obviously to drink himself to death.

"Granted that he were sufficiently human and humane to have been capable of such a love, one would have supposed its effect would have been a plunge into the depths of debauchery, a drowning of sorrow in drink. Surely, nine times out of ten, a man of this type would seek the only anodyne he knows, his accustomed way of escape from reality.

"But no! this astonishing Jonathan took the loss of his David differently, and the *débauché* became the ascetic, instead of submerging his troubled soul beneath a sea of alcohol.

"I tried to get *en rapport* with him.

"He did not so much repulse me as fail to realize

me. I made no impression upon him, and nothing that I said appeared to reach his mind. I think that was wholly unreceptive, as though it had frozen into a solid block of fact—one dreadful fact—*My friend is dead.*

"One day I said to him, 'Look here, Molle. If you don't eat you'll die. Even *your* strength can't last much longer. Come out with me to-night. We'll have supper together in some nice quiet place.'

" '*Eh?*' he replied.

"And when I had repeated what I had said, he again murmured, '*Eh?*'—and that was as far as I could get with him.

"I completely failed to make him realize that I, more than any man, could understand how he suffered: I, who had lost every one and everything; I, whose mind, like his, had suddenly died.

"With a word of sympathy on my lips, and genuine sorrow in my heart, I turned and left him.

"But I spoke to him once again, and got an answer.

"For my evening walk, I strolled to the cemetery to visit the grave of David Edwards, just to lay a flower and say a word of farewell to a dead comrade.

"A foolish thing, of course, and one I often wonder at—this connecting of the freed and soaring spirit with the poor corrupting clay, and its last resting-place.

"But poor humanity must have its concrete symbols. . . .

"And there was Jean Molle before me lying prone upon the grave.

"I went to raise him up. His left hand was buried quite deeply into the ground, and in his right hand was the knife with which he had stabbed himself.

"As I turned him over, to see if anything could yet be done to save him, I saw that the hand that had been buried clutched an earth-stained letter.

" 'What has happened?' I asked, bewildered.

"Molle opened his eyes.

" 'I cannot get it down to him,' he moaned. . . . 'Oh, David, my friend, my friend! . . . I did not mean to do it. . . . Can you hear me, David, and will you believe me? . . . I did not even know that a knife was in my hand, when you came to me that last night in the barrack-room, and I struck you, David. . . .'

"I tried to staunch the blood that flowed from his bared breast.

" '*Get him the letter,*' he whispered, '*I cannot reach to* . . .' and died.

"I buried the letter. . . . Doubtless Edwards received it. . . ."

IV

THE McSNORRT REMINISCENT

I

"I SAY, citizens," quoth Digby Geste, as his brothers entered the barrack-room, "Ludwig'll . . ."

"Ludwiggle?" enquired Michael. "Who's he?"

Digby sighed. "As I was about to say, Ludwig'll . . ."

"You *did* say Ludwiggle," pointed out John.

Digby ignored his younger brother.

Addressing Michael, he said firmly, "Ludwig'll . . ."

"He's got this Ludwiggle on the brain," observed Michael. "What's his surname—Hornswoggle?"

"Yes, obviously; what else could it be?" accommodated Digby in a soothing voice, and continued, "Well, Ludwig Hornswoggle'll clean our kit to-night. In fact he's very keen on getting the job, and keener still on the threepence he'll earn by it. Thinking of marrying, I believe, and wants to get a few sticks of furniture for the home."

"Good for Ludwiggle," agreed Michael. "We'll go to Mustapha's and improve the shining hour, and our shining Arabic."

Le Légionnaire Ludwig Müller alias Hornswoggle, having received payment in advance, and a
promise that it would be recovered if the work were
not satisfactorily done, settled down to the evening's
labours, as the boys, having brushed each other's
coats, took their caps.

"Good-bye, Ludwiggle," observed Michael, as
they left the barrack-room. "You speak English,
don't you?"

"Yes, yes, I speak it much," replied Müller. "I
haf been waiter in London."

" '*Thig or glear?*' " murmured Digby.

"Well then," replied Michael, "you will achieve
a just and accurate perception of what I would fain
indicate when I say that you have had payment *a
priori*, and if we are unable to approve the result of
your industry and application, both intensive and ex-
tensive, you'll get some *a posteriori* too."

"Yes, and *a forteriori* also, Ludwiggle. Now
excogitate the esoteric implications of those few ill-
chosen words."

Ludwig Müller grinned and waggled his hands.

§ 2

"Good heavens, listen," said Michael, suddenly
seizing the arms of his brothers, between whom he
was walking, as they passed a low café in the Spanish quarter.

"Rough-house," observed Digby, as a man came flying backward through the doorway. "That is what the instructed call being thrown out on your ear," observed John.

"I thought I heard English," said Michael.

"Scotch," said Digby, "or did I smell it?"

"Only the soda," corrected John. . . . By Jove, it *is* English," he added, as a bull voice roared above the din.

"Is there a man among ye has the Gaelic? . . . Is there a man among ye can speak English even? . . . Is there a man among ye at all? Ye gang o' lasceevious auld de'ils, decked oot like weemin, in spite o' yer hairy long whuskers, full beards and full skirts, ye deceitful besoms. Whuskers and petticoats wi' the vices o' both and the virtues o' neither. I'll sorrt ye."

And there were sounds of alarums and excursions within.

The door opened, and a *légionnaire* came out laughing—a Frenchman called Blanc, once a Captain in his country's Mercantile Marine.

"Ho, ho, *ce bon* McSnorrt," he chuckled.

"Hullo, there's a compatriot of yours in there," he added, on catching sight of the brothers. "Perhaps you could get him back to Barracks. I can't. He's not coming out of there till some one speaks to him in Gaelic, has danced the sword-dance or sung a *Chanson Ecosse* about Scots who have bled at the same time and place as Monsieur Guillaume Wallace."

Blanc laughed again.

"He's taken a dislike to Arabs, Jews and Spaniards to-night, because they can't talk Gaelic, and he'll kill a few in there unless they kill him first. . . . Well, I've done my best with the old fool."

A few questions elicited the information that *ce bon* McSnorrt was a Scot with a perfectly unpronounceable name—really more a sneeze than a name, explained Blanc,—something between McIlwraith and Colquohoun, who had, long ago, been re-named "McSnorrt" by an English *légionnaire* calling himself Jean Boule. He had taken his discharge three times, and each time had re-enlisted destitute, after a period of peace, retrenchment, and reform, during which he had, according to his own account, been Chief Engineer on great liners.

Apparently he was the pride and joy of his officers in the day of battle, and their despair, disgrace and utter curse, in the piping times of peace. On more than one occasion, nothing but his decorations and glorious fighting record could have saved him from the Zephyrs or a firing-party. According to Blanc, he had been very bad in the days of his friend Jean Boule, and ten times worse since the removal, by the hand of death, of that gentleman's restraining influence.

Followed by his brothers, Beau Geste pushed open the door and entered the wine-shop.

Brandishing an empty bottle, a red man—red of hair, beard, nose and eye—enormous and powerfully built, was threatening an audience of grave and wondering Arabs and grinning, sneering, or scowling Spaniards, Jews, and nondescripts, while he bitterly and passionately harangued them on the shortcomings, impropriety, and general unsuitability of native dress; on their inability to sing the songs that he approved, and their complete ignorance of Gaelic.

Inasmuch as his address concluded with the firm assurance that no man should leave the building until he had cast off his unseemly garb, danced a sword-dance, sung "Annie Laurie," and spoken Gaelic, there appeared to be every probability of serious trouble.

Even as the boys entered, a big, powerful, and truculent-looking Spaniard set down his glass with a loud bang on the zinc bar, lit a cigarette, spat in the direction of the self-constituted censor of local morals, manners and customs, and strode toward the door.

As the McSnorrt gripped him by the arm, he whipped out a knife. Quick as he was, the drunken Scot was quicker. Seizing the upraised hand, the McSnorrt forced the man's arm downward and backward, and then, with a mighty heave and lift, swung round and flung him, like a sack of straw, against the swing-doors—and the subsequent proceedings interested him no more.

There was a general movement and ugly murmurings, as knives were drawn and empty bottles seized, preparatory to a concerted rush.

"Speak Gaelic, ye ignorant and contumeelious spawn of Gehenna, ye dommed dirrty, degraded, derelict descendants o' the Duke of Hell," roared the McSnorrt, in reply to cries of "Stab him," "Get behind him," or "Throw a knife in his ear," and general exhortations of all to sundry that they should do drastic things with promptitude and despatch.

"Hi, comrade, hae ye the Gaelic yersel'?" shouted Michael, as he thrust through the encircling company of murderous blackguards, choice specimens of a cosmopolitan and criminal underworld.

"Not a worrd, laddie, an' I was never further norrth, ye'll ken, than my ain fair city o' Glesgie. Not a worrd, an' I doot if ever I hearrd one. . . . But the soond of yon lovely tongue wad be sweeter in ma ears than that o' the bonnie pibroch itself. . . . Oh, to hear the skirrl o' the bonnie, bonnie bag-pipes playing 'Lochaber no more,' or the 'Flowers of the Forest' in this meeserable land o' dule and drought. No, I hae na the Gaelic, but I'm goin' to hearr it the nicht. An' no man leaves this den o' thieves until I do, yersel's included."

"Then listen," replied Michael, " 'listen, my little

one, and you shall hear,' " and in fluent Arabic he continued, "You are a filthy drunken disgrace to the most decent, self-respecting, thrifty and sober people in the world.   You are a noisy ruffian, debauched, beastly and detestable, a shame and a reproach to the white race, and to the Foreign Legion."

Michael paused for breath.

"How did you like that?" he inquired.   "Pretty good Gaelic, eh?"

"Graand, man!   Gie's your hand.   Och, the bonnie, bonnie Gaelic.   It minds me o' when I was a wee laddie, and paddled i' the burrn. . . . Or the Clyde at Greenock, anyhow."

And the McSnorrt swallowed hard.

"Oh, cheer up, wee Macgregor," begged Digby. "Listen."

And at the top of his voice he tunefully declared that Maxwelton's braes were bonnie.

Scarcely had he uttered the name of Miss Laurie, and the gift of her promise true, than the McSnorrt burst into tears, and was led weeping away—away back to Barracks, to the strains of "Loch Lomond," and the promptings of a somewhat vituperative-seeming Gaelic.

§ 3

Every fifth day is "pay-day," the great day when a soldier of the Legion has five *sous* to spend, and can spend it with untrammelled recklessness.

It was a Fifth Day at eventide, and the McSnorrt, established as usual in the Canteen, was rapidly recovering from the drear and dreadful drought of the four previous days, when chill penury failed to repress his noble rage.

Warmed by wine, the McSnorrt was expanding, mellowing and waxing genial, shedding moroseness like a garment, and finding joy, relief, and satisfaction in self-expression. Speech bubbled up within this usually inarticulate man, and he spake with tongues; also he remembered his love of the Gaelic, as he caught sight of the three boys who had come to his rescue in the wine-shop last pay-day.

With a roar and a shout and a wave of one mighty paw, while the other banged a bottle heavily upon the table, he attracted the attention of the Geste brothers and bade them come, and in return for their Gaelic, hear words of wisdom and delight from a great and good man who had drunk exactly 3,000 gallons of whiskey before the three of them had been born.

Nothing loth, the brothers gathered round the veteran reprobate, a man with a vivid imagination, an inexhaustible fund of strange experience, and, on the rare occasions when not possessed of a dumb devil, a copious flow of potent speech.

Ere long, the party was joined by Maris and Cordier, friends of the brothers, and practised users of the English tongue.

Michael, Digby and John, finishing a brief argument as to whether one Robinson, the Carven-faced
Man, should be written down a liar, and if not,
should be esteemed something of a knave, were anon
aware that the McSnorrt, ancient mariner that he
was, had fixed them with a glittering eye and was
unfolding a round, if not unvarnished, tale of which
they had missed the beginning.

"Aye . . . aye, this Mr. Bute-Arrol was a well-
kenned and highly respected man. Last of a great
shipping firm he was, and an ornament to Glasgow
as he walked aboot it, a fine big upstanding man with
the sea in his eyes, and the sun-bronze on his face.

"More like a ship's captain than a shipping-owner,
he was, and well he might be, for he had sailed the
seven seas, and travelled far and wide. Aye, and
Mr. Bute-Arrol, partner in the Bell, Brown, Scott
and Bute-Arrol's 'Loch' Line, was a man of parrts
and education. . . . Hobbies he had. . . . Nane
of yer fule hobbies o' collectin' stamps, or moths, or
trouser-buttons, or doin' fret-work or photography,
but scienteefic and literary, ye ken.

"And, I say, scienteefic. There was botany and
orchids, that cost him a fortune, from South America
to New Guinea, and trees and shrubs in his grounds
such as ye'd have to go to Kew Gardens to see the
like of.

"And then there was zoology and all sorts of
weird beasties, snakes and lizards and fishes, chame-

leons and similar molluscs, and brachycephalous
orrnithorhincusses; marvellous-coloured bugs, bee-
tles, salamanders, iguanas and all such-like lepidop-
tera and hagiologies. He'd got conservatories and
an aviary and an insect-house and a reptile-house,
all kept as warm as the tropics, while Christians went
blue-nosed with the Glasgow east wind and whiskey.

"Aye, he was a man of interests, this Mr. Bute-
Arrol, and three of his greatest were early gold coins,
scarce First Editions of bukes, and rare poisons. . . .
Yon disreppitable and unneighbourly family of
Borrgias. . . . That lassie they ca'ed Madame
Brinvilliers, famous poisoners of history—he'd quite
a library of them, and the men that hunted him his
orchids, humming-birds, butterflies and such *bichus*,
had to bring him poisoned arrows o' the heathen,
and the little darts they puff through the long blow-
pipes. *Sumpitans*, I think they ca' them. And he'd
be extra douce wi' any hunter or agent or captain
who'd send him, or bring him, specimens o' yon
wourali stuff fra' South America, or *dhatura* fra' the
East, *stropanthus* from Africa, and dozens of other
such unwholesome food-stuffs from China to Peru—
things ye'd never hear of unless ye went there, and
then likely not—and all unknown to the British
Pharmacopœia.

"Aye, he was a grraand man, and I'm tellin' ye
he had grraand hobbies, and great ideas.

"Aye, and something else he had, and that was a

great enemy, a successful rival in love, which was bad, and a successful rival in business which was waur. McRattery his name was, and if ye'd say Bute-Arrol was the finest figure o' a man, a citizen, a gentleman, a pillar o' law, order and property, and ornament o' the Kirk in all Glasgow ye might perhaps add, 'Unless it's yon Mr. McRattery.'

"A pair they were, but not a pair that would ever run in harness, ye ken, nor side by side, nor in the same direction.

"Rivals and enemies, from their school-days at Fettes, to the prime o' manhood. What the one had, the other must have more of; what the one did, the other must outdo; what the one was, the other must be in higher degree. Aye, what the one wanted, the other must get first.

"And McRattery put the crown on his life's work o' rivalry, thwarting and competition, by cutting in and getting Mary MacDonald just when Bute-Arrol decided that it was time he had a son to follow him, and had marked bonnie Mary down for the high honour and advancement of becoming Mrs. Bute-Arrol.

"Big men they were both, wise and patient and clever, learned and able and dour, ill men to cross, wilful and set in their ways, and neither to haud nor to bind when once started on a course. And perhaps, after all, McRattery was the bigger man, for not only had he beaten Bute-Arrol in love and war, but he had fought fair, and *sans rancune,* as these French havering bletherers say.

"Fight he would, while there was breath in his body, but he bore no malice, and would always fight fair; and ye couldna say the same o' Bute-Arrol.

"*He'd* fight fair wi' the steepulation that a's fair in love and war. An' he *did* bear malice. He was a good hater, and he wasna the man to stultify himself wi' impotent hatred, either. An' McRattery marryin' Mary MacDonald was a turnin'-point in Bute-Arrol's career. Aye, the down-turnin' point, for he grew more and more dour, and then soured and warped.

"And then two things happened which turned bad to worse, and that was very bad indeed.

"The first of these was the death of Mrs. McRattery, that had been his beloved Mary MacDonald; and the second was McRattery beating him over a huge Admiralty contract.

"What made Mary's death more terrible to him, was his firm belief that her life could have been saved. He had a mind like Aberdeen granite, and hard as granite was his belief, his certainty, that if Mary had been Mrs. Bute-Arrol instead of Mrs. McRattery, she'd have lived to four-score.

" 'Yon meeserable money-grubbing McRattery simply *let* her die—or else she died wilfully, bein' sick sorry and tired at the sight of her husband's ugly face, and the sound of his croakin' voice. Why; had

the creature been a man, he would have defied and
fought Death himself—and kept her alive, despite
the Devil and all the Imps of Hell. No, she
shouldn't have died if she'd been Mary Bute-Arrol,
and she wouldn't have wanted to, forbye.'

"That was the way he talked. But when McRattery undercut him with a big contract for the Navy,
he didn't talk at all.

"He never said another word against McRattery.

"On the contrary, if anybody at the Club criticised
the man, Bute-Arrol wouldna let it pass, if it were
unfair. And, whiles, he would take an opportunity
o' publicly speaking worrds o' praise concernin'
McRattery; and though he made no overtures nor
approaches to his rival, it got aboot that auld Wullie
Bute-Arrol's bark was waur than his bite, and that
he had naethin' against Eckie McRattery in spite
of a'.

"Weel, ye ken hoo things get roond, and in time
McRattery got to hear that Bute-Arrol wouldna
hear a worrd against him. And one day, when he
said, daffing-like, at his own table, that yon Bute-
Arrol was a thrawn diel and an ill cur to turn from
his bone, a crony said:

" 'Nay, dinna misca' the man, Eckie, for I heard
him only yesterday at the Club uphaudin' and de-
fendin' ye like a brither, and sayin' ye were a man
that had earrned and desairved every penny o' your

fortune, and every step o' your success . . .' and the like.

"An' McRattery, being the man he was, made to out-do Bute-Arrol in generosity, as he had out-done him in business and in love.

"Aye, aye, it's a queer worrld," mused the Mc-Snorrt, gazing pensively into his empty glass and slowly shaking his huge red head.

It was noticeable that—in talking to the Geste brothers—he talked less and less like a Clyde-side docker from Glasgow, and more like the educated man he was.

"Aye, a queer worrld," he continued, when his glass was replenished, "an' one o' its queer sights was seen when William Bute-Arrol sat down at a banquet as one of the guests of Alexander Buchanan McRattery—the guest of honour on his host's right hand.

"I can tell ye aboot that banquet at first hand, for I've talked many a time an' oft wi' a man who was there, Sir Andrew Anderson he was, and a great and wealthy marine engineer before he retired. He died at the age of 90, when I was a lad, and many a good turn he did me, had I but had the sense to ha' taken advantage o' them.

"According to his account, it was a richt merry and successfu' dinner, and ye'd have thought that McRattery and Bute-Arrol had been life-long friends instead o' rivals and enemies.

"For McRattery fairly laid himself out to charm and captivate Bute-Arrol, and Bute-Arrol fairly laid himself out to be pleased and pleasant.

"That dinner-table was a battlefield o' magnanimity. Each o' the two big men strivin' to out-do the other in generosity and great-hearted forgiveness and forgetting o' what there was to forgive and forget.

"They drank each other's health and each made a little speech full o' kindness and compliment to the other, and when they had come to the coffee and liqueurs and big cigar stage, and men leant back in their chairs and unbuttoned their minds socially and right sociably, there was no pair o' cronies that chatted more easily and freely than the generous-hearted Eckie McRattery and his one-time rival and enemy Wullie Bute-Arrol.

"And McRattery must needs strike a match and light Bute-Arrol's cigarette for him, and Bute-Arrol must clip a cigar for McRattery—more like loving brothers than life-long rivals and enemies ye'd believe.

"And as it happened, auld Andrew Anderson was watchin' and wonderin', as McRattery, with his cigar in one hand and a match in the other, laughed long and loud at some sly quip or jest, or mayhap sculduddery, o' Bute-Arrol's.

"And that hearty merry laugh was the last sound poor McRattery made in this worrld, for still shakin'

wi' laughter, he put his cigar to his lips, lit it, took
one long satisfyin' draught, slowly poured it out fra
his smilin' lips, and then gave a start, and, with a
terrible expression on his face, gazed around him
and died.

"Died there in his chair wi'oot a worrd. His head
just fell on to his shoulder, and he sank heavily
against his neighbour—William Bute-Arrol.

"O' coorse they all sprang to their feet and dashed
water in his face, opened the windows, fanned him,
tried to make him drink brandy and did sic-like
things, until the doctor came and said he was dead.
For dead he was—cut off in the prime of his health
and strength, and no healthier, heartier, stronger
man had walked the streets of Glesgae that day.

"An inquest there was, and the two best doctors in
the city confessed themselves puzzled and defeated.

"Deceased had a heart as sound as a bell, they
said, and not an organ that wasna perfect.

"Naturally, the immediate supposition was that
he'd eaten somethin' that had disagreed with him.
But how should he have eaten or drunk something
that had disagreed with him to the point o' killin'
him, when not anither man at the table had felt the
slightest qualm o' pain, ill-health or discomfort?

"The contents of the stomach bein' analysed,
showed absolutely no trace o' anything deeleterious,
and the cause o' death was a fair mystery. Apart
from the offeecial and scienteefic investigation, the

guests themsel's worked it out that he had not tasted a thing from soup to coffee that others had not shared.

"And when some auld fule spoke of suicide, he had but to be asked why Alexander Buchanan Mc-Rattery, in boisterous spirits, rude health, and at the height of his success and fortune, should commit suicide, and at such a time and place. And more-over, what of the Analyst's report on the absolutely normal and innocuous contents o' the stomach?

"No, it was a mystery, unfathomable and com-plete.

"It was a nine-days' wonder, too, and the town talked of nothing else, but this awfu' tragedy that cast real gloom over the dead man's wide circle o' freends and acquaintances.

"And none more sorrowfu' and sympathetic than his new friend and old enemy, William Bute-Arrol.

"Aye, an' it was practical sympathy too, for, in order, perhaps, to show how deeply he had been affected by McRattery's death at his very side, nay, in his arms, at the very banquet given to celebrate and demonstrate their reconciliation, Bute-Arrol had adopted McRattery's orphan child.

"What were the worrkin's of his mind when he thought o' doin' sic a thing? Who shall presume to fathom the dark mysterious depths of the human mind? Aye, and ye might ask the question anither way, or rather ask a different question a'thgither.

Who shall dare presume to fathom and unnerstand the worrkings o' Providence? God moves in a meesterious way His wonders to perforrm.

"Weel, whatever was the man's motive—whether it were a gesture to catch the public eye; whether it were a salve to his conscience; or whether he had some dark design upon the child, and thoughts o' carryin' vengeance against his father even beyond the grave—no-one will ever know.

"But see the result, ponder the ways of the A'mighty, and turrn fra your wickedness. . . ."

The McSnorrt paused and drank deeply.

"Especially drink," he added, wiping his bearded lips with the back of a vast and hairy hand.

"See what happened," he continued.

"Now Alexander Buchanan McRattery's son Uchtred, aged aboot five or six years when Bute-Arrol adopted him—wi' the willing and even thankful agreement o' the Executor, a child-hatin' plausible scoundrel, who later defaulted and went to prison—was a healthy and active young limb o' Satan, wi' an enquirin' mind and busy fingers.

"Folk who liked childer said he was an enterprisin' and original laddie; and those who didn't like childer said he was a mischievous and meddlesome young deil.

"But every one thoct it was graand to see the way he and dour Bute-Arrol got on togither, walkin' hand in hand aboot the grounds o' the big hoose, or the boy slippin' awa' doon fra the nursery to get a bit fruit or sweetie or jeely-piece, at dessert.

"Whiles he'd sit curled up in a chair and watch Bute-Arrol with solemn big eyes, and Bute-Arrol'd sit sippin' his porrt and thinkin' his deep thoughts as he stared at the child.

"An' mind ye, the child was fond of him, there's no denyin', and was the only one in that hoose from the butler to the sixth gardener's under-gardener that wasna afeard o' the man.

"No one ever saw Bute-Arrol caress the child, any more than they saw the opposite or heard an unkind worrd; but it was clear enough that the little lad was happy, and had taken no scunner at his dour unsmilin' guardian.

"When the late McRattery's Executor absconded to South America and finished what the ruinous strike in the ship-yard had begun, folk wondered if the boy was goin' to become Bute-Arrol's heir— and some of Bute-Arrol's relations had disturrbin' thoughts.

"There was other folk—but ye ken what folk are—professed the opeenion that Bute-Arrol deleeberately turrned a very blind eye on the doin's o' the said Executor, and had more than a finger in the McRattery strike.

"But what I started to tell ye was this—the boy lived happy and contented with his governess in Bute-Arrol's hoose, and had the free run of it, an'

of the grounds too. And while it was a false and
maleecious slander to say he was wantonly mischievous, there's nae denyin' he could poke and pry and
investigate with the best—an' what normal healthy
boy will not?

"An' one day he found something.

"It was in a most attractive and wunnerful box
in a big room that opened oot o' his guardian's bedroom—a sort o' combined dressin'-room and study
that Bute-Arrol used more than any o' his fine
graand rooms doonstairs. There was a huge great
desk in it, and this big old bureau, and a fine safe,
and twa-three wardrobes and some big deep arm-
chairs, and Bute-Arrol would smoke his ceegar there
in his dressing-gown late at night, an' he'd read an'
write there more than in his great library.

"Weel, prowlin' round this room, as he loved to
do, fingerin' this an' that, the boy spied this fine box.

"Chinese it was, ebony and ivory and mother o'
pearl, with bands o' brass, brass corners and a brass
lock,—and to crown a', a key in the lock. Ye'll
imagine it wasna long before the laddie had that
box open, and sniffed its lovely scent o' sandal-wood,
and pried into every compartment and drawer,
amusin' himself, absorbed and happy, for an hoor
that went like a minnut.

"He did no harm, and he kept nothing for himself, and the one thing he took oot, he only took
that he might do something with it for his guardian

—just the little childish ploy that a wee laddie would think of. He guessed that the box had come oot o' the safe or the bureau, had been left out by mistake, and would disappear again when his guardian came home and entered the room.

"That night the boy slippit doon and watched over the bannisters o' the stairs until the right moment, and then, in his wee dressin'-gown and bedroom slippers, marched into the big dinin'-room where Bute-Arrol sat all by his lane, the butler havin' set his wine in front o' him and gone for the coffee.

" 'Hullo, Uncle,' called the little lad. 'Can I have some grapes?'

"Bute-Arrol, unsmilin', nodded at the child.

" 'Help yersel',' he growled, and the boy marched round the table, and then to the big sideboard, spyin' oot the land.

"As the butler came in, carryin' a big silver tray on which were coffee and a box o' ceegars, Bute-Arrol took a ceegar, laid it on the cloth beside his plate, and helped himself to coffee—which he took with hot milk, cream and sugar. While he did so, the wee laddie came behind his chair, and picked up the ceegar.

" 'Can I have some coffee, Uncle?' he asked.

" 'Ye canna,' Bute-Arrol replied, 'but ye can hae a sup o' milk.'

" 'Pooh! Wha wants milk?' replied the child. 'I'll hae a glass o' wine.'

" 'Ye willna,' said Bute-Arrol, and picked up the ceegar that the boy had laid down again, beside his plate.

"The butler put match-box and ash-tray on the table, as usual, and went out.

"Bute-Arrol put the ceegar to his lips, lit it, and took a puff or two.

"He then leant back in his chair, and, wi' an awful look o' fright an' terror on his face, stared at the laughing wee laddie who held out a gold ceegar-piercer in his hand—a thing like a wee pencil-case that ye press at the top, and a sharp hollow steel piercer pushes out of it and into the ceegar.

" 'I did the ceegar for ye, Uncle,' laughed the child gleefully.

"Bute-Arrol groaned.

" '*The judgment of God*,' he whispered, and died —poisoned with the instrument he had used to poison the boy's father."

The McSnorrt paused dramatically, and his hearers, who had ceased to smoke and to drink, sat silent.

"How d'you know all this?" asked Beau Geste at last.

"Ma real name's Uchtred Buchanan McRattery," replied the McSnorrt.

V

MAD MURPHY'S MIRACLE

I

LORD MONTAIGLE, like King Bruce of Scotland, sat himself down in a lonely mood to think—the more lonely because he was in the crowded ball-room of the world-famous Majestic Hotel in the hub of the metropolis which is the hub of the universe.

What was he doing there at his time of life, he asked himself. Rotten new-fangled rubbish—this modern dancing and dance-music. . . . Jazz! . . . Damned row. . . .

Well, at his hostess's earnest request, he had looked in, and now he'd jolly well look out again. . . . Run along to his club and finish the day in peace and quiet and comfort with a book, and a cigar, and a drink—and so to bed.

Hullo, here was dear old Pop, more widely known as Sir Popham Ronceval. Lady Anstruther had dragged *him* here, too, eh!

As the music stopped, Sir Popham Ronceval seated himself in the arm-chair beside that of his old friend, among the palms, near the band.

"Hear oneself speak, now that row's stopped,"

he observed. "What are you doing here, Monty?"

"Same as you, Pop—going away. . . . Coming?"

"Only just arrived. Let's stick out another dance,
and then I'm with you."

Lord Montaigle suppressed a yawn.

"Sad about Tommy Vane," observed his friend,
almost casually, though a look of concern shadowed
his handsome eyes.

"What about him?" asked Lord Montaigle, his
rubicund and cheery countenance unresponsive as
yet, to the other's concern.

"Died this morning . . ."

"*No?* Did he? . . . Well, nothing very sad
about that—not for him, anyhow. Nor for Long
John. Best day's work Tommy Vane ever did, I
should say," pondered Lord Montaigle.

"Oh, I dunno. . . . I was rather fond of old
Tommy," said Sir Popham Ronceval—"when he
wasn't mad, that is."

"When he wasn't!" objected his friend. "But he
was. . . . Born mad, lived mad, died mad—like his
father before him—and his grandfather, too, and
his great-grandfather, by all accounts."

"His father shot himself, didn't he?" mused Sir
Popham.

"Yes, and *his* father was killed by the man he
attacked. Attacked the feller in his own smoking-
room, and he knocked Vane out with a bronze figure,
or ornament, or something, that stood handy. And

Tommy's great-grandfather was hanged—on a silken rope—for unjustifiable homicide."

"Poor old Tommy," repeated the baronet.

"What did he die of?" asked Montaigle.

"Razor-blade," was the short reply. "Just that."

Lord Montaigle nodded his head slowly, and made no further comment than:

"There's a son somewhere, isn't there?"

"*A* son," agreed the other, with meaning emphasis, and added: "Not Tommy's."

Montaigle smiled.

"Long John, eh? . . . The wild Irishman. . . . Aren't we a pair of scandal-mongering old devils?"

"Look here, Claud, I wouldn't talk like this to any other living soul. I'm Long John's *executor*, and I don't mind telling you for a fact what everybody else knows for a guess . . ."

"Guessed it myself," admitted Montaigle. "I saw the boy once at Speech Day—Long John to the very life! . . . Tall, red-haired, blue-eyed, freckled, regular red Celt."

"Yes, I suppose Long John will come home now. . . . Now there's no fear of his murdering Tommy Vane."

"I doubt it. Why should he? He's got a splendid place in East Africa, and it isn't as though Lady Vane were alive," replied Ronceval.

"Died when the boy was born, didn't she?" asked Montaigle.

"Yes. . . . Long John nearly went out of his
mind. . . . I tell you I had all I could do to get
him away. He was all for shooting Tommy Vane
first, and himself afterwards. Rotten position for
me. I was the friend of both of them. Promised
Long John I'd keep an eye on the boy. . . . Her
boy. . . . *His* boy."

"What became of him?" inquired Lord Montaigle.

"Wish I could tell you. . . . He was going up
to Oxford for his first term, and never got there.
Simply vanished into thin air. Tommy Vane didn't
give a damn. But I was frightfully worried. . . .
I wish to God I knew what happened to him. . . .
I would . . ."

A burst of music from the band cut short the
gossip. . . .

§ 2

Beau Geste strode into the barrack-room at Ain
Dula, between Douargala and El Rasa, in search of
his brothers Digby and John. In his well-fitting,
dark blue tunic, with its red facings, green-topped,
red-fringed epaulettes, his smart white-covered *képi*,
brilliantly-polished buttons, belt and bayonet, well-
ironed white trousers, and highly-polished boots, he
was as smart a figure of a soldier as any in his regiment, famous in the 19th Army Corps for its
smartness.

Digby was lying upon his bed, clad in a white shirt and trousers, and engrossed in the study of Arabic, while John sat on the opposite cot writing a letter to Isobel.

Both looked up as Beau Geste approached.

"Ho, pups," quoth he. "Rise up, and stand to attention. Thumbs in a line with the seams of the pyjamas, the weight of the body resting on the chin strap. . . . And listen. . . . My orders to you are *'Keep an eye on "Mad Murphy,"* as they call him. The poor chap's up against it badly. I've just had a dose of him. I left him on the bench there by the *entrée de la redoute.'* "

"Poor beggar gets madder every day," observed Digby. "He'll be as mad as John soon."

"Well, two of a kind never agree," observed John, "so you go and play with him, Dig . . . and keep him out of *le Village Nègre.* . . . I'm writing to Isobel."

"Righto!" agreed Digby, and, rising from his bed, began to dress.

"He's got as far as talking to himself aloud," continued Beau, "and, unlike most mad people, he knows he's mad, or very nearly so. His great terror, among a thousand terrors, is that he'll go quite finally insane, and kill somebody—probably his best friend. He's just begged me to drive my bayonet through his throat if he ever so much as raises his fist or snarls at me."

"And you want *me* to go and play with him,"
observed Digby. "Both of you lend me your rifles—
I've only got one."

"What we want is a scrap," observed John. "Poor
old Mad Murphy and all the other loonies would
soon work their *cafard* off on the Touareg, if they
came for us."

"Yes, scrapping is the prescribed cure for *cafard,*"
agreed Beau. "A bayonet charge must be a wonderful soother. . . . Meantime Mad Murphy is to
be kept from using his bayonet on himself or anyone
else. . . ."

"We *are* our brother's keeper. We *are*, we *are*,
we *are*," chanted Digby, as he buckled on his belt,
and straightened his tunic.

§ 3

Mad Murphy was sitting alone on the bench outside the entrance to the fort, his blazing red head
supported upon his clenched fists, his blazing blue
eyes glaring at the ground in front of him. His
mouth was set in a grim line, and a heavy frown
marred his haggard, handsome face.

Digby Geste seated himself on the bench without
speaking, leant forward with his elbows on his knees,
took his head between his clenched fists, frowned
heavily, set his mouth grimly, and stared ferociously
at the ground in front of him.

By and by Mad Murphy sat up and stared at his neighbour.

"Go and moult somewhere else," he growled. . . . "I'm dangerous. . . . I'm going mad."

"So am I," replied Digby. "I'm dangerous, too. Please don't let me bite you. . . . Mad as a hatter."

Mad Murphy stared at him, suspicion mingling with anger in his glare.

"Wonder why hatters *are* mad," continued Digby.

"Go mad making hats for fools like you, perhaps," suggested Murphy.

"Why, of course," agreed Digby. "Who's *your* hatter? . . . Madame la République at the moment, of course. . . . She must be *quite* mad, or she'd make you and me Generals at once. . . . Then there's March hares. Why are *they* mad? March too much, I suppose, like us. I think I'll be a won't-march hare in future, then Lejaune'll get mad. Yes, I can honestly say it was marching made me mad. . . . Lots of times."

Silence.

"La Cigale is a grasshopper, I'm a hare; what are you going to be? A hatter? Depends on what drove you mad, of course. What was it, if one might ask?"

"Are you being funny?" growled Mad Murphy.

"I should think so," replied Digby. "I feel very funny. Mad, you know. Like a hare. By Jove, though, I'm not so sure that I *will* be a hare. La

Cigale is a grasshopper, and that makes him hop about on all fours, as you know. It would be a frightful thing if I became a March hare, and simply couldn't stop marching. That would make Lejaune just as mad as if I wouldn't march at all. It's a problem."

Murphy eyed him with less of suspicion and something of concern.

"Any madness in your family?" he asked.

"No," replied Digby. "None apparent, I believe. I'm the first—'hare apparent,' so to speak."

"You are lucky, then," said Murphy. "If you take a grip on yourself, there's some hope for you. My trouble is that I come of diseased, rotten, tainted, filthy, mad stock. . . . Father a mad beast who tortured my mother. . . . Isn't any man mad who ill-treats or hurts a woman in any way?"

"Obviously a criminal lunatic," agreed Digby.

"I've a good mind to go and shoot him before I shoot myself," continued Mad Murphy. "I would, if my mother were alive. She died in giving birth to me. I'm a pretty thing for her to have given her life for, good God!"

"She'd probably think so," observed Digby, and there was now no simulated insanity in his voice.

"Think so?" said Murphy. "She's dead I tell you."

"Nobody's dead," said Digby.

"No," agreed Murphy, "not *really* dead . . ."

and fell into a moody silence, which Digby broke
with the remark:

"But, of course, your father may have had a
whang on the head, or some illness. I believe some
forms of meningitis leave you a bit balmy on the
crumpet, and batty in the belfry."

"Illness be damned!" spat Murphy; "he is a
madman, I tell you. A criminal lunatic. . . . *And*,
my lad, so was my grandfather—mad and evil.
Best thing he ever did was when he shot himself.
. . . And if that's not enough for you, may I mention that my great-grandfather was a homicidal
maniac, and was killed by his best friend, whom he
murderously assaulted?"

Digby's face grew yet more thoughtful. This
was a pretty tale indeed.

"And if you'd like a little more family history,
his father, after a quiet sojourn in Newgate Gaol,
was hanged on Tyburn tree—and for a very dirty
crime. Not even a decent highwayman job. How's
that for a family record? And you want to know
what drove me mad, do you? Nothing! I was
born mad . . . mad for generations. . . . *'Unto
the third and fourth generation of them that hate
Me.'* . . . Haven't I some cause to hate Him?"

Silence.

"Look here, Murphy. You're evidently not up
to date. Don't you know that this heredity business
is an absolutely exploded fallacy? Nothing in it at

all. A child isn't tuberculous because its parents are, but because it grows up in the same conditions that made them tuberculous. . . . We inherit family likenesses, traits, tastes, and habits sometimes, and *only* sometimes, but we don't inherit microbes, and mental and physical diseases. . . .

"You yourself admit that nothing has driven you mad, and, so far as I can see, you are just a poor, weak, feeble ass who is simply inducing the very thing he fears. . . . *Fears*—that's it. You aren't so much an ass as a coward. . . . A cowardly ass, shall we say."

"Begod, you'd better not," growled Murphy, rising to his feet.

"Oh, sit down, man," said Digby. "It's too hot to fight. Besides, an ass, if that's what you're going to be, couldn't fight a hare. It would be all round him. Though, to tell the truth, I think you're more like a broody hen than an ass, really. Yes, you sit here all huddled up, and frightfully concerned with yourself, exactly like a broody hen in a dust-hole, counting her itchings before they are scratched. Yes, a broody hen. We'll be the Hare and Hen. Good name for a public-house! Let's leave the Legion and open one. . . .

"Isn't there a fable about them? The hare taught us—not to sleep on our posts. Not that one *could* sleep on a post, if you come to think of it."

Murphy sat down again, a very puzzled man.

"Talk sense," he requested.

"I can't," replied Digby. "I'm *mad.*"

"You were talking sense enough just now—about heredity," objected Murphy.

"Oh, yes, that was sense all right," admitted Digby. "There is no such thing as hereditary taint."

"And will you then tell me, you damned fool," shouted Murphy, "why I'm the sixth in direct line of homicidal maniacs, of beastly, bloodthirsty madmen; evil, malignant, murderous lunatics? Heredity! Isn't six generations enough for you? It *may* be sixty, for all I know."

"I don't care if it's six hundred," interrupted Digby. "All I know is I wouldn't make the six hundred and first. That's just weak-mindedness, not madness. . . . Just giving way to an *idée fixe,* and deliberately carrying on a family tradition—like that of going into the Army or Navy. Now, *I'm* a proper madman—off my own bat—not a miserable copy-cat like you want to be. If your people have been madmen, why not start something original, and be a sane person? My people have all been sane for six generations—or sixty—or six hundred perhaps, but *I'm* going to be mad. Would you mind addressing me as Monsieur M. Hare, in future?"

"I say, old chap, do you *really* think you're going dotty?" asked Murphy, with anxious concern.

"Well, it's like this," replied Digby. "I've been watching you a lot lately, you know, ever since your

detachment joined ours at Douargala, and I fluctu-
ate with *you*. When you give way to this madness,
I do, and when you pull yourself together, I buck
up like anything. I wish you'd help me. Can't
you drop this heredity idea?"

"Look here, Jones," said Murphy, laying his
hand upon Digby's knee, "you're sane enough—if
you don't give way. You must pull yourself together, and keep a tight hold on things. Now,
listen—you're all right—tell me . . . what would
you have done in case like this? Just when I left
school, I realized I was in love with the most glorious, wonderful girl in the whole world. The best,
and loveliest, and dearest, and sweetest woman that
ever lived . . ."

"Her name's Isobel," observed Digby.

"No, *Mary*—Mary Ronceval, daughter of Sir
Popham Ronceval, my guardian. . . . I was up in
town getting some kit . . . on my way to Oxford
. . . and went to a dance at their house. . . . And
do you know what devilish thing I did? Could you
imagine it; guess it; dream it? I lost my head in
the moonlit garden, and told her that she was all the
world—and all heaven—to me, and that I had loved
her for years. . . . And I kissed her, and heard her
say that she had always loved *me* . . . !

"How's that, for the last of a line of malignant
maniacs—foul, homicidal madmen? . . . Oh, God,
Mary! Mary!" . . .

And Mad Murphy bowed his head, and covered his face.

Digby Geste swallowed. . . . Had it been he and Isobel! . . .

"And so you bolted to the Legion!" he said, and, rising, laid his hand on Murphy's shaking shoulder.

"Keep sane, for her sake, old chap," continued Digby. "You *can,* you *can!* Of course you can; and go back to her when you've conquered. . . . I and my brothers will help you, and you can help me to . . ."

"*Sixth* of the line," groaned Murphy. "*Sixth* to my certain knowledge. . . . Homicidal maniacs . . ."

§ 4

Lieutenant Debussy was *au fond* a kindly person, though a strict disciplinarian, and very popular with his men, especially when on active service. They then saw far more of him than they did in barracks.

As he stepped, that evening, from his lighted room, mud-walled, mud-floored, and furnished with nothing but a table, a chair, a bag, and a radio set, he saw three of his *légionnaires*—three brothers, Englishmen, of whom he approved.

. . ."*Ah, mes enfants,*" said he, as they sprang to attention. "I've just been listening to something which would interest you—a band playing in one of your London hotels. . . . Would you like to hear it for a few minutes? I shall be gone for about half an hour. Have it for ten minutes each. . . . All most irregular, improper, and contrary to discipline, so don't get caught."

And, with a laugh, the gay and debonair young man descended the steps into the courtyard of this outpost that he commanded.

"*Quick!* Fetch Mad Murphy," whispered Beau Geste, as their hands dropped from the salute. "Do him a world of good. 'His need is greater than ours.'"

"Rather," agreed John. "Let him have the whole half-hour. We three can 'keep *cave*.' . . ."

§ 5

But Mad Murphy did not have his full half-hour.

For a few minutes he listened with a tortured smile on his face, as his foot unconsciously beat time to the music.

The music stopped, and with its stopping the chatter and applause of the crowd on the Majestic's dance-floor came through the headphones with a distinctness which to the listening exile painfully bridged the gulf between London and the desert around him.

"Rotten position for *me*," said a voice above the murmur of the ballroom. "I was the friend of both of them. Promised Long John I'd keep an eye on the boy. . . . Her boy . . . *His* boy."

"What became of him?"

"Wish I could tell you. . . . He was going up to Oxford for his first term, and never got there. Simply vanished into thin air. Tommy Vane didn't—"

And then he started up.

The smile left his face, and a look of astounded wonder and bewilderment took its place. Soon his face wore the expression of a man gazing at the foreman of a jury, whose *"Guilty"* or *"Not Guilty,* my Lord," means life or death to him. He paled beneath his tan, gasped, and suddenly cried:

"God in Heaven! . . . Long John . . . *Sir John Fitzgerald* . . . the great sportsman and big-game shot. *My father! . . . Mary! . . .*"

He swayed, staggered, sagged at the knees, and, to the consternation of the watching Digby Geste, burst into tears.

VI

BURIED TREASURE

I

"POOR old Cigale's pretty bad these days," said John Geste to his brothers Michael and Digby as he stepped into a tent of the standing camp some ninety kilometres south of Douargala.

"Yes," replied Digby, as he rose to help his brother remove and stow his kit in the tiny space which was allotted to each of the twelve men who lived in the little tent that could uncomfortably accommodate eight.

"Moon getting to the full," observed Michael. "We shall have to keep an eye on the poor old chap. What's his latest?"

"Seeing ghosts," replied John. "He's just been telling me all about it in the Guard Tent. When he was on sentry last night, he saw somebody approaching him. Such a very remarkable and extraordinary somebody that, instead of challenging, he rubbed his eyes and stared again. He told me all this in the most rational and convincing manner. It was really almost impossible to do anything but believe. He said:

"'When I looked again I hardly knew what to

do. There undoubtedly was a man coming towards me out of the desert, from the direction of the ruins. Nothing strange in that, you may say, but the man was a soldier in uniform. And the uniform was not of this regiment, nor of this army, nor of this country—nor of this century—no, nor of this thousand years. His helmet was of shining metal, with ear-pieces and neck-shield, but no visor—rather like a pompier's helmet, but with a horsehair crest and plume, and he had a gleaming cuirass of the same metal. In fact, I thought, for a moment, that he was a trooper of the Dragoon Guards until I saw that he carried a spear, at the slope, across his right shoulder, and for side-arms had a short sword— broad, but not much longer than a dagger. Under his cuirass he wore a sort of tunic that came down to his knees, and over this hung a fringe of broad strips of metal on leather. He wore metal greaves on his shins and sandals on his feet.

" 'In fact, he was a Roman soldier marching on patrol or doing sentry-go on his beat. For one foolish moment I thought of enemy tricks and stratagems and also of practical jokes, but then I realized that not only could I see him as plainly as I see you now, but that I could see *through* him. No, he was not nebulous and misty like a cloud of steam; his outline was perfectly clear-cut, but, as he approached me, he came between me and one of the pillars of the ruins, and though I could see him perfectly clearly and distinctly, I could also see the pillar.

" 'I was in something of a quandary. As you know, I try to do my duty to the very best of my poor ability, and aim at being the perfect private soldier. But there is nothing laid down in regulations on the subject of the conduct of a sentry when approached by a ghost.

" 'In the Regulations it says, "*Anyone* approaching," and at once the question arises as to whether a ghost is anyone. You see, it is the ghost *of* some-one, and therefore cannot *be* someone, can it? . . .'

"Thus spake the good Cigale," continued John, "and I assured him that personally I should not turn out the Guard nor rouse the camp to repel ghosts."

"No," agreed Digby. "I don't think I should, either. Sure to be a catch in it somewhere. The moment the Sergeant of the Guard came, the dirty dog would disappear—the ghost, I mean—and then you'd be for it.

"On the other hand," he continued, "if you didn't challenge him, he might go straight into the General's tent and give the old dear the fright of his life—and then you'd be for it again."

"Very rightly," agreed Michael. "What good would the General be at running a scrap next day, if he'd had a Roman soldier tickling him in the tummy with the butt-end of a spear all night?"

"True," mused John. "It's a problem. There

ought to be a section in the Regulations. They
certainly provide for most other things."

"And supposing it were the ghost of a most lovely
houri approaching the General's tent?" asked Digby.
"Should it be left to the sentry's indiscretion? And
suppose the General came out and caught him turning her away—or turning unto her the other cheek
also—"

"It's weird, though," Michael broke in upon these
musings. "You can be absolutely certain that La
Cigale thought he saw a Roman soldier, and if you
think you see a thing, you *do* see it."

"What's that?" inquired Digby incredulously.
"If I think I see a pimple on the end of your nose,
I *do* see one?"

"Yes, you do, if you really think it. There is an
image of it on the retina of your eye—and what
is that but seeing?"

"He did more than see him, too," put in John.
"He had a long conversation with him. They com-
pared notes as to their respective regiments—the
Third Legion, and the French Foreign Legion."

"By Jove, that's interesting!" observed Beau
Geste. "I should have liked to hear them."

"I wonder if you'd have heard the ghost?" said
Digby. "Of course, if you *thought* you heard him,
you *would* have heard him, eh?

"I say," he added. "I just thought I heard you
ask me to have a cigarette. Therefore I *did* hear it."

"Yes," agreed Michael. "And you thought you saw me give you one. Therefore I did give you one. Smoke it."

The tent-flap was pulled aside, and La Cigale entered.

"Come along, old chap! Splendid! We were just talking about you and your interesting experience with the Roman legionary," Beau continued.

"Yes, yes," replied Cigale. "A charming fellow. We had a most interesting conversation. His *dépôt* was here, and he'd served everywhere from Egypt to Britain, had sun-stroke twice in Africa, and frost-bite twice when stationed on The Wall, as he called it—Hadrian's Wall, that would be, between England and Scotland.

"He actually spoke of the Belgæ, and must have been stationed quite near my home at one time. A most intelligent chap, and with that education which comes from travel and experience. A little rocky on Roman history, I found, but who would expect a private soldier to be an authority on history—even that of his own country?"

§ 2

La Cigale fell silent and mused awhile, breaking thereafter into mutterings, disjointed and fragmentary.

"Most interesting fellow. Rome in Africa, five

centuries; France in Africa, one century; the sun
the unconquerable enemy of both. Rome did not
assimilate although she conquered. Will France
assimilate, or be herself assimilated?"

And turning to Michael Geste, said:

"He was stationed at Cæsarea once. They called
it 'The Athens of the West.' We talked of Masi-
nissa, the Berber King of Cæsarea and all Numidia.
You will remember he fought against Rome, and
then against Carthage in alliance with Rome. He
was the grandfather of the great Jugurtha.

"We chatted also of his son Juba, who fought for
Pompey in the civil war and committed suicide after
Cæsar defeated him at Thapsus.

"*Most* interesting fellow. He told me that Antony's wife Octavia adopted Juba's little son and
brought him up with Antony's own little daughter by
Cleopatra—young Silene Cleopatra he called her.
Quite a charming little romance he made of it, for
the two kiddies grew up together at the Roman
Court and fell in love with each other—married and
lived happy ever after. They went back to Cæsarea
and he ruled in the house of his fathers. Rather
nice to think about when one considers those cruel
times—"

§ 3

"Oh, for God's sake, shut your jabbering row,"
growled The Treasure, from where he was lying

on his blanket. "Enough to make a dog sick to listen to you."

"Then suppose the dog goes and is sick outside, and doesn't listen," suggested Digby.

"Yes, a charming little story," agreed Michael. "What else did your visitor talk about?"

"Oh, places where he was stationed," replied La Cigale, "and about his Legion. He was frightfully proud of that—like we are of ours. He was in the Third African Legion. 'The Augustine,' he called it. He says it was three centuries in Africa. They only kept one legion in Africa, he tells me, though there were three in Britain. Great fellows, those Romans, for system and organization. What do you think? In this Third Legion of his, the recruiting was almost purely hereditary. Think of that—hereditary drafts. When a man had served his time in the Legion they gave him land on the understanding that he married and settled down there, and sent his sons into the Legion. No wonder there was *esprit de corps* in the Augustine Legion. By the way, they built that place over there in A.D. 100, called it Sagunta Diana, and built it on the ground plan of a Roman camp.

"By Jove, he did a march that I envy him. First they marched right across North Africa, from here to Alexandria. There they embarked in triremes for Italy, and marched to Rome. Thence north, right up Italy, and all across France to a place whence

they could see Britain. Then by transports again
to Dover, whence they marched to London, and
from there through the length of England to
Hadrian's Wall. Twenty times 2,000 paces was
their day's march—all marked off by regular camp-
ing-places.

"He tells me they had a frightful row in camp
outside Alexandria with the Sixth Legion from Judea
—the Ferrata Legion they called it. It seems the
Third Legion hated the others coming into Africa
to relieve them while they did their tour of foreign
service; they looked upon Africa as their own, and
didn't want interlopers in their stations, such as Timgad Lambæsis, Mascula, Verecundia and Sitifis. He
called Timgad *Thamugadi.* I didn't recognize the
word at first, as he pronounced it. He was awfully
interested to hear that I'd been there and could
identify some of the temples in which he had worshipped. It is still in a wonderful state of preser-
vation, as you know. Lambæsis was his favourite
camp, for some reason. He was delighted when I
told him that the Arch of Septimus Severus is almost
as perfect to-day as when he saw it last. That led us
to speak of the Arch of Caracalla. That's at The-
veste—about 200 miles from Carthage, you know.
I'm afraid he began to think I was pulling his leg
when I told him I knew it, as well as his beloved
Temple of Minerva. He got quite excited."

The Treasure growled, cursed, and spat.

"Told you all that, did he?" he said. "Damn fine ghost! Pity he couldn't have told you something useful. Where he'd buried a few bottles of wine, for example. D'you know what there was when you and your ghost was jabberin'? Two village idiots together—that's what there was."

"If you interrupt again I'll put your face in the sand, and sit on your head till you die," murmured John Geste.

"But there wasn't two *crétins*," continued The Treasure. "There was only one barmy lunatic, and he was talkin' to hisself. 'E's talkin' to three others, 'e is, now."

John Geste rose to his feet, and The Treasure scrambled from the tent in haste.

"And this is a *most* interesting thing," continued La Cigale, still staring at the ground between his feet, as was his habit when not on duty or employed. "Very curious, too. He told me about a deserter from the Roman army—the Legionary Tacfrineas he called him, who went over to the enemy, and organized the Berber tribes against Rome. The Third Legion was frightfully sick about it. Of course, it was just as though one of us deserted and joined the Senussi or the Touareg or the Riffs, and taught them our drill and tactics, trained their artillerymen, gave them our plans and passwords and generally made them about ten times as dangerous as they are.

"I'd certainly never heard of this Tacfrineas be-fore, so I couldn't have *imagined* all this, could I?"

And he gazed appealingly at the faces of the three brothers.

"Of course not," said Beau Geste. "Extraordi-narily interesting experience. It must give you great pleasure to think that, out of all the Battalion, it was you whom the Roman soldier chose to visit."

"Oh, yes. Indeed, yes," agreed La Cigale, smil-ing. "I feel quite happy to-day, and can even bear the sight—and smell—of The Treasure. And the Roman soldier has promised to come and visit me again when I am on sentry, and he's going to tell me a great secret. I don't know what it is, but it's something about some gold."

La Cigale fell silent, pondering, and gradually the light of intelligence faded from his eyes, his mouth fell open, and he looked stupid, dull and miserable.

Digby Geste leant over and shook him by the knee.

"Splendid, old chap," he said. "You're a very remarkable man, you know. I envy you. What else did you and the other old *légionnaire* yarn about?"

"Oh, we compared pay, rations, drill, marches and all that sort of thing, you know," replied La Cigale, brightening like a re-lighted lamp. They had the same infernal road-making fatigues that we do.

"Why, he tells me they built one hundred and ninety miles of solid stone road from Thevesti to Carthage. Think of that—*stone!*

"Oh, yes, we exchanged grumbles. They had the same god-forsaken little outposts down in the South and much the same sort of tyranny from 'foreign' N.C.O.'s, of whom they were more afraid than they were of the Centurions themselves. Yes, they had an iron discipline and even severer punishments. In a case where a man here might get *crapaudine*, because there were no cells in which to give him thirty days' solitary confinement, he would have been flogged to death in the Third Legion, or perhaps crucified.

"I say, I *do* hope he comes again. Do you think he will? He gave me the happiest night I've had since I went—went—went—"

La Cigale groaned, and gazed stupidly around.

"Eh?" he asked. "What's this?" and lay down upon his blanket to sleep.

§ 4

La Cigale's *bête noir* was a person whom, in full possession of his faculties, had less understanding and intelligence than La Cigale at his maddest.

He was that curious product of the Paris slums, that seems to be less like a human being than are the criminal denizens of the underworld of any other

city—Eastern or Western, civilized or savage. He
was not so much a typical Paris apache, as an apache
too bestial, degraded, evil and brutish to be typical
even of the Parisian apache. Even the Geste brothers, who could find "tongues in trees, books in the
running brooks, sermons in stones, and good in everything," could find no good in "The Treasure"—as
Sergeant-Major Lejaune, with grim irony, had chris-
tened him. They had, individually and collectively,
done their best, and had completely failed. That
such a creature, personally filthy (inside his uniform), with foulest tongue and foulest habits, degraded and disgusting, a walking pollution and cor-
ruption, should be one's intimate companion at bed
and board, was one of the many things that made life
in the Legion difficult. One had to sleep, eat, march,
and take one's ease (!) cheek by jowl with The
Treasure, and could not escape him.

§ 5

And The Treasure, by nature indescribably objectionable, deliberately made himself as personally and
peculiarly objectionable to La Cigale as he possibly
could. From the store of his vile, foul manners, he
gave the sensitive ex-officer constant experience of
the vilest and foulest of his filthy and revolting
speech. Of his mean, low, injurious tricks, he reserved the worst for La Cigale. When accused by a

non-commissioned officer of some offence, he in-
variably laid the blame upon La Cigale, in the rea-
soned belief and reasonable hope that the poor madman would have either too little wit or too much
chivalry to defend himself and arraign his lying
accuser.

On one occasion, at Ain Sefra, Beau Geste had
seen The Treasure, just before kit inspection, direct
the attention of La Cigale, by a sudden shout and
pointing hand, to something else, while he snatched
a belt from La Cigale's kit and placed it with his
own. This saved him from eight days' prison and
transferred the punishment to the bewildered La
Cigale, who could only stammer to the roaring Sergeant-Major Lejaune that his show-down of kit
had been complete a few seconds before. But it had
earned The Treasure a worse punishment, for the
indignant Beau Geste had soundly and scientifically
hammered him, until he wept and begged for mercy,
with profuse protestations that he had not done it,
but would never do it again.

He never did, but he redoubled his efforts to render La Cigale's life insupportable, and showed something almost approaching intelligence in ascertain-
ing which of his foul habits and fouler words most
annoyed, shocked, disgusted and upset his unhappy
victim.

For Beau Geste, The Treasure entertained a deep
respect, a great fear and a sharp knife, the last-named

to be taken as prescribed (in the back), and when opportunity and occasion should arise. These would have arisen long ago but that his enemy had two brothers and two horrible American friends who rendered an otherwise perfectly simple job not only difficult but extremely dangerous. . . . (Remember poor Bolidar!)

Like almost all of his kind, The Treasure was a drunkard, and there was nothing he would not do for money, inasmuch as money to him was synonymous with liquor. Having been, in private life, a professional pick-pocket and sneak-thief, he was able to keep himself modestly supplied with cash while avoiding the terrible retribution which overtakes the *légionnaire* who robs his comrades.

§ 6

"Do you know, young gentlemen," said John Geste, one afternoon, to his two brothers as they strolled from the parade ground whence they had just been dismissed to the tent where they would now settle down to the cleaning of their kit, "I've had an idea?"

Digby seized John's wrist that he might feel his pulse, and observed:

"An idea, Beau! He's had an idea. Hold him while I fetch some water."

"He's got plenty already," replied Michael unperturbed, "on the brain. Idea's probably drowned by now."

"No, no," said John. "It's still swimming around. It's this: La Cigale is for guard again to-night and simply bubbling with excitement at the thought of seeing his Roman soldier again."

"What! Do you want to go and pal up with him?" interrupted Digby. "Butt in and make up to La Cigale's old pal—severing two loving hearts—green-eyed jealousy—"

"No, the pup only wants to see a ghost," said Michael.

"Well, of course, I would," admitted John. "But what I was going to say, when you two—er—gentlemen began to bray, was this. Poor old Cigale may do anything under the disturbing influences of full moon and a private visit from this Shade."

"Shady business," murmured Digby. "He may go clean off the deep end in his excitement—start showing him round the camp, take him in to gaze upon the slumbering features of Lejaune, or even toddle off with him to visit a two thousand years closed wine shop in the forum at Sagunta Diana. It occurred to me that a few of us three might exchange with fellows who are for guard, and keep an eye on the poor old chap."

"Quite so," agreed Beau Geste. "Good lad. I fancy Lejaune would be only too glad of the chance to smash La Cigale for being a gentleman and an ex-

officer. And if the doctor or the colonel or a court
martial officially pronounced him mad he might be
put in a lunatic asylum. And that would be about
the cruelest and most dreadful thing one could
imagine, for he's half sane half the time, and as sane
as we are occasionally."

"Oh, yes," agreed Digby. "Far saner than some
people—John, for example."

§ 7

In the early moonlit hours of the following morning, John Geste patrolled the beat which adjoined
that of La Cigale, while Michael and Digby took
turns to sit outside the guard tent to watch.

For an hour or so of his tour of sentry go, La
Cigale behaved quite normally.

Suddenly John, marching on his beat towards
where La Cigale stood staring in the direction of
the ruins of Sagunta Diana, saw him spring to attention, present arms, hold himself erect and rigid
as a statue, relax and stand at ease, change his rifle
from his right hand to his left and then, bowing,
warmly shake hands with some person invisible.

"I am so glad you've come again, my friend,"
John heard La Cigale say. "Most kind and charming of you. I'm awfully sorry I can't show myself
as hospitable as I should like to be—but you know
what it is. No, we shan't be disturbed until I'm

relieved. Grand Rounds passed some time ago."

John Geste shivered slightly.

A most uncanny experience. It was perfectly obvious that La Cigale was talking to somebody whom
he could see and hear and touch.

Could it be that ghosts really exist, and are visible
to those who are what is called psychic?

He stared and stared at the place where anyone
would be standing who was talking, face to face, with
La Cigale. Nothing, of course.

He rubbed his eyes and, clasping the blade of the
long bayonet in his hands, leant upon his rifle while
he concentrated his gaze as though peering through
a fog.

Nothing, of course.

But *was* there nothing? Was there a shadow con-
fronting La Cigale? The shadow of a medium-sized
thick-set man leaning upon his spear in the very attitude in which John was leaning upon his bayonet and
rifle.

Or was it pure illusion? All moonshine—a curious optical delusion enormously strengthened by La
Cigale's conduct and the fact that he was talking
so naturally.

Yes, a clear case of hetero-suggestion. Curious,
though, that one's ears could so affect one's eyes that
one could imagine one saw what one imagined one
heard.

Would he hear the Roman soldier's voice in a

moment? If so, he would be perfectly certain that he *could* see the figure of a Roman soldier wearing a helmet like that of a fireman; a moulded breastplate from which depended heavy hangings; metal greaves; and high-laced sandals—a man who bore a longish shield curved at the sides and straight at the top and bottom, on which was painted an eagle, a capital A, and the figure III.

He only *thought* he saw him now, of course, and in a moment he would think he heard his voice. At present there was but one, and hearing it was like listening to a person who is using the telephone in the room in which one is.

.   .   .   .

"Were you really? No! How very interesting!"

.   .   .   .

"Oh, yes; I've been there several times. To think that we have trodden the same streets, entered the very same shops and dwelling-houses, temples and theatres, actually drunk from the same faucet and washed our hands in the same stone trough! I think that one of the most interesting—the most *human* and real—things in all the wonderful Pompeii are those grooves worn in the edges of the troughs where thousands of people for hundreds of years all laid their right hands on the same spot to support themselves as they bent over the trough to put their lips to the faucet from which the water trickled."

.   .   .   .

"Yes, of course you have, many and many a time, and so did I once—just to be one with all those departed Romans."

.   .   .   .

"Yes, that's what makes it so wonderful. Not merely a case of my having been in a place which is only on the site of a place in which you have been. Yes, exactly. The very same actual and identical houses. You and I, my friend, have trodden on the same actual paving-blocks, and have sat upon the same stone seats. I have walked in the very ruts in which the wheels of your chariot rolled as you drove it down the stone-paved High Street of Pompeii, and I have stood in the wine shops in which you have drunk."

.   .   .   .

"Yes, a very funny picture, indeed. It is still there, the colours as perfect as when you saw it last. They've got glass, and a sort of blind over it now, and a custodian to guard it. To think you actually saw it being painted and remember roaring with laughter when Balbus drew your attention to it."

.   .   .   .

"Oh, didn't you? A pity. History says that he was living there about that time."

.   .   .   .

"Yes, you must have hated returning from furlough just then even to the Third Legion."

.   .   .   .

"Well, no, we aren't supposed to do it—and there'd be precious little to be had if we were. One hears tales, of course. There's a place we call Fez where one or two are supposed to have got hold of a little."

.   .   .   .

"Really? By Jove, that would be an interesting find for anybody who unearthed it now. . . ."

.   .   .   .

"*I* could? I'm afraid it wouldn't be of much use to me—though it would be most awfully interesting to see it. There would probably be coins of which no known specimen exists at the present day. Priceless. Oh, yes, they would fetch any sum. . . ."

.   .   .   .

"By Jove, that was hard luck! They don't seem to have changed much, from your day to ours. We call them Bedouin and Touareg. Attack us in much the same way. Stamp us flat occasionally, but discipline always tells. . . ."

.   .   .   .

"Could you really? The very spot? Very kind of you—most charming. I should love to see the coins."

.   .   .   .

"Oh, no, I shouldn't wish to remove it, but if you could spare one or two specimens that are unknown to-day, I should love to have them as souvenirs. I

should not part with them of course. One or two
early Greek gold ones."

.   .   .   .

"Now at once? Really most kind of you. A very
great honour. Oh, no, I wouldn't dream of showing
anybody else. I never betray a confidence. . . ."

.   .   .   .

And then John Geste rushed forward as La Cigale,
throwing his rifle up on his right shoulder, marched
off in the direction of Sagunta Diana. Digby Geste
came hurrying from the direction of the Guard Tent.

Seizing La Cigale's arm, John swung him about.

"What are you doing, man?" he expostulated.
"You can't leave your post like this. You're a pretty
sentry! You don't want to be shot, do you?—not
at dawn by a firing party of your own comrades, at
any rate!"

Digby arrived and seized La Cigale's other arm.

"Come home, Bill Bailey," quoth he. "Setting us
all a nice example, aren't you? And I thought you
were the model *légionnaire*."

"Good God, what am I doing!" stammered La
Cigale and passed his hand across his eyes as the
brothers released him.

"Thank you so much, gentlemen. This absent-
mindedness is terrible. Do you know, a friend of
mine, a most interesting chap, strolled over from his
lines and we fell into conversation. I actually for-

got that I was on sentry. I am getting *so* absent-
minded. When he invited me to come over and—er
—look at something I was just going to walk across
with him. Thank you *so* much."

"All right now?" asked Digby.

"Oh, quite, thank you!" replied La Cigale. "It
was only a momentary aberration. I'd sooner die
than leave my post, of course."

"What became of him?" asked John.

"Oh, he went off without me," replied La Cigale.
"There he goes, look. I hope he's not offended."

§ 8

The brothers stared and stared in the direction of
La Cigale's extended hand.

"See anything, John?" whispered Digby.

"Well, do you know?" answered John, "I couldn't
absolutely swear that I didn't see a nebulous figure.
And the astounding thing is that I saw or thought
I saw something that La Cigale never mentioned."

"The shield?" whispered Digby. "With a capital A and the Roman III, and something at the
top?"

"Did you see it, too?" enquired a voice from behind.

Michael had joined them.

"Clearly," replied Digby. "Did you, Beau?"

"Absolutely distinctly," replied Michael. "I saw a Roman soldier. I could describe every detail of his kit; I could sketch him exactly as he was."

"I, too," affirmed Digby.

"You, John?" asked Michael.

"Couldn't swear to it," replied John. "Cigale was chatting away so naturally with *somebody*—that I couldn't help fancying that I saw the man to whom he was talking. I certainly didn't see anything clearly and definitely like you two seem to have done. And yet I fancied I dimly saw the III A shield. If nobody else had mentioned it I should have thought that I'd dreamed the whole thing."

"Rum business," murmured Digby.

"Not an 'absinthe' business, anyhow," replied Michael, as John and La Cigale turned about and began to pace their respective beats.

"You and I are fey, Digby Geste," smiled Michael, linking his arm through that of his brother as they turned back to the guard-tent.

§ 9

The Treasure lay hid in the black shadow of a crumbling arch watching with wolfish eyes a man who laboured to remove the light, loose sand that had collected at the base of a wall at a point twenty-five paces from a pillar—the fourth of a row that had once supported and adorned the front of a

Temple of Diana. Something approaching excitement stirred the sluggish depths of his evil and avaricious soul as he once more assured himself that he was on the track of something good.

Yesterday—with his back turned to his comrades and an appearance of great absorption in his work—he had listened with close attention as this bloomin' lunatic told his blasted friends, those bestial Englishmen, about how he was going to sneak over to these ruddy ruins and dig out a *cache* of gold coins of which he had got wind. Some poor legionary had hid his little bit of loot there one night and the place had been rushed and sacked at dawn, the next morning. Gold coins, too! Nice, handy, portable form of loot, too! And the dirty double-crosser was only going to take one or two to look at, was he? The sacred liar! Not so *fou* as he pretended, that Cigale. Oh, very tricky. Well, other people might know a few tricks, too! What about letting the swindling silly hound sweat for the stuff, and a better man scoop it when the fool had got it?

§ 10

An hour or so later, La Cigale straightened himself up, gazed around the moonlit ruins in a dazed manner, climbed out of the hole that he had excavated, and made his way towards the camp.

The Treasure crouched back, motionless, in the

darkest shadow, until his comrade had passed, and then, rising, followed him—a large stone in his right hand.

The Treasure was a workman skilled in all branches of his trade—one of which was the throwing of knives and other weapons of offence. The heavy stone, flung at a range of six feet or so, struck the unfortunate Cigale at the base of the skull, and by the time he had recovered consciousness The Treasure had come reluctantly to the conclusion that the accursed, lying, swindling *crétin* had only got a single old coin of some sort, gold, and curiously shaped, about his person. One ancient gold coin, the size of a two-franc piece.

By the time La Cigale had painfully raised himself upon his hands and knees, The Treasure was working feverishly in the excavation that his comrade had recently left.

By the time La Cigale had recovered sufficiently to rise to his feet and gaze uncertainly toward the ruins whence he had come, a dull rumbling, followed by an earth-shaking crash, had startled the watchful sentries of the camp. An undermined pillar had fallen.

The Treasure was seen no more by his unsorrowing comrades.

Buried Treasure.

VII

IF WISHES WERE HORSES . . .

I

THE full moon, a great luminous pearl, and the incredible tropic stars—palely blue diamonds scattered over darkly blue velvet—looked down upon four weary, dirty men who lounged around a small camp-fire beneath a stunted, crooked palm beside a puddle of slimy water, rock-circled, thing-inhabited, malodorous.

One of the men was fair, huge, with huge moustache, a great laugh, great hands, and gross appetite. He looked too dull to be wicked, or successful. Drink had washed him into the Legion.

The second was dark, tiny, the ideal gentleman-jockey in build; pretty, small of mouth, and large of eye. He looked too clever to be trustworthy or determined. Race-horses had carried him to the Legion.

The third was grey, tall, spare and gaunt, a light-cavalry type. His craggy face was sad and weary, bitter, and somewhat cruel. He looked too cynical to be very intelligent or helpful. Vengeance had driven him to the Legion.

The fourth was Digby Geste, typical English gentleman. Brother-love had led him to the Legion.

Around them stretched to the horizon, on every side, the illimitable desert plain, still, mysterious, inimical, its dead level of monotony broken only by an occasional bush or boulder. A select small company of vultures formed a large circle around them, and took an abiding interest in their risings up, and their lyings down—particularly the latter.

A more select and smaller company of human vultures had made their camp a mile or so distant— by the simple process of lying down in their tracks, eating dates, and going to sleep—while one of their number, having wriggled like a snake with incredible flatness, speed and skill to within view of the men around the little camp-fire, squatted behind a boulder and also took an abiding interest in their risings up, and their lyings down, and particularly the latter.

To the vultures, the chance of a meal was something to follow up for days, and to the human vultures the chance of a rifle, worth its weight in silver, was something to follow up for weeks. Should the watcher, one night, see the sentry nod, sit down, lean back, sleep—he would wriggle near, satisfy himself, and then flee like a deer to his fellows. There would be a quick loping run, a close recognisance, a sudden swift rush, a flash of knives, and soon the meal, ready jointed, would await the other vultures.

§ 2

"Suppose the good Archangel Gabriel suddenly alighted here, with easy grace, and, folding his wings, granted us each a wish, what would you have, Zimmerman?" the dark little man suddenly asked the huge, fair one.

"Eh? . . . Me? . . . . Grant me a wish? . . . Like those people in the Grimm fairy tales?" replied Zimmerman, a harmless, worthless waster—once.

"Oh, I don't know. . . . Pick up a diamond as big as my fist. . . . Strike for Berlin, home and beauty then. Take a suite in the Hotel Adlon in the Pariser Platz, do the *Weinrestaurants, tanzlokals,* theatres, beer-halls, night-cafés of the Kurfürstendamm, for a bit. Look up all the boys—and the girls. . . . Oh, ho! Champagne . . . fresh caviare . . . feasting . . . races . . . the tables . . . Peacock Island, Grunewald, Charlottenburg, nightclubs . . . Ho, ho! When I drove my girl down the Unter den Linden, every one would turn and look at us. Then I'd take her down to Monte Carlo, by way of Paris. Nothing wrong with Paris, and Monte Carlo, after you've picked up a diamond as big as your fist. Yes, I'd give her a time she'd remember. Let her see all the shops in Paris and Monte. . . . Let her see me win a pile of hundred-franc notes at the Casino. . . . Let her see me shoot the pigeons."

"She'd *love* that, I'm sure," observed Digby Geste.

"Yes, she would so! . . . *Gott in Himmel!* I'd melt that diamond down. . . .

"What would you do, Gomez? . . . Madrid, a Señorita, and the bull-ring? . . . Carmelitas . . . fandangos, guitars, wine of Oporto and Xeres, serenades?"

"Not a bit of it. I should make straight for England. Get another string together, and train 'em myself."

"Win the Derby, Oaks, and the Grand National, all in the same year, what? . . ."

"Yes . . . I'd have my stables all white tiles, mahogany, porcelain and silver plate—the talk of the country-side—and my horses the talk of England, the talk of the world. . . . Ascot . . . Goodwood . . . Newmarket . . . Longchamps Auteuil . . ."

He sighed heavily.

"Well, thank the good God for tobacco, even French tobacco, until Gabriel comes," guffawed Zimmerman.

"What would be *your* line, Jones?" he added, turning to Digby Geste.

Digby took his pipe from his mouth, slowly blew a long cloud of smoke, and gazed at the great ball

of gentle light that hung from the velvet dome of
the low sky.

What boon would he ask, if one were to be granted
to him?

It cannot be said that his thoughts turned to
Brandon Abbas, for they were already there.

What would be the loveliest thing his mind could
possibly conceive? What about a drive in the high
dog-cart with Isobel?—through the glorious Devon
countryside; the smart cob doing his comfortable ten
miles an hour; harness jingling; hoof-beats regular
as clockwork; Isobel's hand under his right arm;
Devon lanes; Devon fields and orchards; Devon
moors; glorious—beyond description.

But then he would have to keep at least one eye
on the horse and the road, and that would leave only
one eye for Isobel. . . . When one is driving a
horse, one should drive him properly, with the care
and attention which is one's courtesy to a horse that
is worth driving. . . . Well up to his bit, with
watchful eye and ready hand . . .

No, not a drive. What about two long chairs in
the Bower, side by side, but facing opposite ways,
so that he would have a full view of Isobel's face
. . . nothing for his eyes to do but to watch every
change of expression in *her* wonderful eyes, and
lovely face . . . nothing for his ears to do but note
every change and inflexion and sound of her sweet
voice?

Or what about asking something bigger—something really big? . . . Why not ask that time be pushed forward a few years, and that the three of them be distinguished officers? Beau a Colonel, John and he Majors, going home on leave after a glorious campaign; home to Brandon Abbas and Isobel . . . Isobel . . . Isobel's arms about his neck . . . the little Church in Brandon Park . . . the Chaplain at the altar . . . Beau should give her away . . . John should be best man. . . . Oh, too wonderfully beautiful . . . too terribly glorious . . . too unthinkable. . . .

He turned to Zimmerman.

"What would *I* like best in all the world?" he said. "Oh, I should love, beyond expression, beyond the power of human speech . . . to hit a very bald man on the head with a very long cucumber."

His companions pondered this ambition.

"No, no! Not *a* bald man. Not just *any* bald man. It's *l'Adjudant* Lejaune one would like to hit on the head with a long cucumber," said the Spaniard. "Now, that really would be a deed worth doing! . . . *Smack!* . . . Just when he's bawling his foulest insults. . . . One could die happy after that. Yes, a really great conception, Jones. Can you beat it, Budiski? What would you like?"

"I? . . . I'd ask for nothing better than two minutes with a certain Russian gentleman I know . . .

a perfect little gentleman. A General, in fact," replied the grey-haired, grey-faced man.

"I've followed his career with interest ever since
he was quite a junior officer. . . . I have shot him
once. . . . That's why I am here. . . .

"He came with his half-company to our village
when I was a lad . . . long, long ago. . . . It was
pogrom time, and everybody was accusing everybody,
when they weren't shooting them instead. . . . And
our Russian masters were 'pacifying' that little corner of our country by the excellent Russian method.

"Any Lieutenant was the equal of Julius Cæsar
in respect of his complete ability to 'make a solitude
and call it peace. . . .'

"They banged on our door one night, because ours
was the biggest, and most comfortable house in the
neighbourhood. . . . Ostensibly, because there was
a blood-stained hand-cart in our stables. Of course
there was. . . . It had been put there by the worthy
soul who had used it to remove bleeding carcases
from where they were inconvenient, to where they
were useful evidence against his enemy. . . . Probably—in proof of his hatred of all evil-doing, and
his love of all Jews and Russians—he had shown the
dripping push-cart to the Russian police.

"Anyhow, there it was, and there were the Russian soldiers round our house, in which slept my
father and mother in a front room; my sister Wanda
—a lovely girl of about eighteen—in the next room,

and I and my young brother in a big room at the
back. . . .

"He was a good boy, that young brother of mine.
I was rather fond of him. Perhaps some of you can
understand that?"

Digby Geste nodded his head.

"And we both adored Wanda. She was one of
those simple, gentle, kind natures who, knowing no
evil, are slow to think there is any in others, and
imagine that all men—and women—are like themselves. Not clever, you know, nor accomplished,
nor advanced, nor up-to-date, but just merely simply
something to thank God for, in a world like this."

"Marguerite, before Faust came on the scene, eh?"
said the big German.

The Pole regarded him absent-mindedly, and continued:

"I suppose there is a God of Love—a beneficent
Deity?"

"Of course there is," observed Digby Geste.
"Didn't he create your Wanda?"

"And didn't he watch what followed? . . . I
pulled on an overcoat, and ran downstairs as my
father opened the front door to the soldiers. In five
minutes they were all over the house, and they
brought Wanda and my mother and my young
brother down into the big living-room where the
Lieutenant, his drawn sword in his hand, lolled in a
chair, questioning my father, or rather abusing and

bullying him and shouting accusations to which he would hear no answer.

"I can see that *intérieur* now, the impudent hard-faced rascal in my father's chair. A Sergeant and half a dozen grey-coated, flat-capped soldiers at attention behind him. Other soldiers replenishing the fire, lighting more lamps and candles, ransacking the place for food, drink, and loot . . .

"For the sake of his wife and children, my father was humble, meek, conciliatory, deprecating. It did not take the brave Lieutenant, who was prosecutor, witnesses, judge and jury all in one, many minutes to try the old man, find him guilty, and sentence him to death.

" 'Remove the prisoner,' said he, having delivered sentence. 'Bind him, and take him outside—under a tree with a suitable bough.'

"As my mother and Wanda threw themselves on their knees before this upright judge, a Corporal and four men seized my father, tied a rope round his body, so that his arms were bound to his sides, and led him out into the snow, over which the cold, grey dawn was beginning to break.

"Smiling evilly on the two imploring women, the gentleman leant forward. With his left hand he gave my mother a rough thrust that sent her sprawling, and then, cupping Wanda's chin in his palm, he turned her face up to his, and kissed her on the lips.

"The brave rash boy, my brother Karol, sprang forward, before his two guards could stop him—and even as I shouted, 'Don't, you young fool,' and, with bursting heart, firmly controlled myself for the sake of all of us—he struck the Lieutenant heavily between the eyes, sending that hero over backwards, chair and all.

"Leaping to his feet, as the guards sprang upon my brother, and on me, this brave Russian officer put his sword-point to my brother's throat—and *thrust* . . .

"I fought like a madman . . .

"I hear my mother's screams to this day . . .

"Wanda had fainted.

"The Lieutenant gave orders that she should be carried to her bed, and tied to it securely. Also that I and my mother should be bound.

" 'Take the old hag out to her husband,' he ordered, as they tore her from my brother, who lay bleeding to death among their feet.

"I lost control.

" 'Yes,' I shouted. 'You foul dog! You cowardly, inhuman devil! You *Russian!* Bind an old woman, lest she hurt you! . . . Bind her, and feel safe, you miserable swine!'

"And I contrived to spit on him.

"Calmly he wiped his face, and sat himself down again.

" 'Bring the woman back, Sergeant,' he ordered

quietly, 'and send a man to tell Corporal Kyriloff to fetch the old man back, too. . . . Bring the next prisoner before the Court.'

"I was dragged before his chair, my arms roped to my sides, and my ankles bound together. He eyed me very coldly.

"Always beware of those who, while a seething hell of rage boils within them, eye you coldly, and speak quietly.

" 'You have resisted, insulted, and attempted to kill a Russian Officer in the execution of his duty,' he said quietly. . . . 'You are condemned to death. Your father has already been condemned to death. Your brother has been put to death. . . . But the Court is merciful. Like your ruler, the Great Czar, whom I have the honour to serve, and against whom you Polish scum treasonably plot and rebel, the Court is just—but it is merciful. . . .

" 'Of the five of you, but two shall die, and one is already dead. . . .

" 'Or, at any rate, the dog is dying,' he added, stirring my brother's body with his foot, 'so but one remains.'

"My mother's mind rose triumphant from the abyss of horror, woe, grief, and fear into which it had sunk while they held her back from the body of her dying youngest-born.

" '*Me! Me!*' she cried. 'Kill *me!* . . . They are innocent, innocent . . .'

" 'Gag her, if she speaks again,' growled the Lieutenant, pouring himself out a glass of vodka.

" 'But one remains,' he repeated, smacking his lips. 'Yes, in my mercy, I will hang but one.'

" 'The one who spat upon you,' I said. 'The one who will surely kill you some day, somewhere, somehow, unless you hang him now.'

" 'No, no, my son!' shrieked my mother, and a soldier clapped his great hand upon her mouth.

" 'The Lieutenant will hang me,' said my father with calm dignity.

" 'No, the Lieutenant will not hang you,' replied that Russian dog, 'but hanged you shall most assuredly be.'

"And turning to me, he asked in that cold, cruel voice, so suave and quiet now:

" 'Do you love your dear Mother?'

" 'In a way you could not begin to understand,' I answered.

" 'And that nice, plump, pretty little partridge, your Sister?' he continued.

" 'To a degree that no foul animal could begin to understand,' I replied, hoping to turn all his wrath to me.

"What less could one do?

" 'Ah, that is good,' he smiled. 'Most excellent. . . . And you would save that dear Mother, and beautiful Sister, at any cost, eh?'

" 'From what?' I asked.

" 'Wel-l-l,' he drawled, 'from a certain—un-pleasantness. . . . Your Mother from dying of cold and hunger in a Warsaw prison cell, or perhaps in the Loubianka dungeons, or, possibly, on that little stroll to Siberia. . . . Who shall say? . . .

" 'And the nice plump partridge . . . from being *"the little friend of all the soldiers"* when she begins to bore me. . . .

" 'They *do* bore one, you know,' he drawled, 'even the prettiest of girls—in time. They mope, most of them, and fail to realize their good fortune; or else they are spit-fires, and one has to take—er—*disciplinary* measures.

" 'Well, what about it? Would you like to save them, and your own life, too?'

" 'Yes,' I replied.

" 'Ah, then you *shall.*'

"My little Lieutenant smiled.

" 'When you've done a small job for me, that is,' he added.

" 'How do I know that you would keep your word?' I asked.

" 'I always keep my word,' he replied. 'It is the word of a Russian officer.'

" 'That is the trouble!' I remarked. But nothing could anger him now—outwardly, that is to say.

" 'What do you Polish boors know of the word of a gentleman?' he continued, and then rose to his feet.

" 'Come—we're wasting time,' he said briskly.

'You wish to save your Mother from death, and your Sister from shame, I understand. . . . *Then come and hang your father for me.*' "

§ 3

The others stared aghast at the old man's twitching face. Like most of his countrymen he was a good raconteur, and could dramatize a tale as he told it.

" '*Hang your father*?'" murmured Digby Geste. "Did you say . . ."

"Yes, my friends," continued Budiski. "The Russian Bear stood declared, in all its shocking savagery. Fang and claw were revealed. My little Russian gentleman had dropped his semitransparent mask of civilization. He had been struck by a man, and now he was about to strike back as a beast—the most terrible, relentless, savage, and hypocritical of beasts—the Bear.

"Have any of you ever stood face to face with the bear, and seen it change—change from a rather absurd, stupid, earth-bound thing, somewhat ridiculous —into a monster, a great and terrifying Thing reared upon its hind legs, towering above you, capable of removing your face with one wipe of its paw, capable of removing the front of your body with another? . . ."

The speaker paused, and stared into the embers of the dying fire.

"You hardly believed your ears when I told of it," he continued, turning to Digby Geste.

"Judge then whether we believed our ears when we heard those words, '*Come and hang your father for me.*'

"We thought it was a joke—a typical Russian joke. . . .

"It was—but it was a *practical* joke.

" 'Fetch the girl again,' said my Lieutenant to the Sergeant, and the great brute, a huge Siberian, strode off and returned in a minute with my poor Wanda— weeping, half-fainting in his arms.

" 'Aha, our little plump partridge! . . . Bring her here,' said this officer and gentleman; and, as Wanda sank to the ground, when the Sergeant put her down beside the chair, he added:

" 'Here, wake up, my dear, don't be alarmed. . . . Your brave brother is going to save you,' and he shook her, tearing the shoulder of her nightgown.

" 'Oh, thank God,' she said, and, realizing that her father had been brought back, uttered a cry of joy, and scrambled to her feet to rush to him.

"The Lieutenant pulled her back, tearing her nightgown the more.

" 'Gently, gently, *golubtchick*,' he said, as he drew her to him. 'Your brother hasn't saved you *yet*. . . . He's going to rescue you and dear Mamma from the naughty men, by doing a little job for me.'

"Wanda raised trusting and grateful eyes to the

face of this nobleman—this true *boyar*. My Lieutenant smiled at her, and cupped her chin again.

" 'Yes, sweet child,' he added, as he kissed her.

" '*He's going to hang Papa*' . . . and this time his words became real to us.

"We understood.

" '*No!*' my mother screamed. '*No!*'

" '*What?*' shrieked Wanda.

" '*No, no, no,*' screamed my mother.

" 'Very well,' smiled my Lieutenant, and turning to the Sergeant gave the order:

" 'Take the old woman to the Guard Room just as she is, and the girl to my quarters. Let *her* dress, and take what clothing she wants.'

" 'Stop!' cried my father, as the Corporal and a couple of men began to hustle my mother from the room, and the Sergeant seized Wanda.

" 'Stop. . . . *You will save your mother and sister, my son,*' said our brave old father, a picture of noble dignity. 'You have never disobeyed me, and you will not disobey me now. Do not hesitate for a moment. Are we Russians that we should save ourselves by sacrificing our women? I will show these scum how a *man* can die, and you will live to protect your mother and sister. . . . And perhaps to avenge me.' . . .

" '*No, no, no!*' screamed my mother. 'Take *me!* Take *me!*'

"Wanda shrieked in the Sergeant's arms.

" 'Quick, my son,' urged my father. 'How could we live and face each other . . . *afterwards?* . . . How *could* we? . . . I order you to save your mother and sister. . . . How can you hesitate?'

"I turned to the grinning Lieutenant.

" 'End this joke, I beg of you, your Excellency,' I prayed. 'See, you have killed my brother. If we have done wrong, you have punished us enough. . . . You do not make war on women and old men. . . . Hang me, and let them go. . . . You said that two would be enough—two out of five, and they are innocent. We have never plotted, nor talked sedition, nor raised a hand against the Government. . . . Be merciful. . . .'

" 'Wel-l-l, wel-l-l,' drawled the Lieutenant. 'Mercy is undoubtedly a beautiful thing. I will allow my soft and kindly nature to triumph once again. . . . Yes, yes, my heart shall rule my head. . . . Your adored Mother, and worshipped Sister, shall go free. . . . Your well-beloved and revered father shall *not* be hung.'

" 'God bless you, sir,' I whispered.

" 'No, he shall not be hung, since you intercede for him so movingly,' he continued. *'He shall hang you, instead!'*

"I stared this monster in the face, incredulous— though subconsciously I knew that he meant what he said. . . .

"And for the moment I was even thankful that my mother and my sister were not there.

" 'Well? . . . Come, hurry up! . . . I can't spend the whole night here. Either hang your father, or let him hang you, and thank me for my mercy,' he yawned.

" 'Yes, my son, *hasten*,' said my father. 'Your mother will die of cold . . . And Wanda will . . .'

"Oh, my God. . . .

" 'Father,' I cried, 'let *me* die.'

" 'Silence, my son,' replied the old man. 'Show now of what stuff we sons of Poland are made. . . . You are young and strong, and I look to you to protect your mother and sister—to work for them . . . to comfort them . . . to save them . . . And to *remember* . . . I am old and feeble, and near my end. . . . It is a strong man they need. . . . Obey me for the last time, as you have always obeyed me.'

"And the terrible knowledge grew in my heart that I must drink of this cup. How could I thrust this burden upon my father—this crushing burden, this unbearable cross for him to carry to his grave? For, through every day and hour and minute that he lived, he would have the burning, corroding thought of the deed that he had done. Death would be nothing to it.

"I would choose the harder part. . . .

"But some day I would meet this devilish Russian, face to face. . . .

" 'So be it,' I said. 'Give me your blessing, my father.'

"And the brave old man thanked, praised, and blessed me.

"I turned to the Lieutenant.

" 'If it is possible that you can do this thing,' I said; 'if you *can* look forward to remembering this night upon your death-bed; if your own soldiers will not prove to be human beings, tear you limb from limb, and stamp you into the mud where you belong —I will save my mother and sister.'

"The Lieutenant smiled.

" 'Ah,' he remarked silkily. 'I doubt if *you* will ever spit upon a Russian officer again . . . any more than your dead brother will strike one!'

"He sent two men with orders that my mother and sister be brought back forthwith.

"By the time they arrived, my father was standing beneath the 'suitable' tree, the noose about his neck, the rope dangling from the branch above.

"And God was merciful, for my mother, with a terrible cry of *'Jan! Jan!'* sank down senseless upon the snow.

"I glanced from my mother to Wanda, and saw that her body was hanging inanimate in the arms of the big Sergeant.

"Her eyes were closed.

" *'Now,* my son,' said my father in a firm voice. . . ."

VIII

THE DEVIL AND DIGBY GESTE

I

"LOOK here," said Digby Geste, known locally as *Légionnaire* Thomas Jones No. 18896, "will you kindly endeavour to get into your magnificent brain, Monsieur Tant de Soif, once and for all, the fact that I will *not* drink absinthe with you? . . . Very kind of you, and all that; but I don't like it, and I don't want it, and I'm not going to drink it."

"And would you have me *faire Suisse?*" asked the *Légionnaire* Tant de Soif, as, with trembling hands, he poured an evil-looking fluid from his water-bottle into a tin mug.

"I don't care what you *faire*, you old marvel, so long as you don't *faire* yourself a nuisance. If you do I'll pour that muck out on the sand."

Tant de Soif shuddered.

"Hush!" he begged. "Do not utter such horrible words—even in jest! . . . It is a kind of blasphemy," and he drank deeply from his mug.

"*Horrible* language," he grumbled, wiping his bearded lips with the back of his hand. "Never heard anything like it in all my forty years of soldiering—and I've heard some awful language, too, in the *Marsouins* [1] and the Legion. . . . And so I must *faire Suisse* at last—after fifty years of soldiering! . . ."

"Once again, *faire* what you like, only don't *faire* nuisance. That's just what you are when you're drunk—'a fair nuisance.' "

"Eh? . . . *Mon Dieu!* . . . *To me!* . . . After sixty years of soldiering! . . . What did you say? A *nuisance?* . . . Say it again. . . ."

And, with drunken gravity, old Tant de Soif rose to his feet, drew his sword-bayonet, and advanced upon the admired comrade whom he loved as a son.

"Say it—*hic*—again if you please," he requested.

"*Vous êtes une peste pour tout le monde,*" repeated Digby slowly. "Understand? A nuisance to everybody, when you're drunk."

And, seizing the bayonet with his left hand, he gave the aged gentleman a shove with his right. The bayonet and its owner parted company.

"A nuisance when I'm drunk?" murmured Tant de Soif incredulously, as he sat suddenly down. "And am I to hear *that* said of me, after seventy years of soldiering! . . . Why, I was born drunk— I've lived drunk, and shall *die* drunk! and be a loved and respected centenarian soldier. . . . Yes. . . . The Government will give me a tomb like that of Fraulein Eberhardt, the Spahi Sergeant, at Figuig.

[1] Colonial Infantry.

. . . On it they will write the dignified and simple epitaph, *'One hundred years a soldier.'* "

A tear trickled from the eye of Tant de Soif as he contemplated his apotheosis.

"More likely *'One hundred years drunk,'* you old lunatic," laughed Digby Geste. "That's what you are—the original and authentic Lunatic among the Tombs."

"Undeniably we are in a tomb," replied Tant de Soif, nodding his head thoughtfully, "but it is not *I* who am the lunatic. . . . It is not *I* who am refusing good liquor. . . . No, indeed! . . . Nor have I, in eighty years of soldiering, met a man who *did*. . . . No, not until this night. . . . And now I am in a tomb with him. *I*, Tant de Soif, with a lunatic in the Tomb."

In a tomb they undoubtedly were, and in a place of tombs, built none knew how many centuries before —perhaps on the site of some battlefield, where great men had fallen and received princely sepulture. Or possibly some holy and far-famed *marabout* had dwelt at this tiny oasis, had been buried here by the sorrowing devout; and around his tomb had been laid those of the pious who had wished to sleep near him in death, as they had dwelt near him in life.

In the largest of these tombs the two *légionnaires* had taken up a strategic position for the night. Fastening the still practicable heavy door, and using the

two horizontal tombstones as beds, they had con-
verted the mosque-like *taj* into a barrack-room and a
fort.

The two graves were extraordinarily reminiscent
of a pair of crusader, princely, or episcopal tombs in
a European cathedral—save that no recumbent effigy
adorned the large, flat, oblong stone that formed the
top of each.   Ideal beds—if a little hard—roomy,
level three feet from the ground, and thus well
above the sphere of operations of scorpion, serpent,
and objectionable insect left by pariah dog or wandering beggar.

As though in their heat-warped and horrible ca-
serne at Tokotu, whence they had come on this
patrol, the two soldiers made ready for the night,
and, having cleaned their accoutrements and folded
the clothing they had removed, laid themselves down
upon their cold and silent tombs—their temporary
graves, as Digby Geste described them.   The "night
attire" of the latter consisted of white canvas shoes,
belted canvas trousers, and a short-sleeved white
shirt.   Tant de Soif, for reasons best known to himself, wore only his *képi* and his boots.   He explained,
with convincing clarity, that, in the case of emergency, he was thus protected against the sun (or
moon) at the one end and against sharp stones and
thorns at the other; while, if no emergency arose, all
was still well, as it was obvious to the meanest intelligence that if the head and the feet were kept hot, the

intervening and adjacent tracts must inevitably be benefited and remain in a satisfactory condition.

"So you always sleep in your *képi* to keep your tummy warm, eh?" observed Digby, as he settled his head upon his knapsack.

"And my boots to keep the lumbar regions protected," was the reply. "I have suffered from lumbago, and one cannot be too careful . . . especially when one has no blood in one's veins. . . . I have no blood at all, and, when wounded, I bleed absinthe."

"Valuable gift," murmured his companion sleepily. "Good idea. Every man his own canteen. Like the pelican in the wilderness, or the camel feeding on its own hump. . . . G'night, Gran'pa, and don't you dare speak another word till daylight doth appear. . . ."

Ere he fell asleep the thoughts of Digby Geste wandered. First, to Brandon Abbas, where dwelt the girl who had been his life's sunshine, the sound of whose voice had been his life's music, for a brief sight of whose face he would now have given almost anything—certainly a year of his life.

"Darling Isobel," he murmured. "Darling, Faithful Hound," and smiled. Next he thought of his brothers, Michael and John, at the Fort of Zinderneuf.

"Dear old Beau. . . . Dear old John. . . . Hope all's well with them. . . . Wish to God I could get transferred there.   They must be having a thin time with Lejaune. . . . Wonder if de Beaujolais would listen to me if I asked to be sent there. . . .

"Glad old St. André and Maris, and Cordier are there too.   Decent chaps. . . . Wish Hank and Buddy were—much as I should miss them at Tokotu.

"Wonder if I and old Tant de Soif ought to keep watch and watch? . . . No point in doing so, really. If a raiding-party come, they come—and they get us, anyhow. . . . And it wouldn't be till dawn. . . . I shall be awake by then. . . ."

But Digby Geste was awakened before dawn.

Silence. . . .

Outside the tomb a world of silence—a Universe of Silence, broken only by the occasional sound of a soft, light footstep, almost inaudible.

Silence and stillness, upon which the great full moon looked down . . . upon the illimitable desert, all patined with fine silver, over which the shadows thrown by the few scattered palms and by the ancient domed and minareted mosques lay black as ink.

Into one of these mosques the great moon peeped, and by the light of her own rays beheld, through a narrow unglazed window, two faces—the one innocent, calm, peacefully happy, the other debased, scarred, haunted, contorted in the agony of some miserable nightmare.

The moon watched. . . .

Suddenly at the opposite aperture, appeared the face of another watcher—a horrible face, a terrible face—long, gaunt, bearded, with the shallow, soulless eyes of a beast.

Within the tomb, silence, broken only by the sound of breathing, and an occasional sigh from Digby; from Tant de Soif a groan.

§ 2

An unusually loud groan from the restless veteran awoke his young comrade from a deep dream of peace. The latter raised his head from the knapsack on which it rested.

"What's up, Daddy?" he said, and yawned.

The old man murmured something concerning a *courant d'air*, and the extreme unwholesomeness of ventilation.

With a laugh the boy sat up, stretched and yawned hugely, and, with a remark to the effect that, in his own callow and uninstructed mind, he regarded absinthe as even more unwholesome than fresh air, he spread Tant de Soif's *capote* over him and bade him be of good cheer, for he couldn't much longer survive the troubles of this vale of woe.

Returning to his stony couch, Digby gazed around the moonlit chamber, so chapel-like with its high, narrow "windows," its pair of tombs, high, vaulted

roof, and stone-flagged floor. In the moonlight the
figure of old Tant de Soif might well have been a
stone effigy, as he lay like a warrior taking his rest,
with his martial cloak around him.

The boy closed his eyes.

Darling Isobel. . . .

What was she doing now? . . .

Sleeping, of course. . . . Sleeping in her moonlit, panelled room at Brandon Abbas. . . .

Same jolly old moon that was looking into this
mosque was peeping through the leaded panes of her
casement. Funny if she were awake, too, and wondering whether he were looking at the moon at that
moment. . . .

Darling Isobel! When would he see her again?
Not till his five years were up, anyhow; unless, of
course, they were sent back to Sidi-bel-Abbès and
she came there. . . . Even when their time had
expired they couldn't go back to Brandon Abbas until
that astounding business was cleared up. . . . Beau
running off in that extraordinary way. . . .

And young John, the silly young ass! . . .
Daring to run away from home, too, like his elders
and betters—a child like that. . . . A good year
junior to the twins. . . . Frightful little ass. . . .
That's what happens when the young are released
from proper, repressive discipline. . . . Very 'cute
of him, though, to guess that they had joined the
Legion. . . . Pretty mess he'd have found himself

in if he'd been wrong. . . . Dear old Johnny. . . .
How ghastly if anything happened to him. . . .
Thank God he was with Beau. . . . Beau would
look after him all right. . . . Yes, Beau would look
after him.

Yawns. . . .

Digby Geste slept.

And was awakened later by a blood-curdling yell
—a terrible scream, like that of a wounded horse.
In almost one movement he was on his feet, crouch-
ing between the tombs, his rifle in his hands, his head
turning swiftly from window to window at the
opposite sides of the chamber—the one idea on his
mind being of an Arab raid.

Nothing at either window.

No rifles thrust through the ten-inch aperture,
between the stone sides of the high, narrow openings.
No heavy blows upon the door. . . .

And then he was aware that Tant de Soif was
pointing with trembling hand to the window nearest
to him—the one through which the moon did not
shed her soft light. Bringing his rifle swiftly round,
he "covered" the aperture and waited.

Strange! . . . Why hadn't the devils shot at
them from both windows as they slept? And why
hadn't old Tant de Soif made one jump for his gun?
Why had he screamed like a tortured woman, and
why was he still lying there, trembling from head

to foot?   Old Tant de Soif, with his *Médaille Mili-taire*, brave as a lion?

"Arabs?" whispered Digby.

"No, no," groaned the old soldier.   "Oh, my God! . . . God forgive me . . . forgive me all my wickedness. . . . *Oh, mon Général le bon Dieu*, have mercy on an old soldier. . . . *Première classe . . .*"

"What *is* it, you old fool?" urged Digby, breaking upon the prayer.   "God helps those who help them-selves.   What *is* it, if it isn't Arabs?   A lion, or a . . . rabbit, or what?"

"*Hush!*   Don't blaspheme," whispered Tant de Soif, turning from the window, flinging his arms about Digby, and crushing his bearded face against the boy's breast.

There was no doubt that the old man had had a terrible fright, and, indeed, a terrible shock.   He was sober enough now, and in a state of absolute, utter terror.

There is nothing more infectious than panic, ter-ror, fear—and particularly fear of the utterly unknown.

Perfect love casteth out fear.   So doth perfect anger—and a good deal more quickly.   Digby's anger was certainly perfect—at being awakened; at being made to jump and take cover; at being—well —frightened or at any rate threatened with fright— by this old drunkard.

"What *is* it?" he repeated. "What did you see— or think you saw?" And his free hand was upon Tant de Soif heavily laid, though not in the way of kindness.

But Tant de Soif could say nothing. His teeth were chattering with fright.

It was useless to be angry with the old man. He was most obviously terrified almost to death.

"What *is* it, old chap? What did you see?" Digby asked again, without taking his eyes from the narrow aperture, of which the base or window-sill was some three feet from the ground. "What did you see?"

"*The Devil himself!*" whispered Tant de Soif, and, with a hollow groan, let his head fall heavily back upon the stone.

"Oh—*the Devil?*" replied the incensed Digby. "Is *that* all! . . . I'll show you something worse than the Devil if you wake me up again with your nightmares—you walking whisky-flask; you woolly-witted wine-cask; you bibulous brandy-bottle, you . . ."

"Oh, God!" moaned the old soldier. "Oh, Jesus Christ! Oh, Holy Virgin! Guard me this night. It was *the Devil himself.* The Devil has come for me—at last! . . ."

"Well, he hasn't *got* you yet, has he?" expostulated Digby. "And he won't. . . . But *I* will. *I'll* get you all right, old son, if you wake me up again."

"The Devil has come for me, and I am dying,"

groaned the old soldier as he turned his face again toward the window. "We were mad to come in here. . . . It is a sepulchre. . . . This tomb is my bed, and this bed will be my tomb."

"It'll be all *that*," replied Digby, "if you don't shut up. Go to sleep, you silly old ass. Do you think the Devil's a fool, that he should want *you* in . . ."

An awful scream interrupted the speaker as the lower part of the unglazed "window" was filled by a truly appalling face.

Tant de Soif again flung himself upon his comrade, effectually pinning his arms to his sides.

Digby Geste was a brave man—young, strong, healthy, and devoid of nerves. He felt his blood run cold, his knees weaken, his heart pound furiously, and the cold perspiration start forth upon his skin.

Not one of these symptoms would have been evoked by the sight of the most evil face of any human being, Negro or Arab, looking at him from behind a levelled gun. Rather would Digby Geste's pulse have tingled with the joy of battle as he jerked his rifle forward, and tried to shoot ere he was shot.

But this was face neither of Arab nor of Negro. . . . Nor of any human being.

Tant de Soif looked again, and shrieked again— the dreadful, agonized shriek of a madman.

It was *not* a human face. It was the face of a . . .

the face of a *devil*. . . . The face of *the* Devil!

Yes . . . merciful God . . . from the forehead that overhung the glowing luminiscent eyes—the dreadful, shallow, bestial, devilish eyes—to the bearded chin, the face was fiendish!

The hideous mouth, with its great strong white teeth, opened to speak, and closed again in silence. The hideous lips twitched in a sneering smile, and the whole awful face, long, gaunt, and hairy, leered with a hellish malignity, triumphant, terrible, cruel beyond expression.

But Digby Geste was more afraid of fear than of the Devil. Wrenching himself free from the frenzied clutch of Tant de Soif, he threw his rifle to his shoulder—only to find it torn almost from his hands as Tant de Soif seized it, and scrambling to his knees, fell upon him.

"*Don't! Don't!*" he screamed. "*It is the Devil. . . .* You *cannot* shoot the Devil."

"Watch me," laughed Digby, his own man again, and with a strong thrust sent Tant de Soif sprawling on the ground, instantly raising his rifle as he did so.

But the Devil had gone.

Nothing was to be seen, but the silvered sandhills, and some distant palms.

Digby lowered his rifle and stared aghast. Was this a nightmare? No, he was awake, and here was

Tant de Soif clasping him round the knees, and praying to God and to the Devil impartially.

Was it hypnotism . . . auto-suggestion . . . hetero-suggestion? Was he, for some reason, seeing with his own eyes what this poor drunken old sot, in an attack of delirium tremens, thought he saw with his? Was there something in the physical or psychic atmosphere of this ancient mausoleum that was supernatural or, at any rate, super-normal? *Were* there djinns in these lone desert places?

"*Kneel down and pray! . . . Kneel down and pray!*" gabbled Tant de Soif.

"Stand up and watch, more sense," replied Digby. "There's a time for everything. . . . Get up and get your rifle."

"You can't fight *the Devil*," groaned Tant de Soif.

"There isn't any devil," affirmed Digby.

"Haven't we just *seen* him, you fool?" replied the drunkard.

"And if we can see him we can shoot him. . . . Pull yourself together, you old coward," growled Digby.

"I'm not a coward. I fear nothing human, nothing solid. . . ."

"Pity you don't fear nothing liquid, too. . . . Absinthe, for example. . . ."

Yes, that was all very well, but he, Digby Geste, had never tasted absinthe in his life, and most un-

doubtedly he had seen what Tant de Soif saw. . . .
Seen it clearly and unmistakably, and for at least a
minute. . . . Had seen the dreadful eyes move, the
ghastly mouth smile horribly.

Stooping, he pulled Tant de Soif to his feet.

"Now, then," he said. "Pull yourself together,
you wretched old woman. Put on your overcoat,
and pick up your rifle. Cover that other window,
while I cover this one. . . . If nothing happens I'm
going outside for a scout round. . . . If it's the
Devil, I want to see a bit more of him. . . . Cloven
hoof, and all that. . . ."

But Tant de Soif was past self-help.

"For the love of *God* don't open that door," he
stuttered. "Don't leave me. . . . For the love of
Christ don't leave me. I . . ."

"Look!" he shrieked, and collapsed. The Face
had reappeared at the window. . . . Terrible,
gleaming, yellow eyes. . . . Inhuman, sub-human,
devilish, shallow eyes. . . . Terrible, inhuman
mouth with twitching lips and gleaming teeth. . . .
A gargoyle face, the face of the Devil as portrayed
in ancient books, wood-carvings and gargoyles.

Digby Geste raised his rifle, and the lips parted in
a brutish smile.

Digby Geste stood firm and steady, the foresight
of his weapon pointing between the gleaming eyes—
eyes that shone as though each contained a glowing

core of fire—his forefinger curled about the trigger
—and did not fire.

Undoubtedly he had been frightened. He was
not frightened now, and he refused to panic. He
was not going to blow a hole in the middle of a face
simply because he didn't like the look of it. That
was not the sort of thing that Beau would do. To
shoot first and ask after was to exhibit the fear of
which he was afraid. . . .

Stalemate. . . .

The devilish Face watched him, and he covered
the devilish Face.

Stalemate. . . .

His arms were growing tired. . . .

Why didn't the Thing do something? Did it
calmly await his futile shot, secure in the knowledge
of its immunity? . . . *Was* it a devil? . . . *The*
Devil?

That dreadful, impish, evil face . . . that hairy,
bearded mask of evil . . . ?

Mask! . . . Mask? . . . Was this some Arab
trick to frighten them? . . . To drive them, screaming in terror, from their stronghold?

Absurd! The man could have shot them sleeping.
. . . Perhaps he had no gun.

The great mouth opened.

No, that was a face, and not a mask. Should he
fire? No. One does not shoot an "unarmed,"
unarmoured Face.

Digby Geste lowered his rifle and backed slowly to the door, his eyes fixed upon those other terrible eyes that followed his every movement.

"Tant de Soif!" he called. "Get up and open this door. Tant de Soif—you coward—get up!"

Tant de Soif stirred, struggled to his feet, glanced at the Face, howled, rushed to his comrade, not to obey him, but to get behind him.

Turning his back upon the Face, Digby thrust Tant de Soif aside, knocked up the heavy bar with the butt of his rifle, glanced across the tomb at the motionless, basilisk head, dashed through the doorway, his rifle at the ready, crept round the building, turned the second corner, and there beheld, upreared upon the cloven hooves of its hind legs, a large billy-goat.

IX

THE MULE

I

IT is said that there is good in everyone, and that though the whitest sheep has a black or a grey hair somewhere, there is no black sheep so black that he has not one grey lock, if he cannot boast a white one.

Be that as it may, *le Légionnaire* Xarro, blackest of black sheep, did marvellously conceal the fact if he possessed the faintest redeeming shade of lighter colour.

Although admittedly a black sheep, *le Légionnaire* Xarro was known as "The Mule." This name had been bestowed upon him only partly in tribute to the fact that he was astonishingly mulish, surly, cross-grained, stupid, malevolent and dangerous. For the other part, the name was esteemed appropriate by reason of the fact that the company mules apparently accepted him as a friend and a brother. He was one with them, and they were at one with him. No mule ever kicked, bit, thwarted or disobeyed *le Légionnaire* Xarro. Mules were his friends, if not, as his comrades averred, his relations. A fiendishly cruel man, who delighted to torture other animals, and to

203

devise tortures which he hoped some day to inflict upon Arab men, women and children, he was never cruel to a mule.

Nor was this merely one of those beautiful instances of virtue being its own reward, and kindness begetting kindness. Digby Geste was just as kind to his mule as Xarro was to his, but this did not induce the beast to lose any opportunity of kicking or biting Digby; of slipping his heel-rope and absenting himself without leave; of throwing his load whenever he could; of instigating his fellows to stampede, and generally of being as ungrateful, obnoxious and exasperating as only a mule can.

Digby Geste loved animals, and hated this mule as he had never hated anything before—with good reason—and the more he hated it, the more kindly he treated it. The more kindly he treated it, the more evil it seemed to grow—*seemed*—because no one would care to state categorically that there was room for it to grow more evil. . . .

Yet when this same mule was in the hands of *le Légionnaire* Xarro, it was the Perfect Mule—an animal without moral spot or blemish, wearing in its head-stall the white flower of a blameless life.

It pleased the good Xarro enormously that any peculiarly intractable and unmanageable mule should be handed over to him with the sure and certain knowledge that, while in his hands, it would be entirely docile.

Had *le Légionnaire* Xarro been any other than *le Légionnaire* Xarro, he would have been promoted, and made one of the non-commissioned personnel at a Mounted Infantry *dépôt* where men and mules are trained. He might have become Sergeant-Major or even *Adjudant*, and had a glorious opportunity of exercising his markedly developed traits of cruelty, malevolence, brutality and spite, upon *les légionnaires*, whom he hated collectively and individually.

But, in spite of these qualities, it was quite impossible to promote *ce bon* Xarro. He was too utterly unreliable and untrustworthy; too debauched, depraved and slovenly; too mean, ineffectual and stupid; too bad a soldier, and too good a liar, thief and drunkard.

Nor can it be urged in his favour that he was fond of his mules.

Love is a lovely thing—if it be only love for a mule; but Xarro loved them no more than he did pariah dogs of the *Village Nègre*, wild cats of the rocks, and vultures of the air.

When a mule was hit by a bullet, fell down a precipice, or suffered a broken leg and was butchered to become steaks and cutlets for hungry soldiers, he was inordinately amused, and apparently very pleased.

No, he certainly did not love them, but he understood them, and they understood him, and were perfectly *en rapport*.

It was said—and probably truly—that he had been a muleteer "in real life" (that is to say before he joined the Legion), and had been bred and born among mules, thinking their thoughts, feeling their sensations, needs, desires and sufferings, and, moreover, speaking their language—this last because he uttered words, if such sounds could be called words, which the mules understood.

Digby Geste, watching him, was reminded of what Uncle Hector had told him about *mahouts* in India, who undeniably had an elephant-language which their charges understood and obeyed.

Seated on his mule, Xarro, without movement of hand or heel, could cause his mount to sidle a few paces to the right or to the left, to advance a few steps or to rein back—merely by the use of a single word for each movement. His mule would halt, about-turn, or wheel to the right or left, at a word. More, it would lift a left or right hoof, come to its fore-knees, or lie upon the ground, at Xarro's command.

His particular beast, known as "Satan," was a rare black animal, big beyond the size of large mules, and, save in the hands of Xarro himself, a fitter inmate of a cage in a Zoological Gardens than a place in a mule-lines. Among mules, Satan was as objectionable and detestable as Xarro was among men.

§ 2

We have it on excellent authority that we needs must love the highest when we see it. *Le Légionnaire* Xarro must have been an exception to this golden rule. Definitely he did not love the highest when he saw it. Hating all his officers, non-commissioned officers and comrades, he hated the best most. For scoundrels like Bolidar, Boldini, Guantaio and Vogué (all now away at Zinderneuf) he had quite a mild detestation.

The three English brothers, who called themselves Brown, Jones and Smith respectively, he loathed peculiarly, and of these the one named Jones, who was here at Tokotu, he abhorred most of all. Was he not always merry and bright, laughing and smiling—curse him! As if there were anything whatever to laugh or smile about, in this devilish world! Was he not always pleasant and friendly—damn him!—in contrast to one's own morose ill-humoured surliness? Was he not open and frank and generous—blast him! Was he not popular and cool and unafraid? Was he not rich, a gentleman, an aristocrat? Yes, and after all, what was he, with all his airs and graces, but a damned jewel-thief, hiding from the English police? Who was *he* to give himself airs, and walk in pride?

Pride goeth before a fall. Aha, yes, *a fall!* . . .

A bright idea! . . . And *le Légionnaire* Xarro showed a mouthful of blackened and broken teeth, in an artful and evil grin.

§ 3

"Sunday pants of Holy Moses! What in Hell's that guy Xarro up to *now?*" exclaimed Buddy to his friend Hank one evening, as, having strolled beyond the rough and dirty camp known as *le Village Nègre,* they seated themselves upon the summit of a sand-dune and gazed across the stretch of level country, an unbroken plain of rock, sand, and gravel, which stretched before them.

Unaware of their presence, Xarro and Satan, a couple of hundred metres distant, were engaged upon some mutually diverting exercise. It soon became apparent to the interested watchers that Satan was learning a new trick, or rather was learning to do, instantly and methodically, at the word of command, what he sometimes did at the prompting of idle errant fancy. He was learning to roll—on his back, over and over, to and fro, bent legs waving in the air—as, and when, ordered to do so.

Hank and Buddy who, in their time, had played many parts and been many things to many men, were intrigued.

"Say, that guy and his burro ought to be in vaudeville," quoth Hank.

"Sure thing," agreed Buddy, "Xarro and his Performing Mule."

"And a prize to be given for the first member of the audience as correctly guesses which is the mule."

Their usual laconic silence then descended upon them, and they watched.

Satan stood at attention, Xarro three paces in front of him, both motionless.

Suddenly Xarro uttered a single word of command, and down went Satan as though shot.

Thrice he rolled from left to right and right to left, arose to his feet, and stood like a graven image —of wickedness.

Xarro strolled away, and, from a few yards' distance, threw a word over his shoulder. Instantly the mule rolled, and arose again. Xarro returned, patted the animal's neck, and gave it something from his pocket. Proceeding to the rear of the imaginary rank which Satan adorned, Xarro wheeled about, and again at a few yards' distance uttered a word of command from behind the mule and again Satan rolled.

Xarro now varied the proceedings. Placing his hands on Satan's back he lightly vaulted astride him, and sitting with folded arms bade the mule rein back, right close, left close, advance, about turn, walk march, right wheel, left wheel and halt. He then, once again, uttered the sharp short word of command, and sprang clear as the beast instantly obeyed, threw itself down and rolled thrice upon its back.

"Say, Hank, what d'you know about *that*," murmured Buddy, as the last manœuvre was again repeated. "He surely is the World's Champion Mule-Tamer. What's the idee?"

"Got me guessing, Bud," was the reply. "P'r'aps he plans to get a job lion-taming in a circus, when he's through with the Legion."

"He surely does understand mules," said Buddy. "I've known guys make horses act that way, but I allow he's the first man ever taught a mule to sit up and beg. Wonder how he does it?"

"Power of the human eye over the savage beast," opined Hank.

"Pity he don't try it on the Sergeant-Major then," observed Buddy, rising to his feet, and the two sauntered back to the *poste*.

§ 4

The mule-*peloton* out on a recognizance patrol was taking an "easy" in the shadow of a great rock, or small cliff, that marked the turning point of their journey, and weary men stood easing weary limbs, each at the head of what one would have supposed to be a weary mule.

Not so, however, the four-legged fiend in mule-skin in charge of Digby Geste. The phrase is ambiguous, and so was the situation, inasmuch as the mule appeared at times to be in Digby's charge, and the mule at times to be in charge of Digby.

Suddenly the devil entered into the beast, or else the devil that never left it awoke, and with an energy rarely displayed in a legitimate cause, the perverse animal began to back, to kick, to buck, rear and plunge, as though its soul's salvation depended upon creating the maximum of confusion in the ranks, wrath in the Commandant, and despair in the unfortunate Digby. A torrent of abuse from the Sergeant-Major did nothing to help the matter, though it seemed to amuse and exhilarate the mule who, with a neigh of laughter, bounded the more vigorously and struggled the more violently to be free, free to roam the wide desert o'er, untrammelled and untied.

Genuine hearty mule laughter!

"He saith among the trumpets ha, ha! and he smelleth the battle afar off, the thunder of the captains and the shouting," quoted Digby from the book of Job.

"There will certainly be some thunder from the Captain in a minute, and the Sergeant-Major is undoubtedly shouting," he added, as he clung to the equine-asinine rebel.

The mule, rearing and lashing out with his forefeet, made a noble effort for liberty and self-determination.

But Digby Geste had a word to say to that and the struggle continued.

Giving his rein to his right-hand man, *le Légionnaire* Xarro stepped up to the kicking, struggling mule and quieted it with a word.

"That's the way to handle a mule," he said. "You take mine, and I'll ride this one back. But remember this. You mustn't hit it or touch it with your heel. If you want to steady it, you must just say '*Brrrtsch*'—like that. Understand? Just '*Brrrtsch*'—and especially when we are on that narrow path with a precipice on one side, and a cliff on the other be sure to say '*Brrrtsch*' and it'll prick up its ears, and know you for a friend. See?"

"Thanks very much," replied Digby. "But I'll stick to this Father of Vice."

"Don't be a fool," urged Xarro. "You'll find my mule like a lady's hack."

"Thanks again, very much," replied Digby. "It's very good of you, but I mustn't let this beast get the better of me. I must make it quite clear that it is out with me, and not I with it."

"It'll get away," persisted Xarro, "and you'll do fifty-two days' solitary confinement for a start, if it's lost. You go and take old Satan. He's more like an Arab horse than a mule. And don't forget to say '*Brrrtsch*,' when you want to steady him."

"It's most kind of you, Xarro," said Digby again, "but I really mustn't let this beast defeat me."

"More afraid of Satan, I suppose," jeered Xarro. "Afraid he'll play some trick on you, eh?"

"Put it like that if you wish," replied Digby. "Anyhow, I'll stick to this moke. Thanks all the same."

And with a sneering laugh, Xarro shrugged his shoulders and turned to Satan.

However, although *le Légionnaire* Xarro had not done all that he intended to do, he had done something, for Digby's mule gave no further trouble, either on the narrow and dangerous mountain path or upon the open plain.

§ 5

Digby Geste, alias *le Légionnaire* Thomas Jones, was puzzled. An unsavoury comrade of the name of Xarro whom he particularly disliked was making repeated overtures of friendship, and equally often-repeated suggestions that Digby should ride his mule Satan. It seemed an obsession with the man, and he was particularly urgent when the *peloton* was at a maximum distance from Tokotu, or about to pass through difficult and dangerous mountain country.

But *le Légionnaire* Xarro had made a great mistake. He had dared *le Légionnaire* Jones to ride the mule! He had foolishly said:

"Jones, I'm willing to bet any amount that you

are afraid to ride Satan. You would like to do so, but you refuse because you haven't the pluck."

To which Digby had replied:

"Obviously that must be the reason. It needs a hero like you to ride the old black moke," and neither jeers nor cajolings could induce Digby to do so.

What he did do was frequently and lengthily to wonder what the man's object could be. Doubtless Satan would give anyone but Xarro a great deal of trouble, but he couldn't give Digby more trouble than did the malevolent Son of Sin and Sorrow with whom he was at present afflicted.

One thing was very certain. Xarro—the surly, quarrelsome, insolent Xarro; the malignant, sly, dangerous Xarro; full of ill-will, ill-nature and ill-breeding—was not offering the mule to Digby for Digby's good. It was very puzzling. . . .

But one tragic day the puzzle was solved—quite horribly.

The Mule-Company to which Digby was attached rode out from Tokotu one red-hot morning, on a forty-eight hours' patrol and tactical exercise as Mounted Infantry. On this occasion they were given admirable exercise, for they were followed at a most respectful distance by a Targui scout, and when at night they halted and made their desert bivouac, he rode off with the glad news that rifles were to be had for the snatching; mules to be cap-tured, and Roumis to be hunted down, shot and tortured.

.   .   .   .

A little camp was pitched in the form of a square, the mule-lines in the centre, each man sleeping in his own *tente d'abri* which, being only one foot high, two feet wide, and three feet long, sounds rather more than it is, particularly on occasions of heavy rain, snow, sand-storm or blasting sunshine.

When a unit of the Legion bivouacs, its Commandant's first thought is to choose a place close to water, so that if the force is pinned to the spot, thirst, the greatest enemy of all, shall not fight on the side of the foe.

Each quarter of the force forms one side of a square; mounts all its tents in a line; and then, at the order, *aux murailles,* builds a stone wall some eighteen inches high, parallel to that line. Should that part of the country be devoid of stones suitable to dry-wall building, a trench is dug instead, and the earth thrown up to form a parapet. By the time each of the four divisions of the force has done this, the bivouac is a square perimeter camp, surrounded by four defensible walls or trenches.

This temporary fortress having been constructed, fatigue parties are told off to fetch in a sufficient supply of fuel and water.

When, as upon this occasion, neither is likely to be procurable, each man carries his own supply of both, and unless he wants to go hungry, supplies his personal quota to the cook.

At sunset, the guard is mounted for each of the faces of the camp, to the extent of four to a Company, and each sentry does two hours on guard and four hours off.

In theory, these sentries patrol continually, in a smart and soldier-like manner, and meet other sentries at each end of their respective beats.

Digby Geste, being for guard that night, found himself posted at a corner of the Square, and, had he been less utterly weary, saddle-galled and knee-sore, after a long day's wrestling with a most uncomfortable and refractory mount, he would have enjoyed his two hours of peaceful solitude beneath the glorious moon and incredible great stars, as he gazed out over the silent and illimitable space. . . .

All was very still and very silent. Not even the sound of marching feet disturbed the perfect peace— for no feet marched. Every sentry about the camp was apparently lost in admiration of the wondrous desert night—or more probably in sleep.

Not so Digby Geste. He was on duty, and he had a habit of doing his duty and a little more. He was there to watch, and he was watching—so carefully and so conscientiously, in fact, that he almost thought for a moment that a distant bush moved! Bushes frequently do move, but not when there is no wind blowing, and the air is still as death. Nor in the night-time, when no bird alights nor flies away, causing a branch to quiver and sway.

But then again, moon-light is notoriously deceptive and treacherous, making hovels look like palaces, witches look like fairies and—stationary bushes to look like moving bushes.

But the thing *was* moving. . . . Surely . . . Digby rubbed his eyes.

It must be a trick of moon-light. A bush might conceivably shake when there was no wind blowing, and no big bird alighting nor flying away; for some small nocturnal animal or snake might possibly cause its branches to move. He stared so hard and so long that his eyes watered, and he closed them for a moment. When he opened them again he was instantly convinced that the bush was moving, and moreover that it was *moving along!*

Now, bushes that move in this manner are really interesting phenomena, and Digby was duly interested. Placing the butt of his rifle on a stone, he crossed his arms upon its muzzle, pushed back his *képi*, yawned loudly, and leant his head upon his arms. With one eye open the sentry slept at his post—or apparently the bush thought he did, for it moved several yards nearer—or perhaps the sentry, in turn, thought it did, because he had only one eye open.

Again yawning, he drew his body erect, struck the attitude of "Stand-at ease," and contemplated infin-

ity.   He also contemplated the bush, and, before
very long, was absolutely certain that the bush was
approaching him.   He was about to raise his rifle
when he was overwhelmed with the thought that,
by firing a shot, he would arouse the whole company,
officers, non-commissioned officers and men, all
weary to death and almost preferring death to a
needless awakening.

If he roused them from their sleep without the
best of good reasons, he would become an object of
universal execration, the focus and target of their
ferocious wrath, hatred and contempt.

"I thought I saw a bush move," would be a fine
excuse when brought before the Commandant to
offer any explanation he could find for rousing the
camp and wasting ammunition.   They would say he
had been asleep and had fired off his rifle in a nightmare.

No, the bush was not moving. . . . Not moving
now, perhaps, but it certainly *had* moved, for it was
undoubtedly nearer than when he had first noticed
it. . . . Or was it all moon-shine?

An idea! . . . There was an almost white stone
shining in the moonlight a few yards from the bush.

Digby Geste deliberately turned his back toward
the bush, slowly patrolled his allotted distance, and
returned. . . . The bush had moved.

It was nearer to the stone by a distance about equal

to the length of his beat. While he had been patrolling from his post, the bush had moved forward, and when he had turned about to come back, the bush had halted.

How many other bushes were approaching the camp in similar fashion? Or was this a solitary rifle-thief, intending to crawl into the camp, silently slit the throat of a sleeping man, and crawl away richer by a good Lebel rifle? More likely the idea, since he was making a straight line for him, was to get sufficiently close to a somnolent Digby Geste to rush him and stab him to the heart before he could make a sound.

Nasty man! . . . Whole company asleep. . . . Mustn't make a mistake. . . . Plenty of time for one more patrol—to make sure. . . .

No, a better notion. Digby Geste yawned, stretched himself, sloped his rifle, turned his back upon the mystery bush and marched off. But, at the end of half-a-dozen paces, he swiftly wheeled about —and saw the bush progressing quite quickly in the direction of his post. Raising his rifle Digby fired at the lower part of the bush, and with all the strength of his lungs called:

"*Aux armes! Aux armes!*"

Immediately each one of the chain of sentries fired his rifle at nothing in particular to show that he too was a keen, wakeful and watchful warrior, and bawled *"Aux armes!"* in evidence that he had seen something suspicious, and probably saved the life of every soul in camp.

In less time than it takes to tell, the men were under arms and lining the perimeter of the camp, each man at his own *créneau* loop-hole.

From each of its four sides levelled rifles were ready to pour forth a hail of death upon a charging enemy.

But no enemy charged.

Nothing happened.

In a very few minutes, lightly clad men were grumbling angrily as they shivered in the bitter cold, and demanding the blood of the nervous fool who had brought them from their warm blankets and snug bivouacs.

Making his rounds, the Sergeant of the Guard found that no sentry had fired first until he reached Digby Geste, who promptly confessed to being the offender, or, if the Sergeant liked to put it that way, the saviour of the situation.

"What did you fire at, you half-witted *salo?* You trembling, squint-eyed, frog-faced Afraid-of-the-Dark?"

"At that bush," replied Digby, pointing.

"Oh, you did, did you, *salo?* . . . Is *that* what you are afraid of? Did you think it was going to bite you?"

"I didn't know *what* it might do—when it got

here, Sergeant," replied Digby, standing stiffly at attention.

"When it *got* here? What do you mean, you sodden lunatic?" roared the Sergeant, and, before Digby could reply, an incisive voice cut in sharply with:

"What's all this about?" and the Sergeant and his satellites sprang to attention.

"This is the man who caused all the trouble, *mon Commandant*," answered the Sergeant, saluting. "He confesses that he deliberately fired at a bush."

Major de Beaujolais turned to Digby Geste, little thinking that this Soldier of the Legion was one of the three boys to whom he had told stories of just such nights in the desert, years before, at beautiful Brandon Abbas in England.

"And why did you fire at a bush, might one ask?" he inquired coldly.

"Because it was moving toward me, Monsieur le Majeur," replied Digby.

"Or because you dreamed that it was?" asked de Beaujolais sternly.

"No, Monsieur le Majeur," replied Digby, firmly but respectfully. "The bush moved towards me. I measured its progress by that stone."

"Then go and fetch it," ordered de Beaujolais. "Quickly, *au pas gymnastique*."

With his rifle at the ready, and his heart beating rapidly, Digby doubled out towards the bush.

Arrived near it, he changed his pace to a slow walk
and covered the bush with his rifle.

He reached it.

Nothing happened.

But when, seizing a branch in his left hand, he
pulled, the bush yielded instantly, and with complete
ease he dragged it to where the little group awaited
him.

"Show a light here," ordered Major de Beaujolais, and it was immediately seen that the bush had
been cut off at ground level.

"You have done well, *mon enfant*," he said kindly,
and turning to the Sergeant, added:

"A good thing if all your men were as ready to
shoot at bushes that move at night! This was a spy.
Probably there's a Touareg band somewhere near.
Quite possibly we are surrounded, and shall be attacked at dawn. Double your sentries, and see if
any more of them can spot moving bushes. Bring
this man to me in the morning."

And the Major strode away to give orders for
the doubling of sentries on the other sides of the
camp, and for "stand-to" an hour before dawn.

But at dawn no attack materialized, and the
company struck camp and moved off as though
surrounded by enemies from whom an attack was
imminent.

The retreat from the position was made a useful
tactical exercise, and proved to be particularly so

when, from distant rocks and sandhills, came a
sudden outburst of irregular firing.

Major de Beaujolais appeared quite pleased, and
a look of boredom promptly departed from his handsome face as he stood up in his stirrups, and gazed
coolly around in all directions and indicated that the
company would proceed at its best pace to a not far
distant *ravin* which appeared to offer excellent
shelter for mules, while an adjacent knoll provided
an eligible site for riflemen. From there he would
give his force a lesson in attack as infantry, and
mobile rear-guard tactics as rifle-armed cavalry.

.   .   .   .

In the rear of the company rode Digby Geste, his
happiness faintly clouded by anxiety as to the conduct or misconduct of Mildred, his mule. It would
be quite the wrong time for her to have a fit of self-
determination, to demonstrate, and to try to make
the Sahara a country fit for mules to live in. What
would she do if she were hit without being seriously
wounded? Probably bolt and take an undeserved
place at the head of the column. Just as likely to
bolt in the opposite direction.

Crash! . . . Hullo, someone was down. A few
yards to his right a *légionnaire* had fallen from his
saddle. He had clung to his rein, and the mule had
come to a stand-still beside him. Digby pulled up,
as he realized that the man's efforts to get to his feet
were in vain.

Riding across, while bullets knocked up puffs of dust and sand around him, he saw that the man was Xarro, and that he was hit in the right knee. He was obviously in the greatest agony, and quite helpless. Springing to the ground, and putting his rein over his shoulder, Digby lifted Xarro in his arms, sat him sideways on Satan, who stood steady as a rock, and then lifted Xarro's left foot and leg across the mule, so that he was seated astride and firmly in the saddle.

As Digby thrust Xarro's left foot into the stirrup the wounded man, who appeared about to faint from pain, shock and loss of blood, drooped forward on Satan's neck and groaned:

"*I can't!* . . . *I can't!* . . . Tie me on. . . . for God's sake. . . ."

Easier said than done, with bullets smacking around, and the enemy drawing nearer and nearer, as they dodged from rock to rock and bush to bush.

"Cross your wrists under the mule's neck, quick," cried Digby, and, snatching a weary-looking handkerchief from his pocket, he swiftly and firmly bound Xarro's hands together. Then, slipping the off stirrup-leather from its fastening beneath the saddle-flap, he unbuckled the strap, thrust the end through the girth, through the buckle, and pulled the thick strap tightly across Xarro's left thigh.

He could not now possibly fall from the mule,

even if he fainted, and, provided Satan would canter after the Company, there was no reason why Xarro should not get safely to hospital.

Smack! A bullet had struck Xarro, and another hit Digby's water-bottle. Seizing Satan's rein, he swiftly scrambled on to the back of Mildred, who, with all the incalculable perversity of the mule, had behaved like a perfect lady at a moment when a little misconduct on her part would have been literally fatal.

As he urged the two mules into a canter, he realized that some of the nearest Arabs had ceased firing, and were actually rushing forward to capture them and their mules alive. Live men can be tortured, and live mules can be ridden or sold.

"First catch your hare," quoth Digby as Mildred and Satan surpassed themselves. Never had he known mules to go so fast. Pity there wasn't a Mules' Derby. Was it because Xarro was present?

Hullo! . . . What was this? . . . Two men galloping back from the main body.

Hank and Buddy! . . . Silly asses; they couldn't do any good, and were merely risking their lives for nothing.

The two reined up, dismounted, and, with reins looped over arms, knelt and opened rapid fire on the running Arabs. These having magically disappeared behind bushes, stones, mounds, boulders

or such sufficient cover (for an Arab) as a dead leaf,
Hank and Buddy again jumped on their mules and
cantered after Digby and Xarro.

A few minutes later, still holding Satan's rein,
Digby galloped into the mouth of the nullah, wadi
or *ravin*, in which the other mules stood in groups
of four, the reins of each group being held by the
No. 3 man of the group. A few wounded men sat
or lay on the shady side of the nullah, in the charge
of a medical-orderly or dresser.

The remainder of the Company, strongly and in-
visibly posted, was waiting to give the advancing
Arabs a warm reception.

Leading Satan to where the wounded lay, Digby
called out to the *infirmier*, the medical subordinate:

"This man's wounded in the knee and chest," and
then, reining in, endeavoured to bring Satan to a
stand-still.

But Satan seemed agitated. Perhaps he missed
his master's voice. Perhaps he thought that in his
master's best interests he had better make straight
for Tokotu, and his comfortable mule-lines.

He declined to stop.

Xarro opened a sickly eye and groaned. He was
not as good at bearing pain as he had been at inflicting it.

"Whoa, whoa, Satan!" cried Digby, and, as he
took his right foot from the stirrup, to dismount
from his own mule, he remembered the word, or

sound, that Xarro himself had told him to use, when he wanted to steady Satan.

"Whoa, Satan! . . . *Brrrtsch!* . . ." cried Digby. . . . "*Brrrtsch!* . . ."

Satan pricked his ears, and instantly flung himself down and rolled—as he had been trained to do, at that word of command.

With his last breath Xarro shrieked in agony, as the huge mule rolled upon him thrice.

X

LOW FINANCE

SEATED on his bed in the barrack-room, and doubtfully assisted by the comments of his brothers, Beau Geste was making up his accounts for the month.

Gradually and unintentionally, he had drifted into the trade, business or profession of money-lender. In so doing, he had incurred the most bitter animosity of Monsieur Veidhaas, a gentleman remarkable by reason of the facts that he was at once a Jew, a *légionnaire*, and a financier; and that he could reap a harvest in so poor a soil.

Of the two financiers, Beau Geste had by far the bigger business, and the more rapidly it grew, the more swiftly did that of Monsieur Veidhaas decline; and yet the latter was undoubtedly the better business man.

The explanation of the phenomenon probably lies in the fact that Beau Geste charged no interest whatsoever, whereas Monsieur Veidhaas charged exactly 5,200 per cent per annum. That is to say, he would lend you a *sou* to-day, provided you handed him two *sous* to-day week.

Beau Geste's method of business was to lend any

reasonable amount to any friend who wanted it; his only reservations being that he didn't lend money to assist and encourage drunkenness, nor did he lend a second sum until the first had been returned.

As Monsieur Veidhaas pointed out to him, with gesticulatory hands and screaming voice, this not only wasn't business, but wasn't common honesty and fair play to Monsieur Veidhaas. In fact it was just the low, mean, dirty, silly sort of trick that an Englishman *would* play.

In point of fact, things were even worse than has been stated, for not only did this black-leg financier charge no interest, but he took no security!

The very thought of such conduct sickened Monsieur Veidhaas to the depths of his soul, and indeed, almost to those of his body. He felt physically nauseated when he saw men casually borrowing good copper *sous*, without bond or receipt, and as casually returning them. For, curiously enough, return them they did, in spite of the lack of documentary evidence against them, their own cruel poverty, the absence of security, and the fact that return was never demanded.

Nevertheless, Beau Geste kept account of these loans, varying from a *sou* to a whole franc, because, though he had an unquenchable desire to help and oblige, he had no desire, nor intention either, to be robbed or to encourage cadging.

"Bloated bloodsucker!" accused Digby, sitting

beside him, and watching him cross off the names of men who had paid their debts that day, fifth-day—pay-day—when every man received the sum of 2½d. for five days' labour, whether he deserved it or not.

Hank and Buddy approached, and John Geste moved up, and made room for them on his bed.

"Bank still open for the transaction of business, Bo?" inquired Hank.

"To a valued and respected client, yes," replied Beau Geste. "How much do you want to pay in?"

Hank patted his pockets.

"Say now, that's too bad," he said with heavy concern. "I've come without it. I must have left it where I left me youth and innocence. No matter, I'll draw a bit, instead. I'll draw myself a cheque for fifty centimes."

"Me too, Bo," added Buddy. "If it ain't making what you might call a run on the Bank, like. I'll cover the overdraft next pay-day, and if I'm caught short, I'll sell something of Hank's and make it up."

"Same here, Son," assured Hank. "I can always sell something of Bud's, if it's only his scalp for a pen-wiper, or to Lejaune for a sooveneer to hang at his belt."

"Or we could go hotel-borrowing again," mused Buddy.

"What *is* hotel-borrowing?" inquired Digby Geste. "I've borrowed various things in my life, but I don't remember ever borrowing a hotel."

"No, Son, you ain't got it right," replied Buddy. "Hotel-borrowing ain't borrowing hotels, it's borrowing *from* hotels, like."

"Shouldn't have thought they were prompt and ready lenders," observed Beau Geste.

"No," replied John. "In fact I've always rather loved the expression 'hotel *guest.*' A gentle irony about it!"

"Oh, that's all right," affirmed Digby. "The hotel guessed it could make a bit out of you—and it was right—so what's wrong?"

"Peace, pups," quoth their brother. "How does one induce hotels to lend anything, Bud?"

"Well, they don't rightly know they're doing it, Son," was the answer, "and it's one of them cases of money making money, and 'unto him that hath shall be given.' . . . But if you've got 150 francs, you can borrow quite a lot from hotels."

"At what rate of interest?" asked John.

"None," replied Buddy.

"For what period?" inquired Digby.

"Long as you like," was the answer.

"But why *hotels?*" asked Beau.

"Oh, reasons," answered Buddy. "I'll tell you . . . give you an example, like. Shall I, Hank?"

"Wel-l-l," mused Hank. "Yes-s. . . . You might tell it to *these* boys. They got high principles

and are above temptation.   It wouldn't be likely to
deterioralize them."

And fixing each of the brothers in turn with a calm
ingenuous eye, he added:

"Nobody oughtn't never to indulge in the sport
and pursuit called hotel-borrowing unless they are
strictly honest, particular and high-principled, and
with strong firm character. . . . Oncorruptible."

The three Gestes slowly nodded their heads in
understanding and agreement.

"We was in Monte Carlo," observed Buddy.
"Also we had one hundred and fifty francs, and
there was lots of hotels. . . ."

"Some lovely place, Monte Carlo . . ." remarked Hank.   "Nothing wrong with Monte Carlo
. . . 'cept the people in it."

"That's so," agreed Buddy.   "There's a lot there
that ain't so simple-minded as they oughta be.   Sets
their hearts on things of this world—dross and filthy
looker. . . . And the one hundred and fifty francs
didn't seem to us a right and sensible sum of money,
somehow. . . . If it had been a hundred and fifty
thousand, we could have made ourselves comfortable. . . . We could have gone to the *Imperial
Splendide Continental* and been two of them eccentric and amusin' American millionaires what nobody
minds what they does—as long as they hands it out
in wads. . . . Or if it had been one hundred and
fifty centimes, we could have tramped along to

Marseilles and enlisted in the Legion. . . . As it
was, it was a foolish sum of money."

"Not so foolish either—in a way," mused Hank.

"No," agreed Buddy. "In a manner of speaking
it weren't. . . . You see, it happened, by the kind
and loving mercy of Heaven, to be in two notes.
Being the financiers you are, you'll grasp the fact
that it was thus a hundred-franc note and a fifty-
franc note. . . . Well, we was sitting on a seat on
that sorter River-Front Drive what looks over the
sea, and listenin' to them heroes down below, blowing the back-ends off lame tame pigeons, when Hank
has an idee . . ."

"That's a lie," interrupted Hank, "you miserable
back-bitin', evil-speakin', character-takin', foul-
mouthed little runt. It was *you*."

"Oh, *me*, was it?" replied Bud. "Very well . . .
I had the idee then, that we oughta give the bigger
note to the Society for the Protection of Cruelty to
Animals and use the other fifty to rush us a growler
of beer and then git up and git, and go on walking."

Hank snorted, as Digby murmured:

"Quite so."

And Beau gravely observed:

"I'm sure you did."

"And then Hank had the idee," continued Buddy,
gazing mildly at Hank, who remained watchfully
silent, "of using the money otherwise, so to speak.

"*His* notion was for him to take the hundred-franc

note and me to take the fifty-franc note. . . ."

"It was *your* notion, you anæmic Ananias," shouted Hank, seizing Buddy by the scruff of the neck.

"Very well! . . . *Very* well! . . . It *were* then," agreed Buddy . . . "for us to take the notes and invest them in real estate and begin to lead a higher and a better life as solid citizens. Hank says he wants to turn honest and live respectable—after watching me."

The three Gestes contrived to separate the two Americans and to keep them apart while Buddy developed his exposition of the art of hotel-borrowing.

"Well, as I was saying," he continued, straightening his disarranged clothing.

"Hank says:

"'You march into the *Hotel Imperial Splendide Continental* as though you owned it, and wasn't proud of it. When the head waiter comes to throw you out or show you to a seat, you gaze upon him as though he was mud and you didn't want to tread in it. . . . Then you order a good blow-out and have eggs-and-bacon in it, or pork-and-beans, or something else they haven't got. And then call 'em a ten-cent hash-joint, not fit for a salmon-canning, corned-beef-packing, lumber-king to sit down in. Drink water because you're a rich eccentric millionaire and can afford to, and don't spend more than ten francs. . . . When the waiter brings the bill, pay with the fifty-franc note, and then set and chew a tooth-pick cheerful, until poor Alphonso comes back with the change.

" 'When he does—*don't take it.* . . . Let it lie on the plate while you smiles a kinda sad sooperior amused smile, and gently shakes your head from side to side. Then you says, still amused, but dignified and kinda ironic:

" ' "What's the game, Alphonso—you poor, feeble, flat-footed fish! What do you take me for? A half-witted Wop, or the monkey off the organ?"

" 'Then you tells him to fetch the Head Waiter or the Manager or the Owner if he likes, and sits back calm and sooperior while he does it. . . . When the Head Waiter or the Manager or the Owner arrives, look him up and down slow-like—take a good stare at any cracks in his shoes and then admire where his pants goes baggy at the knees. Then take a interest in any grease-spots on his weskit. Then sorta brace yourself for a stare at his face; give a shudder at the sight of it, and then work downwards again. . . . In course of time, when you've looked him all over, say quiet, in a pompshus and contempshus voice:

" ' "How often d'you get away with *this* frame-up, Son?"

" 'And when he replies that he *nong comprongs,* you say:

" ' "Cut it *right* out, Bo! . . . Can it! . . .
Fergit it—and listen an earful. . . . I just give Mr.
Alphonso Alonzo Fandango Lorenzo a hundred-
franc note, and he's brought me change for a fifty-
franc note, and if you think you can pull that bunk
on me, you got another think coming. . . . See?
. . . So cut out the funny stuff, and get busy with
another fifty francs."

" 'When you said all that, the Head Waiter or
Manager or Owner or whatever It may be, he'll
give you the soft and saucy answer that turneth on
wrath. He'll tell you that your sort of poor bone-
headed hoodlum tries that silly old stale trick in that
hotel, about seven times a day and fourteen on Sun-
days. And right there, you rises to your feet, Bud,
and with all the weight and dignity of an American
Citizen, with Old Glory flying over him, and the
Band playing "Yankee Doodle," you says in a crool,
cold and cutting voice:

" ' "Before I bring in the Police, will you have
the goodness to go to your cashier's desk *and see
whether she has, or has not, a hundred-franc note*
(and right here you draws out your pocketbook)
*numbered 624 in the top left-hand corner and
E11373 in the right-hand corner—and reverse as
usual at the bottom.*"

" 'Nacherally the guy, whether he's Head Waiter,
Manager or Owner, will look foolish in the face and
make a quick hike to the cash-desk. . . . You'll

foller him too, lookin' haughty, but cold and crool.
And right there among the hundred-franc notes, on
the very top or near it, *there will be our old pal
E11373.*'"

"'"How will there, you old fool?' says I to
Hank.

"''Cos I shall have paid it in meself, in another
part of the room, ten minutes before,' replies
Hank. . . ."

"An' lo! it was so," added Buddy.

Silence.

"And you got away with it?" inquired Beau.

"Sure thing," replied Buddy. . . . "Hank walks
into that *Imperial Splendide Continental* and turneth unto the right hand. . . . A quarter of an hour
later, I walks in and turns unto the left hand and
we has our eats. . . . Soon as I seen him go out
again, I calls for my bill, and pays—and behold
Francesco Gorgonzola only brings me change for the
fifty-franc note which I had give him!. . . .

"When the Manager comes, I says:

"'I have not the slightest wish to get Guiseppe
Spaghetti into trouble, nor yet the cashier, so if you'll
be good enough to give me my proper change for my
lill' ole E11373' (consultin' my notebook) 'we'll
say no more about it.'

"Off goes the Manager, while I gazes idly round
and comes back in a minute, most apologetic.

"Me, I'm quite affable and pleasant and we parts the best of friends. . . .

"Well, not being too bad at games of skill and chance—so called becos we has all the skill and the mugs hasn't a chance, we makes that fifty into five hundred and sends fifty of it back to the *Hotel Imperial Splendide Continental* with our love and no explanations.

"Yes, we has quite a good time at Monte Carlo, hotel-borrowing and hotel-repaying; winning at poker and losing at roulette. Quite a good time, we has, and we leaves Monte Carlo owing nobody a *sou*, and not owning one ourselves."

Silence.

"Gee," murmured Hank. "He oughta married that dame Sapphira, but I wouldn't have liked to be the off-spring."

"*Me?*" replied Buddy in hurt surprise. "My second name is George Washington. It was you thought of it, and you what paid in the hundred-franc note that caused all the trouble and dishonesty! . . . If it hadn't been there, there wouldn't been fifty francs profit every time. . . . *You!* . . . Why, you'll prob'ly pinch angels' wing-feathers on Judgment Day and sell 'em in Hell as sooveneers. . . . No, you ain't what *I* call a good, simple, honest man." And Buddy walked away as one too full for further speech.

XI

PRESENTIMENTS

I

WHEN a dam bursts, a mighty flood follows; when a notably silent man talks, he is apt to say a good deal.

Wine sometimes loosens the tongue, particularly if the drinker be habitually abstemious. There are men who talk when they have fever; others when the moon is full, and the desert and night sky a vision of loveliness and a dream of peace; some when the nerves are frayed, so that they must do something or go mad, and talking is the easiest thing to do; others, again, when they are fey, and are well aware that to-morrow's battle will be their last.

Le Légionnaire Max Linden, a forbidding person, so taciturn, so inarticulate, as to be known as the Dumb Devil, was talking to the Geste brothers—and to some purpose. It was the eve of the battle of El Rasa, and Linden affected to be perfectly certain that he would be killed on the morrow.

"Oh, rubbish, man," said Michael Geste; "not one in a hundred of these presentiments is justified."

". . . Begun in blood . . . ended in blood,"

239

growled Linden, raising himself on his elbow, and staring out into the moonlit night. . . . "But that her blood oozed and spread and trickled in the direction of the door, reached it, and slowly, slowly crept underneath it and out on to the white doorstep, I should not be here now . . . here now, awaiting my death from an Arab bullet."

"Cheer up, old bird," said Digby. "Have a cigarette," he added, offering a packet of *caporal.* "I bet you I'll give you another, this time to-morrow, and that you'll smoke it."

"You may stick it in my dead mouth if you like," replied Linden, "before they shovel me under the sand.

"No," he continued, "if her blood had never reached the door, I shouldn't be here now. . . . On the other hand, my father would not have been executed, which would have been a pity. Executed for the murder of my mother."

The brothers eyed each other uncomfortably. No wonder Max Linden was a bitter and tragic-looking desperado, whose rare speech was either a snarl or a growl.

"Your father murdered your mother before your eyes, and was hanged?" murmured Michael Geste, as Linden turned to him and apparently awaited a reply.

"He was hanged for it, anyhow," replied Linden, and he laughed horribly as he added:

"Death on the scaffold was the terror of his life, too. Yes, an absolute obsession, this fear of the rope. And the executioner got him all right. . . . What about *that* for a presentiment coming true? *And I could have saved him.*"

"What about a spot of sleep?" suggested Digby.

"It was all clear enough to the police, when they burst in," continued Linden, ignoring the hint. "It didn't need a Lecoq, nor your Sherlock Holmes, to see what had happened. It leapt to the eye.

"Picture it.

"Old Franz Muller, nosing about the dust-pails and gutters in the early morning, sees a pool of blood on the doorstep of the little house where lives the drunken *mauvais sujet*, Marc Linden. He knocks at the door, tries the handle, peers through the key-hole, kicks heavily, runs round to the window. No sound nor sign from within; and, full of importance, off he goes to the police.

"All in their own good time, they send a man along to see whether there's a word of truth in old Franz Muller's story; or whether there is a spot of red paint on our doorstep, and we peacefully asleep in our beds.

"The man reports that blood has oozed under the front door, spread across the step, trickled down the sides and soaked into the dust.

"The police come, burst open the door and find— what?"

"A woman lies at full length upon the floor, dead. So great a quantity of blood has flowed from her head and neck that, if she was not killed outright at the time, she has bled to death.

"Seated in a wooden arm-chair, and half sprawling across the table, is a man. He is still in a drunken slumber, his head pillowed upon his bent left arm, the hand of which clutches an empty bottle. His right arm, outstretched before him, and resting on the table, points in the direction of the body of the woman. In the man's right hand is a pistol, its muzzle resting on the table. One chamber has been discharged. In a corner of the room, a boy—a stunted undersized boy—lies on the bare floor.

"They thought he was dead, too, until the Police Surgeon discovered that he was only suffering from a severe blow on the head, a dislocated leg and various minor injuries. He was very emaciated, and had a number of old bruises, weals, abrasions and contusions. It was noticed, too, that the eyes of the woman were blackened and that her face showed evidences of brutal injury.

" 'Aha!' said the police, 'a wife-beater; a scoundrelly brute that assaults children in his drunken frenzy; and now he has gone too far. He has deliberately murdered his wife, and perhaps has fatally injured his son!'

"They reconstructed the crime.

"The man had come home drunk, as usual, bringing with him a bottle of cheap and fiery spirit. He had savagely assaulted the woman, beating her insensible, and had then struck and kicked the boy, finally hurling him across the room, where he had lain unconscious and half dead.

"The ruffian had then seated himself at the table to drink. Unfortunately, before he had fallen into this drunken slumber the unhappy woman had recovered consciousness and, clutching at the table, had raised herself to her knees and reproached or defied him, or perhaps had begged him to get help for the injured child. His drunken fury blazing forth again, he had snatched the pistol from his pocket and shot her dead. He had then emptied the bottle at a draught, and fallen forthwith into the sottish, swinish slumber in which they had found him.

"Thus the police. And thus was the accusation of wilful murder framed against my father.

"Nor could a shadow of doubt remain in the mind of any reasonable and unbiassed person who heard the impassioned speech of the prosecuting Counsel, the Advocate-General, who demanded a life for a life, the heaviest of punishments for the foulest of crimes.

"Certainly there was no doubt in the mind of the Judge. How should there be? What would you three have concluded if you had been the three policemen who burst into the room, and saw the body of a slaughtered woman lying in a pool of

blood that had flowed from a wound caused by a
bullet that had severed jugular vein and carotid
artery? What would you have concluded if, facing
the murdered woman, there sat a man, a noted brute
and wife-beater, whose hand clutched the pistol from
which the bullet had been fired?

"What, I ask you?" insisted Linden, seizing the
wrist of Michael Geste in his hot and shaking hand.
"Tell me; what?"

"I should have said that things looked black
against the man," replied Michael Geste, "very
black."

"Would you have sent him to the scaffold if you
had been his Judge?" asked Linden.

"Don't know, I'm sure," was the reply. "Probably. . . . Possibly not. Evidence all circumstantial. . . . We have a different system, you know.
If a jury brought him in guilty of wilful
murder . . ."

"Yes, but it wasn't England, you see," interrupted
Linden, "and we don't assume that every villainous
criminal is innocent. We leave him to prove that he
is—if he can.

"What would *you* have done if you had been the
Judge?" he added, turning to Digby Geste.

"What the Judge did do, I suppose," replied
Digby.

"And you?" continued Linden, turning to John
Geste.

"Oh, I don't know," replied John. "Benefit of the doubt, if there were any doubt; and I suppose there always is a possibility of doubt when there are no witnesses."

"There *was* a witness," said Linden. "Myself . . . I witnessed the whole affair from beginning to end."

"And you could have saved your father," remarked Michael softly. "What a terrible position for you! Poor chap. . . . You'd have had to perjure yourself to have saved him, I suppose? What a ghastly predicament! Did you give evidence against him, or did you refuse to speak?"

"*Aha!*" replied Max Linden, and grinned unpleasantly.

Silence fell on the little group, and three of the four settled themselves for slumber. But Max Linden, sick-souled and devil-driven, had more to say.

"It is pretty generally true," he went on, "that bullies are cowards, and that those who are readiest in inflicting torture are the worst and feeblest in bearing pain.

"When they reconstructed the crime, my father made me, if possible, still more ashamed to be his son.

"As soon as I had recovered sufficiently, they took me back again from the hospital to the house, and put me on a mattress in the corner of the room, just as the police had found me. The body of my poor mother was arranged exactly as it had lain when the police entered the room. My father was seated in his chair, and made to assume the position in which he had been found. The pistol, clutched in his right hand, was laid on the exact spot—marked by a pencil—where it had rested.

"A police agent then enacted my mother's supposed part in the tragedy. First he lay upon the floor as though stunned by a blow. He then seized the edge of the table opposite to my father, dragged himself to his knees, and showed how a bullet, fired from the pistol as it rested on the table, would penetrate the side of his neck while he was in the act of rising from the floor.

"My father shuddered, shrieked, covered his eyes, and then struggled to escape. Alternately he screamed his protestations of innocence and grovelled for mercy. Weeping, he would point out that he could not possibly have done such a thing and know nothing about it; and he called God and all His saints to witness that he did know nothing about it.

"Then, tearful and voluble, he would point out that he was drunk when the police found him, and that if he *had* done it, he had been too drunk to know what he was doing. Surely they would not punish him for a thing done in ignorance and innocence? His only fault was that he had got drunk.

"Then he would call upon the world to witness

that no man, so drunk as he had been, could possibly aim and fire a pistol. But the *Juge d'Instruction* coldly asked him what evidence there was that he had not deliberately murdered his wife and thereafter drunk himself insensible?

"And that was where I came in.

"Sobbing, groaning, weeping, and sweating with fear for his own miserable skin, this creature, this man, this Noblest Work of God, suddenly caught a glimpse of salvation.

"A bright ray of hope shone into the black darkness of his soul.

" 'My son!' he cried, 'my son! He was in the room throughout the night! He can tell you what happened, *Monsieur le Juge.*'

"They took my evidence, and I gave it freely up to a certain point. I said:

" 'For as long as I can remember, my father has been a drunkard and a brute, living God knows how, and by any means but honest work. Times without number, I have seen him thrash my mother unmercifully, with a stick, with the buckle-end of a heavy belt, with a whip, and with his fist. Times without number, I have seen him knock her senseless with a single blow, and then kick her as she lay. More times than I can tell, he has flogged me, either for no reason whatsoever, or because he had sent me out to steal and I had brought back nothing. It has been his habit, when in funds, to bring in good food

—fish and meat and vegetables—and to stand over my mother while she cooked it. He would then eat the meal himself, while we had nothing but stale bread, and not enough of that. Frequently the rich food and bottle of wine would put him into such high good humour that he would observe that we had no need to eat dry bread, for we could wet it; and that there was no necessity for us to drink cold water, since there was no reason why we should not warm it. . . .

" 'On the night of my mother's death, he came home neither more nor less drunk than usual, bringing with him a bottle of liquor, but no food.

" 'He demanded *soupe* and bread.

" 'When my mother told him that there was no food of any sort in the house, and that we had that day tasted nothing whatsoever but a cup of re-boiled coffee-grounds, he knocked her down, and then kicked her until she managed to pull herself together and rise to her feet. He then announced that he would "feed me to rights." Since I wanted food, he'd feed me with a stick.

" 'As I tried to dodge past him and escape from the house, he kicked me with all his strength, and then, picking me up from the floor, flung me across the room, so that I struck the wall and fell in a corner. He then got the stick, and, as my mother threw herself between him and me, he struck her repeatedly with all his strength, until she fell to the ground near the table. Having kicked her several times, he seated himself at the table and drank from the bottle.

" 'I think I then became unconscious for a time. When I recovered consciousness, my father was drinking from the bottle, and my mother was making feeble efforts to lift her head from the ground and raise herself upon her elbow.

" 'What I saw after that I will never tell. Not though I am *tortured* will I say one word; not though I spend the rest of my life in prison will I add another syllable.'

"Naturally, the police thought that I was reluctant to give testimony which would instantly destroy any chance my father would have of escaping the scaffold; and, while respecting the filial feelings of an unhappy boy, most miserably situated, they drew their own conclusions. Naturally, too, it was perfectly clear to them that my mother could not have committed suicide, inasmuch as the pistol was in my father's hand. Moreover, had it been a case of suicide, I, of course, should have testified to the manner of her death, and removed all suspicion from my father.

"Still protesting his innocence, weeping, shrieking and struggling, my father was taken back to prison, charged with the wilful murder of his wife."

§ 2

Linden bowed his head upon his hands and fell silent.

"Look here, you've talked enough for to-night, old chap," said Michael. "Lie down, and try and get to sleep."

"Oh, let me talk, let me talk, now I have started," groaned Linden. "Let me finish, anyhow. I shall be under the sand this time to-morrow—shot, as my mother was shot, through the face and neck. I want to tell the truth about my father. . . . Let me get it off my chest. . . . I must tell somebody. . . . Let me go on."

"Why, of course," agreed Michael, "talk as much as you like."

"Yes, rather," added Digby; "if it will do you any good, we'll listen all night. But you've really told us everything, you know. . . . Poor old chap! . . . Rough luck. . . ."

"Awful hard lines," murmured John. "Some people *do* have frightful tragedies in their lives. . . . But doesn't it make it worse for you, to rake it all up again? . . . And as my brother says, you've really told us all about it."

"Oh, have I?" replied Linden, again grinning unpleasantly. "Listen.

"Between the Examining Magistrate's preliminary investigations and the Court trial, I begged and prayed and implored that I might be allowed to have an interview with my father in his prison cell.

"And one day I found myself alone with the man who had made my life, and that of my mother, a hell upon earth.

"In the most revolting manner, he fawned upon me, kissing me repeatedly, and straining me to his breast.

" 'My son! My son!' he snivelled, 'my saviour! You'll be famous throughout Europe as the boy who saved his innocent father's life. . . . How wonderful are the ways of God! Wonderful and yet terrible—for I have always had this awful fear of the scaffold, and now I have stood within its very shadow. The thought has been my nightmare and presentiment from childhood, and here I sit within a dozen yards of the dreadful thing itself. But my own beloved son has come to save me! . . . My little Max has come to tell me all that happened on that dreadful night when his poor dear mother took her life.'

"And again he thrust his beastly and tear-bedewed face against mine.

" 'Yes, father,' I replied, 'that is just what I have come to do. Listen:

" 'You nearly committed two murders that night. It was not *your* fault that you did not first kick your own beloved little Max to death, and then his poor dear mother. As a matter of fact, you beat them

both insensible. The mother recovered first, thought
her child was dead—as he lay there, white and still,
where his loving father had flung him.'

" 'And thinking so, she took her life. . . . She
took her own life. . . . *She committed suicide,*'
gabbled my father.

" 'Listen,' I repeated. 'The half-murdered
woman, regaining consciousness, despairing, dazed,
beside herself with agony and grief, stared at what
she thought to be the body of her murdered child,
and then at the sodden brutal face of the bestial
ruffianly sot whom she supported by her unceasing
labours, and who repaid her love and generosity as
a wild animal would not have done. . . . It was a
terrible look, and would to God that the eyes of the
swinish drunkard could have encountered it.'

" 'But they could not! But they could not!'
yelped my father. 'He was drunk, he was insensible; the poor fellow was helpless in a state of stupor,
dead to the world . . . innocent, *unconscious.*'

" 'Quite unconscious,' I agreed, 'drunk and incapable. Entirely unable to see that terrible stare
from the woman who had loved him. Nor could
he see her, after many failures and superhuman
effort, rise to her hands and knees and drag herself
to her feet.'

" 'But *you* saw, *you* saw!' cried my father.

" 'Oh, yes, I saw everything,' I reassured him.
'I saw her drag herself to the cupboard where you

hide your pistol. I saw her stagger from the cupboard with the pistol in her hand, and I saw her
crawl into a chair, fainting, and apparently about to
die.'

" 'Yes, yes, yes,' urged my father, 'and then *she
shot herself*, eh? Thank God! Praise God that my
own precious boy saw it all, and can save his innocent
father from this horrible false charge!'

" 'Listen,' I said a third time. 'How long my
mother sat there, I do not know, but, after a time,
she got to her feet once more, went and drank water,
and then, with one hand holding the pistol and the
other supporting her against the wall, she stood and
peered at me.

" ' "Dead!" she whispered. "*My little Max,
dead!*" and turned again and looked at you, dear
father. . . . I would willingly have died if I could
have made you meet that look. It would have
haunted you, sleeping and waking, to your grave.'

" 'But you were *not* dead,' interrupted my father.
'Why did you not speak to her? Why did you pretend?'

" 'Because I thought she was going to shoot you,
dear father,' I replied. 'Going to shoot you, in the
belief that you had killed me. Not for worlds would
I have let her see that I was alive. I was dazed and
half-delirious, but I had my wits sufficiently about
me to realize that mother was (thank God!) about
to shoot you, and that I could swear that I had seen

you commit suicide! So I lay still as the dead, in
that dark corner, my eyes half-closed, and looking
like the corpse I almost was.'

" 'And *then?* And *then?*' begged my father.

" 'And then my mother made her maimed and
broken way across to where you sat and snored, your
head upon your left arm, your left hand clutching
the bottle, your right hand and arm extended across
the narrow table. . . . And, to my astonishment,
what did she do but carefully, painfully, gently,
slowly, open your right hand and clasp it about the
handle of the revolver, your forefinger through the
trigger-guard, and resting on the trigger.

" 'And then my brain cleared somewhat, and my
heart beat fast with joy, for I realized that my brave
and clever mother was going to make *you* commit
suicide! *You* were going to be found with your
pistol in your hand and such brains as you have
scattered about the room! . . . I almost moved and
spoke. I nearly cried *"Bravo,* mother!" and blessed
her name.

" 'And, wide-eyed, I watched as she went round
to the opposite side of the table and knelt facing
you . . . watched to see her take your right hand
in hers and bend it round so that the pistol touched
your loathsome face . . . watched to see her press
your forefinger when the muzzle of the pistol was
against your temple, or your eye, or thrust into your
open slavering mouth. . . .

" 'She took your right hand in both of hers, and, to my puzzled amazement, presented the pistol—the butt of which rested on the table as you gripped it—*straight at her own neck.*

" 'Even as my amazement turned to horror and I screamed aloud, *"Don't, mother! Don't!"* she must have pressed your forefinger with her two thumbs.

" 'There was a deafening report, and she fell back.

" 'Even as she died, she seemed to be trying to get farther from the table. . . .

" 'And then, too late, I understood. Thinking me dead, she had come to join me, leaving you, the murderer of her child, to explain as best you could the corpses, the blood, the discharged revolver clutched in your hand.'

" '*Devilish! Devilish!*' whispered my father. 'The vile hag. . . . But God looks after the innocent; and my child was there and saw it all—to testify truly that his dear father was the victim of a horrible plot.'

" 'Yes, dear father,' I replied. 'Your child was there, and saw it all, and has truly testified.' "

"My father was now anxious to be rid of me, and could scarcely contain himself until he could communicate with the lawyer charged with his defence. From this gentleman I soon received a visit in hospital.

" 'Well, well,' quoth he, standing beside my bed and rubbing his hands. 'What is this, what is this, my silent young gentleman? You've found your tongue with a vengeance! . . . Now tell me again very carefully all that you told your father,' he continued as he opened his bag, took out a large notebook, and seated himself on my bed.

" 'Now my little man,' he smiled, smug and self-satisfied, 'let us have it.'

"I gazed with blank incomprehension upon the smug face of the lawyer. *Found* my tongue with a vengeance, had I? On the contrary, I had lost it with a very real vengeance.

" 'Sir?' I stammered.

" 'Come on,' he encouraged, 'and be very careful and exact, especially about your mother putting the pistol in your father's hand and pressing the trigger.'

" 'About my mother doing *what*, sir?' I faltered.

" 'You heard what I said,' he snapped.

" 'Yes, sir,' I agreed. 'I heard what you said, but I don't know what you are talking about.'

" 'Your father has just told me,' was the reply, slow and patient, clear and impressive, 'that you have admitted to him that you witnessed the whole affair, and did not, as you previously stated, lie unconscious until you awoke to find your mother dead. He says you told him how you saw your mother put the pistol in his hand, and then deliberately shoot herself.'

"I smiled with pale amusement.

" 'My father seems to have been dreaming, sir,' I said.

"The lawyer stared at me in amazement.

" '*Dreaming?* . . . *Dreaming?* . . .' he said, at length. 'What do you mean? Are you implying that the whole story is a tissue of lies?'

" '*I* called it a dream, sir,' I answered meekly.

"The lawyer stared the harder.

" 'A wonderfully coherent and circumstantial *dream*,' he said. . . . 'Astonishing amount of detail . . . don't you think so?'

" 'My father didn't tell it to me, sir,' I said simply.

" 'Well, I'll tell it you now, my young friend.' . . . And he proceeded to give a very full and accurate repetition of what I had told my father.

" 'A really marvellous dream, sir,' I remarked, when he had finished.

" 'And haven't you dreamed the same dream yourself?' he asked.

" 'I *never* dream, sir,' I replied.

" 'Couldn't you dream that dream to-night?' he suggested, with a subtle smile and a would-be hypnotic gaze.

" 'I *never* dream, sir,' I repeated, and matched his subtle smile."

The three brothers stared incredulous at *le Légionnaire* Max Linden, their young faces expressing a variety of emotions—wonderment, contempt, pity.

"But did they confront you with your father?"

"Oh, yes," replied Linden, "and he, having faithfully repeated the story I had told him, flung himself at my feet, and implored me to corroborate it; begged me to speak the truth; besought me to save him; shrieked to me that he was innocent, *and I alone could prove it.*"

"And what did you do?" asked Michael Geste, as Linden fell silent.

"I saw the wraith of my mother standing behind him, and turning to the Advocate-General, who was present, I tapped my forehead and smiled."

" 'Dreaming again, eh?' " growled the great man.

" 'Yes, sir,' I agreed, 'he is still dreaming.'

"And so my father's presentiment came true."

"Excuse me," asked Michael Geste, as *le Légionnaire* Max Linden lay back and prepared to sleep, "but was the tale you told your father *true*, or did you actually invent it with the object of torturing him?"

"*Aha,*" grinned *le Légionnaire* Linden, and composed himself to slumber.

On the following day his own presentiment came true, and he died on the battlefield of El Rasa. A bullet struck him in the neck, and, as no one had any time to attend to him, he bled to death.

XII

DREAMS COME TRUE

I

"HAVE you come across an extraordinary bird whom they call The Apostle?" asked Digby suddenly, as the three brothers sat in the *Jardin Publique*, and rested their weary bones, after a week of murderous manœuvres, marching, counter-marching, skirmishing, attacking and trench-digging, during each day of which they had been burnt almost unbearably by the sun, and, during each night, soaked and chilled by a cold, relentless rain.

"What's he like?" asked Michael.

"An Apostle," replied Digby.

"What's an Apostle like?" inquired John.

"Don't pretend an ignorance and innocence beyond your years," requested Digby. "It is perfectly well known to any student of German oleographs that an Apostle has a mild and beautiful face, enriched by limpid and liquid eyes like those of a camel; a long-ish, curly but well-trimmed, golden beard; long hair, curling in ringlets about his shoulders; and an expression of relentless benignity."

"And a halo," added Michael.

"Well, this chap has to make a *képi* do for a halo," said Digby. "But I really think that, back in the old Home Town, he must have been a professional sitter."

"What d'you mean—a sitter?" inquired John.

"It's the opposite of professional stander," replied Digby. "A person who makes a business of standing drinks. . . . There is no such person; but a professional sitter is a person who makes a practice of sitting for a photograph. Surely you've seen the Beach Bathing Girl, laughing like two tickled hyenas, waving a hand in the air; the Brother-in-Law of the Murdered Man, marked with a cross, who had nothing to do with it; the Mother of Nineteen, who might have reared twenty only he swallowed a very bad penny; the Channel Aspirant, who had to give up toward the evening of the third day, owing to currents in the bun they gave her; the Very Respectable Man in Shirt Sleeves who won the Football Forecast Competition at the 297th attempt, and is going to buy his wife (inset) a mangle, because they've never had a cross word competition in their lives . . ."

"Shut up," growled Michael.

"Certainly, Sir," agreed Digby. "And The Apostle must have made his living sitting for the pictures that adorn the books on which Good Children are brought up."

"Nearly finished?" inquired Michael, "because if

so, I believe I know the chap you mean, only he was pointed out to me as the Dreamer. He's a friend of Cordier, who, as a doctor and psychologist, is deeply interested in him."

"Oh, yes," said John. "I know the Dreamer. Most extraordinary creature. Preaches, dreams and sees visions."

"Yes, by Jove, I remember now. Some one called him *Le Reveur*."

"Well, what do you think of him?"

"I *don't* think of him," said Michael. "I prefer not to. He gives me the creeps."

"That's interesting," put in John.

"Why?" inquired his brothers.

"Well, I was on a fatigue with him, and after some hours, and quite a long talk, I really didn't know whether I liked or loathed him; nor whether he was quite charming or—not quite charming; almost sinister in fact."

"That's the word," observed Digby. "Sinister. . . . You feel he's a most interesting and delightful chap, and then suddenly you come up against something which is, as you say, almost sinister."

"Unwholesome, what?" suggested Michael. "Bizarre, abnormal, got a mad streak in him."

"Streak is a good word, too," agreed Digby. "You may conceivably have encountered the expression Streaky Bacon. He's like that. A nice expanse of fat white piety and virtue, and then a hard red streak of something lurid."

"A wretched and vulgar simile," commented Michael. "But I know what you mean. He's certainly of less homogeneous structure, more conglomerate, of more diverse elements compact. . . ."

"Yes, Papa," agreed Digby hastily. "In short, a weird bloke. Let's cultivate him for our collection."

"Or collect him for our cultivation," added John, as they arose to return to Barracks.

§ 2

Le Légionnaire Maximilien Gontran, as he called himself, seated at a table in the Canteen, held a circle of his admirers spell-bound by his eloquence—a thing he loved to do, and which he could do at will. He was describing one of those astoundingly vivid and circumstantial dreams that had won him the sobriquet of "The Dreamer," while his unusual appearance, manner and conduct had won him that of "The Apostle."

As the three brothers approached, warmly welcomed by their friends Maris, Cordier and St. André, Gontran paused to bow courteously and suggest refreshment. He then resumed his well-told and realistic account of his latest dream.

"No, I couldn't tell you what place it was," he said, "save that I got the impression of a kind of

Cathedral Chapter-House, or some such place; nor
could I say for certain whether it was part of a
Catholic or a Protestant foundation. It might have
been the Vatican, Canterbury Cathedral, Nôtre
Dame, St. Paul's or St. Mark's. It may have been
in Seville, St. Petersburg, New York, Athens or
Bruges, but it was a magnificently ornate interior of
lace-like ancient stone carving, lace-like old wooden
carving, jewel-like mediæval stained-glass, all mel-
lowed and harmonized with the patina of Time.

"In this great room, with its marble pavement,
from which grew great pillars branching and ex-
foliating in the dim recesses of the groined and lofty
roof, was a great old table from the refectory of
some monastery. It was surrounded by great old
carven chairs, each worthy to be a Bishop's throne.
And in these chairs, about this table, sat a great company of Princes of the Church, over whom presided
the most wonderful and venerable figure of that
most wonderful and venerable Ecclesiastical Court.
A Prince Bishop, Cardinal, Archbishop or Pope. I
can see his face now, old ivory, aquiline, austere,
beautiful, beneath the silver hair and golden mitre.

"His vestments, stiff with brocade, precious metals
and more precious stones, were the most wonderful
that I have ever seen; even more costly ornate and
marvellous than those of the constellation of lesser
lights that shone around him.

"I can see the faces of those others, too. One was

that of a strong—perhaps headstrong and violent—
man; a face that could flush to dull purple with
anger; a face of heavy brows, heavy jaw and heavy
looks. When opposed by one of his colleagues, he
bared strong even teeth and covered them again
reluctantly.

"Next him, in purple and gold and finest lawn,
with a great jewel upon his white forefinger, sat a
gentle, quiet creature who, in silken tones, angered
and goaded the strong and violent man, with honeyed
words and mocking smiles. A subtle, wily man, a
very fox of Æsop.

"And on his other side, a pompous dullard, diseased with egoism and conceit, a man who thought,
if he did not actually say, 'God and I in our wisdom
have decided and ordained . . .'

"And others there were of the great and good—
and successful. And they talked about it and about,
while the High Priest in the high chair slowly
nodded his august head in agreement, or pursed his
thin lips in even more august disapproval.

"What they discussed with such intensity of feeling, such veiled acrimony and bitterness, I do not
know; but I rather fancy that some liturgical practice
was in process of revision; the proposal of some
modification of ritual was being defended and attacked; some alteration in the long-established forms
of ancient prayers. I know not what—but it was
abundantly clear that while some evidently thought

the proposals would afford the Almighty consider-
able satisfaction, others were of an adamantine
certainty that Almighty God would be frightfully
put out about it. One man—if one may use the
mere word 'man' without irreverence—arrayed in
clothing more beautiful and costly than that of a
great Queen at a State Ball, spoke most eloquently
of Progress, of the necessity of the Church's parallel
growth and development with that of the development of the mentality and education of the nation.
A good and learned man, he said that when the
nation was a child, it thought and prayed as a child,
but that now it was attaining to lusty youth and in-
cipient manhood, it would no longer think and pray
as a child, and the Church must realize the fact.

"As he resumed his seat, after a most moving
peroration, the beautiful and saintly figure at the
head of the table slowly nodded its noble and most
venerable head. And even as it did so, another
Prelate sprang to his feet, and with clenched fist and
blazing eye, called down the curse of God, the
rebuke of the High Priest, and in culmination, the
disapproval of the Prime Minister, on the impious
head of him who would dare to lay defiling, dese-
crating and sacrilegious hands upon the most treas-
ured, the most beloved, the most sacred heritage and
possession of the People. If such a dreadful thing
were done, they would not believe their very eyes

when they opened that book which so rarely left their hands. They would not believe their ears when they detected a change in the service of those Churches which they daily thronged. And when the awful truth at last dawned clearly on their shocked and shattered souls, they would swarm forth into the streets and market-places in their millions, and with tongues of men and angels, they would—er— do all sorts of things.

"And as this impassioned Defender of the Faith sank back exhausted upon the velvet cushions of his Throne, and wiped the foam from his lips with an embroidered handkerchief of finest lawn, a little wicket opened in the vast oaken double doors of this great Chapter-House. The little wicket, not five feet high, nor three feet wide, opened, and through it stooped the figure of a man—a common coatless working-man, wearing overalls and an apron, and carrying, slung over his shoulder, one of those flat straw baskets in which carpenters carry their tools. From its ends protruded saws, hammers, and the handles of other such implements used by those who work in wood.

"Humbly, quietly, treading as softly and silently as the contact of his hobnailed boots with that wonderful marble pavement permitted, the workman, with averted eyes and meekest mien, made his unobtrusive way toward a piece of unfinished work in the far distant corner of the Hall. There, in silence, absorption, and obscurity, he went about his business of measurement and then of boring into some rotten wood. In fact, he had settled to his work of restoration before the Lords Spiritual had properly recovered from the shock of his intrusion.

The High Priest at the head of the table, as became a Leader, was the first to give voice to the indignant astonishment of the august assembly. But it was the headstrong and violent Prelate who first took action. Even as the High Priest, cried with a stern note in his beautiful silvern voice:

"'Go hence! Depart! . . . You intrude. . . . This is not the time for you to enter here,' . . . the strong-faced Prelate, rising from his throne, strode across to where the carpenter worked engrossed, his back turned upon that judicial Court of Princes of the Church.

"Seizing the intrusive workman by the arm, he swung him about, and with an angry glare and display of strong white teeth, shouted:

"'Here, what's the meaning of this? Who are you, that you should come into the presence of the Lords Spiritual themselves, even while they deliberate on high matters of the Church—actually while they debate changes in the Form of Worship of Almighty God! . . . Who are you, sir?'

"A sweet and gentle smile wreathed the lips of the carpenter.

"'I am Jesus Christ,' he said softly. . . ."

Le Légionnaire Maximilien Gontran, known as the
Apostle, and also as the Dreamer, laughed, and then
emptied his glass, while the Geste boys eyed him
critically.

§ 3

The patrol under Corporal Heintz, twenty-four
hours out from Douargala, sprawled wearily about
that great man's feet, as they rested in the providen-
tial shadow of a great rock in that thirsty land.

There were present, the Geste brothers and most
of their *escouade*, Maris, Cordier, St. André, Hank,
Buddy, Boldini, Brandt, Haff, Delarey and a few
others, including La Cigale, old Tant de Soif and
Gontran—who distinguished himself next day and
was soon afterwards promoted Corporal.

To become the equal and even the superior of
Corporal Heintz was the dream of Gontran's life,
for he hated Heintz with an unspeakable, unappeas-
able, almost unbearable hatred. If there were, in
the whole world, another hatred that equalled it, it
was the hatred of Corporal Heintz for Gontran.

"Well, Apostle," growled Heintz with a bitter,
vicious sneer, as he looked down, from where he was
seated on a big stone, at the prostrate form of Gontran. "Had any more dreams lately?"

"Not lately, Corporal Heintz," replied *le Légionnaire* Maximilien Gontran, softly, as he turned his

large mild eyes toward the hard, handsome face of his enemy.

"Not lately, eh?" mocked the other. "Then I must see if I can't give you something to dream about. I wonder if you'd dream better in the cells or *en crapaudine*. . . . Tell us one that you *haven't* dreamed lately. . . ."

"I'll tell you one I once dreamed about a bully," replied Gontran, sitting up suddenly, and looking Heintz squarely in the face. "Two, in fact, if you'd care to hear them. I do not know whether you ever went to school, Corporal Heintz. . . . Yes? . . . Indeed! . . . So did I, and they sent me when I was very young—far too young, in fact. I first went to school on my third birthday, and I went in fear and trembling unbelievable, for the schoolmaster was a known bully and brute, who ruled his unhappy charges with a rod of iron, or rather with a rod of pliant cane, that left blue weals and bruises on their tender bodies. He did not spare the rod, but he spoiled the child, by making him a trembling little coward, an arrant little liar. What child, who thinks he can escape torture by means of deception, will not deceive? This brutal bully, this cruel sadistic savage, enjoyed beating children and thrashed them, not 'for their own good,' but for his own enjoyment, and made them furtive, treacherous, cowardly and untruthful. He also made their days a misery, their nights a terror, and their lives a burden. I can see

him now, with his flaming red beard, red hair, red
nose and cold greenish eye, a great powerful, vin-
dictive ruffian of whom our parents were as much
afraid as we were.

"It was no Academy for the Sons of Gentlemen,
our school, but a log hut in a forest, a mile or so
from our village, and there can be but few buildings
in this world from which more screams of agony had
rung out.   One reads of tortures, tortures of the
Chinese and of the Holy Inquisition; one has seen
photographs of the bodies of our poor fellows tortured and mutilated by the Arabs; but, you know, I
doubt if any tortured person suffers more from steel,
or cord, or red-hot iron, than does a tender child
from the stinging, biting cuts of a swishy cane
applied by a master hand.

"To me, at any rate, it was a refinement of agony
ineffable, and I suffered it daily for years, dreamed
of it nightly for centuries, and tried to find the
courage to commit suicide.   But *tout lasse, tout casse,
tout passe,* and at length I was free, and went out
into the great world where I grew big and strong.

"Oh, yes, I'm very strong, Corporal Heintz, and
most patiently I developed and trained my strength,
as the earnest pupil of a great and famous professional Strong Man.

"And then came this dream of which I started to
tell you.

"I dreamed that one fine morning I re-visited the

village of my birth, spent a delightful hour with my
dear old parents, and then took a stroll through the
forest to the scene of my happy school-days—those
days which we are told are the very happiest of our
lives. Nothing had changed in the five or six years
of my absence; not even the sound of agonized
shrieks as I drew near the building; not even the
sound of cutting blows upon bare flesh as I drew near
the open windows of the schoolhouse; not even the
savage grin of enjoyment upon the vile face of my
erstwhile preceptor . . .

"With my blood boiling, my nerves tingling and
my fists clenching and unclenching, I flung open the
door, and strode into the room, smelt the old familiar
smell, saw the rows of strained white faces, heard
the stifled sobbing of a cruelly beaten child.

" 'You dog,' I said quietly. 'You brutal, savage,
snarling cur.'

"And as he whirled upon me, I struck with all
my strength, and he went down, down across the
whipping-bench, over which he had held me a thousand times. And I saw fear in that brute's eyes as
he rose to his feet, and again I smashed my fist
between them, with all my strength.

"When he could stagger to his feet no more, I
flung him across that whipping-bench on which my
young life and soul and nature had been warped, and
taking his own cane, I flogged him until I was too
weary to raise my hand again.

"And as I resumed my coat, I told him that I would keep in closest touch with certain of his pupils, and that if ever I heard of his striking one of his pupils a single blow, I would visit him again and give him a punishment compared with which this would be as nothing.

"Wasn't that a fine dream, Corporal Heintz? Oh! *I am a good hater and I always repay! I always repay!*"

"I suppose it was a true dream," observed Michael Geste.

"Yes," replied Gontran. "A day dream—and quite true."

"You spoke of two," observed La Cigale, who had shuddered and covered his face with his hands during Gontran's description of the sufferings of the children. "What was the other, might one ask? Did you dream that some scoundrelly ruffian was punished in that one also?"

"Ah, a curious dream," murmured Gontran, eyeing Corporal Heintz. "Very curious. . . . *'Wage du zu irren und zu träumen,'* as Schiller says. . . . 'Dare to err and to dream.' . . . Yes, there was a scoundrel in this one also, and I think one may say he was punished. . . . A woman too. . . ."

"Do you never have beautiful dreams of drink?" inquired Tant de Soif. "I once dreamed that I was swimming in a river of wine. Lovely. . . . Wonderful. Every night I go to sleep hoping that I may dream it again."

"I suppose you drank while you swam?" inquired Boldini.

"No, I swam while I drank," replied Tant de Soif, "and I drank so much and so fast that I choked and woke up, to find that it had come on to rain, and that a stream of dirty water was pouring from a roof-gutter into my open mouth. Fancy dreaming of wine, and waking to water."

"That is life in epitome, my friend," observed La Cigale, "to find your wine is water. Tell us your other dream," he added, turning to Gontran.

"Oh, it was nothing . . . nothing much. There are really only a few varieties of dream. They all belong to one or other of about half a dozen kinds. This was quite a stock one—the old triangular dream, you know; two men and a woman. She was a remarkable girl. Of course, all women are remarkable, I know. But she was doubly so, for the simple reason that she was two women."

"So you had two wives, bigamist?" growled the Corporal.

"I did not say that she was my wife—and after all, I'm only telling a *dream*, am I not, Corporal Heintz?

"Yes, she was a gentle, timid, soft little thing, meek and nervous and humble, full of gratitude for your smile, fearful and anxious and cringing at your scowl."

"Proper sort for a wife," smiled Boldini, and licked his lips.

"And yet there was a core of granite at the heart of this soft clay; there was steel somewhere beneath the silk."

"Perhaps she had a heart of gold," sneered Boldini. "Gold's hard enough, and hard to come by."

"Excellent," smiled Gontran. "What a very clever man you are! It must have been her heart of gold that one occasionally came upon beneath that tender softness. Quite so; for she was good. Oh, unutterably good and sweet—the sweetest nature, the sweetest disposition, the sweetest temper—oh, incurably sweet. How would you like to eat honey all day long? And think of the flies such honey attracts. There was one fly in particular. . . . To pursue the simile a little far, he got honey on his wings and couldn't fly away. . . . Sticky stuff, honey. . . . And he got it in his heart, and certainly in his voice. Oh, honeyed words, I assure you. The husband listened secretly.

"He was a gentle soul, this Lover . . . made for love. . . . Undoubtedly in a previous incarnation he had been a Provençal *jongleur*, a wandering minstrel of love, going from castle to castle, and from Court to Court; singing of love; making love; a very warrior in the lists of love; right welcome at King

René's Court of Love; slender, willowy, white-handed, large-eyed, long-haired, golden-bearded—oh, a great lover.

"And she, pleased and smiling, always pleased and smiling, but discreet. . . . Oh, yes, always discreet. . . . And virtuous. . . . Or so the Husband hoped. And believed—sometimes. And sometimes he did not. When he was with them he believed, as he gazed upon that lovely Madonna face, and looked into the soulful, gentle eyes of his sweet-mouthed friend; but when his affairs took him away, as periodically they did, and he must leave his Mountain Forest châlet for days at a time, he did *not* believe; and a dark cloud of jealousy gradually overspread the heaven of his soul.

"Jealousy, to change the metaphor, that purest poison, that deadliest and most damnable distillation of the Devil. . . . And the poison spread and spread until his mind was rotted and corrupted, his conscience paralysed, his better nature dead.

"And as poisoned love was metamorphosed into hideous hate, he watched and schemed and plotted and laid traps. And worse—he made opportunities for them. He would say to his friend:

" 'This time to-morrow night I shall be on the Rhine again, gazing on moon-lit schloss and vine-yard, and thinking of my girl, lonely at home here. Pass the cottage on your night round, comrade, and try the door and window. She is young and careless, and thinks no evil. She does not believe the world holds thieves and robbers and evil men.'

"And the young forester would eagerly agree. What had he to guard one-millionth part as precious as little love-faced Heart-of-Gold?

"And the Husband would take an impassioned farewell of his Dutiful Beautiful, and bid her not to mope in loneliness during his week of absence. Why should she not go and visit Frau Englehardt, and take some dainty for her invalid and aged husband? Young Fritz would see her safely home if she lingered after nightfall.

"And departing, he would swiftly return—and watch.

"And one night he was rewarded—or punished, for he saw her sauntering beneath the trees with her Lover, strolling hand-in-hand in the moonlight, and lingering in the black patches of darkest shadow.

"At the door of the cottage they stood and spoke awhile, and then she drew him in and closed the door. Would a light appear, and if so in which room? With teeth embedded in the knuckle which he gnawed, the Husband waited . . . waited . . . waited. And a light appeared. They had lit the lamp in the sitting-room downstairs.

"Cautiously he crept to the window. Blind and curtain were drawn and he could see nothing. Later, the Lover emerged and strode off into the forest, whistling, his gun upon his shoulder. Scarcely could the Husband refrain from rushing to the house, taking down his own gun from where it hung upon the wall, and stealing off to waylay him on his round. But that would be crude—and dangerous; and it was just possible that he was wrong, his suspicions unfounded. He would make absolutely sure—and then his vengeance should be dreadful.

"But it would be a poor game to alienate his wife, lose his friend, and put a noose about his own neck, for nothing at all—put himself within the shadow of the prison—of the gallows—because of a suspicion that might be as baseless as the airy fabric of a dream.

"*Prison! Gallows!* Unpleasant words, and conjuring up unpleasant thoughts in the mind of one who already had a guilty secret—one who already knew what it was to feel uncomfortable at the approach of a *gendarme*, to feel a certain apprehension whenever there came a sudden and heavy knock upon the door. Such a sinister and sullen sound, ominous and foreboding.

"So he waited . . . waited . . . waited through that night, seated with his back against a tree, his eyes upon his moonlit silent house, wherein the light had disappeared from the sitting-room, appeared in the bedroom, and suddenly gone out. And later, the Lover returned from his round, whistling merrily until he was near the house, when he fell silent and walked delicately, making no noise with his iron-shod boots.

"The Husband rose to his feet and stiffened like a hunting-dog that sees its prey. The forester entered by the little garden-gate, and crept silently to the door. The Husband, in the shadow of his tree, took a step forward, and the faint sound of the intake of his breath was audible.

"The door did not open. Nor did the window. No light appeared within the house, and the Lover strolled silently away.

"At a short distance from the house, he turned, bared his head, extended both arms in the direction of the upstairs window, and stood as though in adjuration and in prayer. Then, wafting a kiss in the direction in which he gazed, he suddenly turned and strode swiftly away.

"Nothing much in all that, you will say. And so the Husband said—for a time. But, being of a jealous nature, he could neither let well alone nor ill, if ill it were—until, one night, returning two days before he was expected, he found his house silent, empty and deserted.

"Stunned and incredulous, he seized his gun, and strode out of that unbearable and mocking house, and, with murder in his heart, rushed through the forest, bareheaded and distraught. He realized that his feet were carrying him in the direction of the cottage where dwelt the *garde-champêtre*, and his aged parents.

"Why? She would not be there. They would have fled.

"But she *was* there, serene and calm, sitting with her lover in the porch, while, in the room above, the old mother ministered to her sick husband, the invalid for whom the girl had brought some delicacy. Coolly she greeted her husband, and told him that he was just in time to take her home, instead of Fritz, who had kindly offered to do so.

"'But why the gun?' jeered the Lover. 'Going rabbit-shooting in the dark?'

"'Yes, I'm going to shoot a rabbit,' replied the Husband, in a deadly quiet voice, 'and quite probably in the dark.'

"Thereafter his mind dwelt much on shooting, but he feared the law. He feared what his wife might suspect, and say, and do, if suddenly her lover disappeared. For he knew, in his heart, though never a word had been spoken, that his wife was but too well aware of his jealousy and his hatred; and he suspected that the forester knew of it, too.

"With amusement? With contempt? Would they laugh at him together behind his back, adding vilest insult to foulest injury? The thought was unbearable, and his soured suspicious mind was all but unhinged.

"One day, the dark recesses of his mind were bril-

liantly illuminated by a lurid idea, and he could
scarcely await the hour for translating thought into
action—the action that would give completest proof
and every excuse and right for committing a *crime
passionel*. The law would pardon the deed, and
public opinion condone it. Proof, confession, punishment. Punishment for them both. The utmost
penalty of the law—the unwritten law.

"Having made his usual preparations for a journey, and requested his wife to put a change of clothing and a parcel of food in his rucksack, he announced his departure for Cologne, and his intention
of returning on the fifth day at earliest.

"'There is no time earlier than the earliest, is
there?' observed his wife, with her enigmatic smile;
and bade him a sufficiently fond farewell.

"He returned the next night, and once again
watched and waited for the passing of Fritz, the
garde-champêtre. This time he waylaid and ac-
costed him, a quarter of a mile from the house; and,
as though even more in sorrow than in anger, in
wounded misery than in savage and vengeful wrath
—accused him of being the Lover of his wife.

"It was the young forester who was angry, and
angry that the woman should be accused, that a
single word should be uttered against her, a single
breath of suspicion tarnish her good name. Of himself he said nothing—his sole reply was to condemn
the unbelievable baseness and villainy of the mind

that could think such thoughts, the man who could speak such words of his innocent wife—and such a wife.

"Oh, it was well acted, clever and very plausible, and when the Husband bade him cease to speak of the woman, and to answer the charge brought against himself, he replied:

" 'Why waste my time and trouble, madman? But take note that I am merely *suspected* of a vile thing, and that by only one man—if you are a man. Whereas you have done—actually *done*—a most vile and awful thing.'

"The Husband recoiled in alarm.

" *'What have I done?'* he cried.

" 'Fouled your own nest, bird of ill-omen,' was the reply. 'Falsely and filthily accused the sweetest and most innocent of women. Spat your stinking poison at a star of Heaven, immeasurably above you. Yes, and it falls back upon your own most beastly face.'

"The Husband laughed.

" 'Why all this heat?' he asked softly, 'since you are not her lover?'

" 'Because she is an innocent woman, you diseased hound, and I will not hear her name befouled, not even by you. Nay, *especially* by you, who should be her sure shield and strong protection. You, the very man who should strike dead the lying scoundrel who spoke evil. . . .'

" 'Or did evil, eh?' interrupted the Husband. 'Strike him dead, you said.'

" 'I did, and I repeat it,' replied the forester. '*Evil* in connection with that true, sweet, innocent woman!'

" 'She is innocent, eh?' interrupted the Husband again.

" 'You know it.'

" 'And you? Are you innocent?'

" 'You know it.'

" 'Good. Then you shall prove it. Refuse to do what I now order you to do, and I shall know, *know*, once and for all, that you are a liar, a coward, and a thief, and that she is a . . .'

"The forester raised his clenched fist, and the Husband sprang back.

" 'Blows prove nothing,' he cried. 'Fists are not arguments. Come with me, and we shall see what we shall see—or hear . . . *Innocent*, is she!'

"And with a bitter laugh he strode in the direction of his house, followed by the forester.

"Silently opening the little garden gate, he laid a finger on his lips and whispered:

" 'Make a sound, and it is a certain proof of guilt. Come.'

"And taking the key from his pocket, he crept to the door, and silently unlocked it.

" 'Follow me,' he whispered almost inaudibly, and drew the Lover into the house.

"There, in the darkness, behind the closed door, they stood. The Husband, shaking with jealous rage, and scarcely able to keep his twitching hands from the throat of the man whom he hated beyond telling or belief; the Lover, sorely bewildered and disturbed, but strong to protect and defend the woman whom he loved.

"Thus they stood, silent in the noiseless darkness, till suddenly the Husband, in low, tense whisper, bade the Lover mount the stairs and open the door of the room where the woman slept.

" 'Go up, you dog,' he whispered, 'softly open the door, and say, "*Lisette, it is I. I am here, Lisette, it is I, Fritz*"—and we shall hear what she replies! Innocent, is she! We shall see.'

" 'I do not know the door,' answered the Lover. 'I have never set foot upon those stairs.'

" 'Liar!' whispered the Husband. 'Coward! Liar again! You dare not. You are afraid of what she will say. You dare not stand there in the dark, knowing that I am behind you with my hunting-knife against your back, and say, "*Lisette, it is I, Fritz. I have come to you.*" No, you know too well what she will answer. "*You are late, my beloved*" . . . or "*And I am waiting, my sweetheart Fritz.*" . . . Eh? That's about what we should hear, isn't it? Very awkward with the point of this between your shoulder-blades, eh? . . . No, you don't know the way to that door, do you?'

" 'No,' replied the Lover. 'Show me the way. Creep softly, and open the door yourself. Then stand behind me, place the point of your knife just where you will, and I will call, "*Lisette, it is I, Fritz. I have come to you,*" and abide the result. Lead on.'

" 'Bluff and bravado,' growled the Husband, softly. 'We shall see.'

" 'Lead on,' whispered the Lover, and slowly, stealthily, silently the two went up the stair. At the top, the Husband, seizing the Lover's wrist, crossed a little landing at the end of which a small window, vaguely outlined by starshine and the feeble fleeting light of a lean, cloud-haunted moon, was visible.

" 'This is the door,' he breathed, then directed the Lover's hand toward the latch, swiftly stepped behind him and drew his knife.

"After a brief fumbling at the latch, the Lover opened the door, and with low insistent voice called '*Lisette, Lisette.*'

"And again:

" '*Lisette, Lisette.*'

"There was a faint sound of movement from the bed, and the Lover felt a pressure on the left side of his broad back.

" '*Lisette,*' he called urgently.

" '*What? Who's that?*' came a woman's voice from the pitchy darkness of the room.

"The pressure increased behind the forester's heart, and he fancied he felt the knife-point against his skin.

" *'It is I, Lisette,'* he said. *'It is I, Fritz. I have come to you, Lisette.'*

"Dead silence in the blank black darkness.

"No reply. No movement. No sound—even of breathing.

"The pressure increased, and no doubt remained as to whether the knife-point pricked the Lover's skin.

" *'Lisette,'* he said again. *'Speak to me, Lisette . . . Say something. It is I, Fritz. Standing here in the doorway of your room. Speak, Lisette.'*

"Silence.

"Aching, unbearable silence and suspense.

" *'Say something, Lisette. Speak to me.'*

"Silence.

"And then suddenly, at what seemed to be the very end of Time itself, a voice came out of the darkness.

" *'You, is it, Fritz?'* spoke the woman. *'And you have opened the door of my room, and are standing there. Ah! . . . Then listen, Fritz. And when I have spoken, you will know what to do.'*

"The voice ceased, but not the increasing pressure behind the young man's heart.

" *'I am listening, Lisette,'* he said.

"And Lisette spoke again.

" '*On the 25th day of June of last year, at about 9 o'clock in the evening . . .*'

"The pressure suddenly relaxed—the knife was no longer touching the young man's back.

" '. . . *a man was sitting on a log in the forest near the waterfall. He had sold his winter's wood-carving that day, and returning homeward had sat him down to rest and to gloat upon the money he had got for it.*

" '*By a curious chance two people saw him—one of them from some distance, but not from so far away that there could be any possibility of mistake as to who sat there with the last rays of the setting sun shining full upon him—nor any possibility of mistake as to who was the other person who saw him, and who crept stealthily upon him from behind.* THAT *man was . . .*'

" 'That's enough,' roared a bull voice in the darkness, and almost in Fritz's ear.

"Dead silence.

"And then the voice of the Husband, a little shaky, false and falsetto, gabbled unconvincingly,

" 'Ha, ha, ha! What do you think of this for a joke, my love? Fritz and I thought we'd play a little trick on you. I met him in the forest on my way home. He said, "*Let's go and give little Lisette a fright.*" '

" '*Oh, you are there too, are you, Karl?*' replied

a cool voice from the darkness. And I swear there was a smile in the voice.

"*'I think it was a splendid joke . . . a wonderful little trick for Fritz, of all people, to suggest. And now the little Lisette has had her fright, eh? Or is it the little Lisette who has had the fright?'*

"'Get out of this, you, quick,' growled the Husband, and gave the Lover a thrust that sent him headlong down the stairs.

"Rising to his feet, the young forester debated for a moment as to whether he should return in triumph and demand an apology, in the name of Lisette, from that evil-thinking, unworthy animal above. But natural delicacy joined with instinct and with wisdom to forbid. Rarely are peacemakers really blessed who come between husband and wife. . . . And the young man, bewildered, indignant, angry and sore at heart, quietly went his way.

"And then for the Husband there followed a period of hell upon earth that made the recent months of misery seem like halcyon days of peace and joy. He had shown his hand, and Lisette had shown her knowledge—her knowledge of a deed which he had hitherto supposed no human eye had witnessed. He had shown his hand, insulting and alienating his friend, insulting and alienating his wife, and had proved nothing, gained nothing. Gained nothing, save a dreadful Fear, a Fear that dogged him by day and gripped him by night.

"How much did Lisette know?

"Everything, of course.

"How otherwise did she know the very hour at which old Caspar Knutzen met his death. Had she followed and watched as he dragged the frail old body to the mouth of the old disused mine and thrust it over the edge? It mattered not, since she had witnessed the crime.

"What a woman—to live with that secret in her heart and to say nothing! But had she said nothing? Had she told her lover? And if she had not told him, would she tell him now, in revenge for this unpardonable offence, the insult of the unforgivable accusation he had made against her and Fritz?

"In what a morass of fear, horror and suspense had he to walk? If she had not told Fritz up to that very day, she might tell him on the morrow. After any quarrel she might run to him with this story of the murder.

"Did Fritz eye him queerly nowadays?

"Was there special meaning and triumph, as well as contempt and scorn, in the glance which he gave him?

"And if she did tell Fritz, what was there to prevent their getting him sent to the scaffold that they might be free to marry? Or, for fear that that might look like interested collusion, why should not

Lisette denounce him to the world, go to the Police
and, after his execution, marry Fritz quietly, in due
course?

"And if she had not yet breathed a word about it
to any living soul, might she not still use this awful
secret for her own ends? Use it to secure his acquiescence and compliance? Perhaps use it to make
him agree to her divorcing him?

"Ah, divorce! Could he not divorce *her*, with the
help of perjured witnesses?

"The Husband was well aware that there are base
scoundrels who rid themselves of women, from
whom they wish to be free, by taking action against
them in the Divorce Court, and putting them in the
position of having either to defend their good name
and remain tied to the foul beast, who has accused
them; or of gaining their freedom at the cost of
leaving the perjured liar's filthy accusations unre-
futed.

"But what would he gain, even if she and Fritz
were willing to remain undefended, and he succeeded in divorcing her? They would marry and
she would surely tell Fritz the husband what she
might not have told Fritz the lover. And Fritz,
of course, would use the knowledge to punish him
for the lies and insults of the divorce.

"And meanwhile, how much longer could he go
on living in the same house with this woman whom
he dared not look in the face? This woman whom

he had so injured and insulted, even while she knew this dreadful thing, and had said no word. And how could he continue to meet this Fritz daily, this Fritz whom he had insulted and accused, and who might, at any moment, learn that he was a murderer, might indeed know it already. How much longer could he go on living here, awaiting the heavy hand that would one day fall upon his shoulder; awaiting the heavy knock that would one day fall upon his door; fearing every stranger who approached him; fearing the sound of every foot that followed him in the forest or the town.

"Flight?

"And if he fled? Whither? And where would he be secure? For the arm of the law is long, and the voice of the murdered dead is loud, as it crieth for vengeance from the unconsecrated grave.

"What to do? How many people knew? Almost certainly no more than Lisette and Fritz. Quite probably Lisette alone. And if Lisette alone knew, and anything—happened to—Lisette, then *no one* would know, and all would be well, and the Husband could struggle out of this fearful morass, shake its mud from his feet, and walk forth a free man.

"But then again, how could one live without Lisette, the beautiful, the sweet, the charming—and maddening—Lisette?

"Well, better to live without her, a free man, than live without her in prison, or die without her, on the scaffold. Lisette was dear, but life was dearer, and self-preservation is man's first law.

"Yes, it looked as though the dear Lisette might have to die, but clearly the first thing was to find out whether the good Fritz had been told of the fatal secret. . . . And if he had, why then it might prove a fatal secret indeed—for Fritz.

"How one's mind did run on! And how one thing led to another—two more murders to cover one!

"Meanwhile Fritz, the *garde-champêtre*, lived in a state of unhappiness far removed indeed from the guilty misery of Karl, but almost as far from his former condition of light-hearted contentment and *joie-de-vivre*. Why had that ill-conditioned cur behaved so, and spoilt everything between him and Lisette; made them self-conscious and uncomfortable? Nothing could ever be the same again, now that this hog had wallowed in the dainty dream-garden of their delight.

"Life was spoilt and defiled, and instead of rising in the morning with a song in his heart and thoughts of a glimpse of Lisette, a word with Lisette, perhaps a walk with Lisette, he must now avoid her, and slink shame-facedly past the cottage that had been the lode-stone of his thoughts, the haven of his dreams, the shrine of his dear love.

"And what was the meaning of that astounding

bedroom scene, that drama played in darkness?
What had Lisette meant, and why had her reference
to a man seated on a log so suddenly changed a
blustering and menacing bully into a frightened
fool?

"How had Lisette known that Karl was standing
there? Woman's quick wit and intuition telling her
that her friend Fritz would not have come to her
thus? . . . Had she guessed; and instantly realized
the plot and trap? Possibly she had heard them
whispering below. Anyhow, the cunning blackguard
had had his lesson; the evil-minded dog come
whimpering to heel.

"But everything was spoilt and a heavy, dirty hand
had roughly and rudely brushed the bloom from
life's fairest and sweetest fruit. Why was it that
women such as Lisette married such men as this Karl
the Miller?

"What a man, what an animal, to be the husband
and owner of Lisette! How could she possibly
tolerate him, much less love him?

"No, if truth were told, the man whom Lisette
loved was . . ."

"*That's enough*," suddenly roared Corporal
Heintz. "Fall in. Stir yourselves, *salands*. . . ."

And the weary squad dragged itself to its feet, and
painfully heaved its *sacs* to its shoulders.

§ 4

On the following night, as the squad sat about the camp fire, digesting the indigestible and smoking the unsmokeable, Michael Geste requested *le Légionnaire* Gontran to continue the story of his remarkable dream concerning the miller and the forester.

"It certainly was some dream," observed Hank to his friend.

"You've said something," replied Buddy. "If I could dream like that, I'd dream you was a lovely girl, old Hoss; or else that you was rich and had a generous nature. Nothing ain't impossible in dreams."

"Which is the true dream, and which the true reality—that of the sleeping night, or this of the waking day?" asked La Cigale.

"How did the dream go on?" replied *le Légionnaire* Gontran to Michael Geste. "Oh, I dreamed that the woman died. . . . Yes, in my dream I saw that unhappy lover, Fritz, receive a letter. It was handed to him by a neighbour's half-witted son, who, on being asked later whether a woman gave it to him said 'Yes,' and on being asked again if a man gave it to him, also said 'Yes.'

"The letter was in the handwriting of Lisette. It seemed to have been written in a state of some agitation and in great haste, and it bade him come to

her at ten o'clock that night, for speak to him she
must—and in the absence of her husband. The
latter had again gone away that day, saying he would
be absent for three nights at least. She relied on
Fritz to come to her; she knew that he would come,
for she needed his help, and there was something
that must be done and done quickly.

"Beneath the signature of Lisette was an urgent
appeal. It seemed that she had started to write with
discretion and restraint, and at the last moment her
feelings had overcome her. Terror, anxiety and the
very fear of death had broken the bonds of prudence.
She had written:

"*'Come and advise me and help me. He is so
strange and terrible, and I feel that I am in the
greatest danger. I truly believe that I'm being
poisoned. What shall I do? Where can I go?
Help me, Fritz.'*

"You may imagine the state of mind in which the
Lover spent the hours which intervened. They were
the longest through which he had ever lived.

"At ten o'clock that night, he approached the dark
and silent house, opened the little garden gate, crept
to the door, and tapped softly.

"No answer. No movement within.

"Again he tapped, and again without response.

"In conjunction with the fact that no light burned
in the sitting-room, this was vaguely disquieting,
though not alarming.

"He tried the latch of the door, and found that the door was not fastened. Should he walk in? She had bidden him come at ten o'clock, and the hour had struck.

"He entered warily, closed the door behind him, and softly called '*Lisette, Lisette.*'

"He struck a match, and entered the living-room. It was, as he had expected, empty, though he had half hoped to see her sitting there in the dark, awaiting him.

"Similarly deserted was the kitchen at the back of the sitting-room.

"With swiftly beating heart, he went to the foot of the well-remembered stairs on which he had set foot but once, and called her name. Again he called, more loudly; and yet again, receiving no reply.

"What could be the meaning of this? Was it a trap, some new and devilish ingenuity of her husband? Should he go up? No. How explain his presence there, if Karl sprang out upon him, or were lurking, awaiting him in the bedroom?

"But she had sent for him. She had implored him to be there at ten o'clock, and time was passing. Should he not go up? Yes. Lisette would not send for him and then go out of the cottage.

"And if it were a trap, let the good Karl see what he had got in his trap! He would not be the first setter of traps that had caught a Tartar—not the first spider whose net had caught a wasp.

"Yes, he would go up, and if the worst happened, things could be no worse, apparently, for Lisette, and might, indeed, be made very much better.

"The Lover climbed the stairs, and was confronted by a closed door. Upon this he knocked again and again, receiving no answer.

"He then tried the door, and found that this also was unfastened. Opening it, he whispered *'Lisette!'* and louder and louder said *'Lisette! Lisette!'* She could not have gone to bed and be sleeping so heavily that his voice failed to wake her.

"Of course she would not have gone to bed after having begged him to come to her at ten o'clock. Could she possibly have gone out into the forest to meet him, and have missed him in the darkness? Almost impossible.

"With fear clutching at his heart, he struck a match. A terrible cry burst from his lips, and dropping the match, he covered his stricken eyes with shaking hands. On the bed lay Lisette—dead. Murdered. Most violently and brutally murdered.

"The reactions of the human mind to sudden emergency or shock are strange and unaccountable, and are not to be foretold. His first impulse was to flee from that dreadful spot. The next was to fling himself upon the bed and shield in his embrace that dear defiled and injured body; coax it back to life and movement with his caresses.

"What he *did* do, was to strike a match and

fumble at the lamp with trembling fingers, the while waves of nausea, grief, and rage shook him from head to foot. Having succeeded in lighting the lamp, he took a grip upon his courage, and then, turning to the bed, repressed his shuddering horror and strove to do what might be done.

"Hopeless and useless. A hunting-knife had done its dreadful work too well, in heart and throat; and all that the stunned, incredulous and broken-hearted man could do, was to pray that he might be vouch-safed sufficient length of life and health and strength to become the instrument of vengeance.

"It was thus the Police found him—the Police who, it appeared, had been anonymously warned to surround and enter the house at the hour of ten-thirty, if they wished to prevent the perpetration of a terrible crime, involving robbery and murder, in the absence of the miller—a crime arranged for the hour of eleven.

"There they found him, his hands stained with blood—a picture, at any rate to the Police, of guilt as well as of horror at the deed he had committed. Nor was the Sergeant of Gendarmes disposed to change his opinion when he noticed that every drawer in the room was opened and ransacked; and that a box, evidently dragged from beneath the bed, had been burst open.

"To the fierce questions and demands of the Police, Fritz could give no satisfactory reply. He could but protest his innocence and swear that he had *happened* to enter the house, had *happened* to go upstairs. . . .

" 'Oh, quite so . . .' the Police had observed, nodding its collective head. 'And had *happened* to go into the poor woman's bedroom, and had *happened* to find her robbed and murdered. A likely story.'

"And why, pray, had he gone to the house at all, at that time of night?,

"And in reply to that awkward question, the prisoner had preserved a dogged silence.

"But the case proved to be far less simple than had, at first sight, appeared, and the Police were mystified. Though they had caught him in the very act—in the ransacked room itself, where was the loot? Where were the money and poor jewellery that had undoubtedly been taken from drawer and box? Though he had been caught red-handed indeed, his hands red with the murdered woman's blood, where was the weapon, and what the motive?

"And another most extraordinary feature of the case—where was the husband? He had absolutely disappeared—vanished from off the face of the earth.

"And was it literally from off the face of the earth, and was he now under the earth in some secret grave dug for him by this monster?

"And then again Fritz the forester was most certainly not a monster, but a most worthy young man of excellent education, known good character and unimpeachable virtue. Hitherto, at any rate. But you never knew, you never knew. And the Police shook its head darkly. Nevertheless the Police was mystified.

"But heart-broken Fritz the forester, in his dank dark cell, was not mystified. He knew, with absolute certainty, as if he had seen it all, that Karl had murdered Lisette, and with superhuman devilish cunning had contrived to divert suspicion, blame, and accusation upon the friend of whom he was jealous.

"Karl had never been the same man since that night of mad accusation and infamous attempt at proof. He had gone from bad to worse, and quite obviously had rendered Lisette's life unbearable, until at length she had been driven, in fear of her life, to write Fritz the letter that had brought him to the house that terrible night.

"Obviously her husband, having told her that he was going away from home again, had spied upon her and had either caught her in the act of getting the letter to the half-witted go-between, or had intercepted it *en route*. He had then waited as long as he dared, had most foully and brutally murdered the poor girl, and had taken all the money and jewellery that was in the house, leaving the bedroom in calculated disorder.

"He had then gone off in the darkness, sent his

anonymous message to the Police and escaped.

"A neat plot, and worthy of the Devil himself. But not quite successful, for the four absent elements saved Fritz's life—probably because he valued it so little—absence of motive, absence of stolen property, absence of weapon, and absence of the husband whom it was decided could not have been murdered and disposed of—at any rate by the prisoner—between the time he was last seen alive and the time of the arrest. Fortunately for Fritz, his movements and whereabouts were known throughout the earlier part of that evening.

"So, finally, Fritz was discharged with a stain upon his character—a stain indelible; and in despair he left his home, his beloved forest and his native land, and joined the Legion of the Self-condemned. . . ."

The Dreamer fell silent.

"And is he in the Legion still?" asked Michael Geste.

"He dreams that he is," was the reply.

"And do you dream that he is?" asked John.

"I dream that I dream that he is," replied Gontran, turning his curious, pale, unsmiling eyes upon the boy.

II

Life at Zinderneuf was life in death, and not infrequently death in life. As *le Légionnaire* Gontran observed, it was like nothing on earth, but was indeed most remarkably like something in Hell— one of Hell's punishment cells, where the Devil sends defaulting fiends from his Penal Battalions when other means have failed to repress them. But *le Légionnaire* Gontran had great compensations, for he had been promoted Corporal.

On the day on which he stood forth, a Corporal revealed, with two chevrons upon his cuff, he had gone in search of Corporal Heintz. And tapping the two red chevrons upon his sleeve had said:

"Ha, ha, my friend, now we shall see what we shall see."

But the triumph of Corporal Gontran had been brief, his grim and menacing complacence short-lived, for the last official act of the Commandant, Captain Renouf, on the very day that he shot himself, was to promote Corporal Heintz to Sergeant. So a Sergeant, pending confirmation in orders, Heintz became. And a Sergeant can make himself quite as painfully unpleasant to a Corporal as a Corporal can to a *légionnaire*. He can get him reduced to the ranks, for example. Meanwhile he can punish him with confinement to Barracks, or with *salle de police* and he can get him sent to prison. Without punishing him at all, he can make his life a burden, a misery and a shame, by undermining his authority and making him ridiculous before the men of his *escouade*. And he can legally and officially hold him responsible for every fault committed by every man of the room of which he is in charge.

It is probable that, on the whole, Sergeant Heintz made life even more unbearable for Corporal Gontran than had Corporal Heintz for *le Légionnaire* Gontran. He quickly succeeded in turning the unfavourable attention of *l'adjudant* Lejaune upon the unfortunate man. To show forth their proper zeal beneath the watchful eye of *l'adjudant* Lejaune, Sergeant Dupré and Corporal Boldini, friends of Sergeant Heintz, joined enthusiastically with him in discovering cause for dissatisfaction with the work of Corporal Gontran.

One fortunate result of this state of affairs was that neither Heintz nor Gontran had much time for bullying other people and became almost popular.

But Sergeant Heintz overdid it, and, one night, Corporal Gontran dreamed another dream, and when on the following day, according to his wont, Sergeant Heintz jeeringly inquired as to whether he had dreamed anything of interest lately, Corporal Gontran replied that he had indeed. And something, moreover, of personal interest to the good Sergeant himself.

It was a curious dream, and in two parts.

In the first of these, the Dreamer had dreamed of a most regrettable and deplorable event, which was nothing less than the premature demise of Sergeant Heintz himself.

Yes, he had seen him die.

"And how, might one inquire?" sneered Sergeant Heintz, moistening dry lips.

"Well, in this curious dream of mine, Sergeant, you were stabbed, just here and just here," and Corporal Gontran indicated his heart and his throat. "Yes, you were stabbed in the heart and in the throat, and you bled to death. When the murder was discovered it was too late to do anything for you. You were dead—oh, quite dead."

"And the second part of this interesting dream?" asked Sergeant Heintz, as listening men, lounging outside the Guard Room, edged nearer and nearer.

"Oh, very vague—you know what dreams are, Sergeant Heintz—but somehow mixed up with the first one. As far as I can remember, it was mainly about a *légionnaire* who had a mission in life."

"What, to shirk work, and give trouble to his superiors?" inquired Heintz.

"No, no. So far as I can remember, it was something more difficult than that. It was to inflict punishment rather than to get it. In fact, to inflict punishment without getting it. Yes, that was it. I remember it quite clearly now, that part of it. Yes, this *légionnaire* had to kill a man."

"Murder, eh?" sneered Sergeant Heintz. "Sort of thing you would dream about."

"Well—not so much murder him as execute him. Take the law into his own hands, or, one might say, assist the law—do what the law had failed to do. Carry out the death sentence which the law would most certainly and most righteously have passed upon him had not the bestial and cowardly Judas fled beyond the reach of its arm.

"Oh, yes, an execution. That was his mission. And he not unnaturally wanted to live awhile, to enjoy the satisfaction that his good deed would bring him. . . . But in my dream—and I remember this part most clearly—it seemed that he had come to the conclusion that it really did not matter whether he lived or not, once he had fulfilled his task, done his duty by the community and mankind in general, punished an unspeakable villain, and avenged the best and sweetest soul that ever graced this world. . . ."

"Quite a dream, in effect," interrupted Sergeant Heintz, his livid face twitching.

"Yes, Sergeant Heintz," continued Corporal Gontran. "Quite a dream. And making it perfectly clear that this *légionnaire* had most finally and firmly decided that he had done wrong and acted foolishly, in waiting for an opportunity to execute justice without himself falling beneath the sword of justice. . . . Yes, he saw the error of his ways, in that he had not immediately done his duty and carried out his mission most cheerfully—as soon as he found the man—and willingly offered his life as the price of that privilege. Why, man, he had prayed—prayed most fervently—that he might live to be the instrument of vengeance upon that foul, savage beast, that treacherous, base, brutal . . ."

As he spoke Corporal Gontran thrust his suffused face close to that of Sergeant Heintz, raised his clenched fists, and slavered at the mouth.

Clearly a case of *cafard*—the man was going mad —and Corporal Boldini, seizing his arm, pulled him roughly away.

"I'll give you something to dream about," growled Sergeant Heintz, "and before long, I'll put you where you'll stop dreaming altogether."

§ 2

That night, a night so unbearably and dangerously hot that but few could sleep, Beau Geste and his brother John sat side by side beneath the desert stars, and talked of Digby, away at Tokotu, of Brandon Abbas, and of old, happy, far-off things.

After a time they fell silent, and from the darkness of the black shadow in which they sat against the wall, idly watched the occasional comings and goings of their comrades, commenting from time to time upon their more salient characteristics.

"Who's that with Boldini?" murmured Beau as two men passed in the moonlight, their heads together in whispered converse.

"That weed Bolidar. They're very thick these days," replied John.

As he spoke, Sergeant Heintz approached, and Bolidar slunk away into the shadows. Heintz gave Bolidar a sharp order, and as he hurried off to fulfil it, another man, descending steps that led down from the roof, approached.

"The Lover and the Husband," murmured John. "Which is which?"

"Neither of them really knows much of love, I think," replied Beau.

Corporal Gontran and Sergeant Heintz met in front of the brothers, and a few yards from where they were sitting.

"Get to your room and dream, you dog," growled Sergeant Heintz. "Dream while you have yet time. Dream you're on the scaffold and . . ."

"I'm dreaming now, Sergeant Heintz. I'm dreaming *now*, you cesspool of sin," and, drawing his sword-bayonet, he stabbed Sergeant Heintz in the left breast.

"*Lisette!*" he shouted, and as the stricken man staggered back, sagged at the knees and fell to the ground, Corporal Gontran struck again, driving the bayonet through the Sergeant's throat.

"*Lisette!*" he cried a second time, and as the astonished brothers sprang forward, he whipped out an automatic pistol.

"Stand still," he shouted, "or I'll shoot you both.

Stand to attention until I tell you to move," and he covered them alternately with the automatic.

"Keep still, John," murmured Beau, in English. "He's quite mad and won't care whom he shoots. Wait till I say 'Now,' and then jump to the right as I jump to the left. . . . *Wait*, though."

"Good," whispered John. "You duck and collar him low, and I'll jump for his pistol."

Corporal Gontran kicked Sergeant Heintz heavily.

"Can you hear, you dog?" he shouted. "Or are you dead? *'Quite a dream in effect,'* eh?"

And then, with an incredible change of voice, he said, softly, as he placed the muzzle of the pistol to his temple and gazed upward at the stars,

"Je viens, ma Lisette."

THE END

CPSIA information can be obtained at www.ICGtesting.com
Printed in the USA
LVOW08s1159300714

396584LV00034B/255/P